REVENGE

A Psychological Thriller

Marilyn Benner Sowyak

Cover design by: Martellia@Fiverr.com

ISBN: 979-8-9885998-3-8

Printed in the United States of America

Contents

Chapter 1

Blanchard House

BLANCHARD HOUSE

THE ELEGANT DINING room, adorned with exquisite tapestries and ornate handcrafted woodwork, created an ambiance of refined luxury. The massive chandelier bathed the room in a warm glow, casting dancing shadows on the walls and adding to the enchantment of the evening.

As the soft melody of Mozart's music floated through the air, Maggie Blanchard's heart filled with overwhelming gratitude. The family had undergone deep trauma and transformation over the past six months within the walls of the Blanchard House. The giant mansion seemed to have developed a soul as it protected them, weaving its magic like a warm hug, healing wounds and uniting souls.

The chef, a thin, graceful man, bowed at the waist at the head of the table beside Maggie's husband, Kerrington Blanchard. It was the signal that the cuisine was ready to be consumed.

Kerrington was indeed dashing. His prematurely gray hair contrasted nicely against his tan, well-cared-for skin and made for a handsome impression. When he looked her way, his bright blue sparkling eyes and smile melted her heart, as always. Sometimes, it was hard for Maggie to realize he was a billionaire twenty times over and carried a powerful reputation on Wall Street. Often called a Corporate Raider and, at times, a White Knight, he never let it go to his head. Despite his mighty reputation at heart, Kerrington was genuinely gentle and kind and went to great lengths to keep Maggie and his family safe from harm. He still took her breath away when he came near her, and she thanked God daily for sending him her way.

Maggie glanced across the table at Benny Maxwell, her friend from the hospital. He was smart, sassy, and filled with an enormous energy that made doctors all but fall on their knees, begging to have him assigned to their area. Benny stood proud at five-five and was lean from demanding work. He kept his long black hair braided and hanging down his back. Willow had called him her handsome knight in shining armor.

Fate had knitted Maggie and Benny tightly together as if it had taken its invisible hand and tied the string personally, bonding their friendship for life.

The two became fast friends in the ER as they struggled to keep people alive during years of staffing shortages and overcrowded hallways. Then, destiny forced their friendship to endure a wild, terrifying trauma at the hands of a serial killer. Not a year later, an enormous tragedy united them once again when Willow, Benny's wife and Maggie's best friend, was kidnapped and then murdered.

Maggie's heartstrings tugged at Willow's memory. She left behind a beautiful young daughter, Dorrie, who looked exactly like her–an appealing blend of Asian, Caucasian, and Black. Maggie smiled, taking in Dorrie's long, straight black hair that shimmered in the candlelight. Yes. God had given them back a piece of Willow.

In due time, Kerrington, Maggie, and Benny adopted Dorrie. Unconventional? Yes. But none of them was willing to let go of her. The success of their willingness to live together as a family was visible in the happiness that glowed on Dorrie's face. Most beautiful of all, that morning, she had trotted happily down the stairs, asking if they could go shopping – and she had called Maggie, *"Mom."*

Living in Blanchard House's loving spirit was as comforting as being wrapped in a warm blanket. It had cared for Dorrie during her crisis, pulling her through. Secret eyes throughout the house always made sure she wanted for nothing: the au pair, the housekeepers, the butler, and the security officers. Every teardrop Dorrie shed was reported so Maggie, Benny, and Kerrington could immediately address and soothe their child's sorrow.

Maggie looked around the table at everyone else seated at the table.

Kerrington was sitting next to His sister, Annella Wryn. The beloved blond bombshell was America's favorite A-List movie actor. "Well, guys," Annella announced unexpectedly, holding her crystal glass of red wine up in a toast. "I'm off to Rome soon. I finally found the role I've always wanted to play."

"Rome?" her husband, Glenn Sloan, who was a physician in the emergency department, held an outraged tone. "I need you here. You've done enough movies."

Annella, as they all did, looked at him in shock. "It's too late to change, Glenn. The contract is signed, sealed, and delivered."

"I don't care what it is. You're not going. We've had this discussion. I don't like you being away from me."

"Could we kindly not have this type of discussion at the dinner table?" Kerrington said calmly.

"Why not?" Glenn soured back.

"Because I asked you."

Glenn rolled his eyes, ignoring Kerrington's request. "You're not going, Annella, and that is my final word."

"No, it's not," Annella replied, embarrassment was written all over her face.

Maggie and Benny looked at each other. Glenn had obviously had too much to drink. The whites of his eyes were red, and a furrowed frown draped his typically handsome smiling face. They had both worked with him in the ER for years and knew him well. His behavior was steady and predictable. It was so out of character for him to behave rudely, and Maggie had seen him in many situations with unruly and even beastly patients. He always kept his cool. As a well-seasoned emergency medicine physician, people looked to him to lead.

Annella continued to eat her meal when Glenn slammed his hand down beside her plate.

"May I eat my dessert in the movie room?" Dorrie asked, clearly uncomfortable.

Maggie nodded and tried to send her a comforting smile.

"You're drunk, my good man," Kerrington said. "Please leave the table.

I'll not have you address my sister disrespectfully, and I certainly do not want my child to be harmed by your behavior. Please don't make me ask security for assistance."

Glenn stood, threw his napkin on his seat, and left the room.

"Annella, if we could talk after dinner."

"I think we need to. I apologize. All of you. I don't know what's gotten into Glenn. His temper is off these days."

The rest of dinner remained quiet, with chatter that was hard for everyone to come by.

***

AS THE EVENING continued over dessert, Maggie wondered what was going on with Glenn. He was always in control. Yes. Things had gotten tense after he'd been shot in the head last year. Maybe returning to the ER so soon, with the added pressure of being the medical director, had pushed him too far. She wondered if he possibly had PTSD.

Without warning, a deafening explosion shattered the room, followed by a long rumbling tremor and vibration on the floor. Dorrie bolted into the room and went straight into Maggie's arms. "The whole house is shaking," she cried out. In an instant, fear gripped everyone as Maggie's terror mirrored her daughter's.

The threatening mighty tremor lasted less than a minute. Maggie watched the chandelier sway, its crystals tinkling softly against one another even after the rumbling ceased. Then, just as suddenly as it started, the house fell into an eerie stillness.

Maggie caught Kerrington's eyes, then Benny's. Concern danced in the air over the secret they shared. Buried deep beneath the earth, at the back of the estate, was a hidden laboratory they had failed to destroy as they promised each other. Had their worst fears come to life?

Without hesitation, Kerrington excused himself and fled the room, his steps quickening into a run as he made his way across the great lawn heading to the rear of the estate. Maggie cast a worried glance in Benny's direction.

They were the only ones in the house who knew about the three-story Level III biohazardous laboratory, other than Kerrington.

Maggie and Benny accidentally discovered the lab last year, and Maggie was livid when she confronted Kerrington about it.

"Why do we have such a thing on the property where we will be raising our children?" Maggie had asked, furious with Kerrington for the first time in their marriage.

"I didn't build it," Kerrington explained, trying to diminish his role in creating the lab. "I inherited it from my great-great-grandfather, William. From what I've been told, he was a brilliant man with a deep passion for discovery, science, and medicine. He spent a vast amount of money developing the lab so he could enjoy tinkering in it."

"He's dead. So, why is it still here? Projects are going on actively as we speak, Kerrington. It's yours. You own it."

"I have no control, Maggie," Kerrington said, looking trapped yet still making an earnest effort to keep eyes level with hers. "I'm trying to get rid of it, but all my efforts have seemingly ended in endless litigation that has gone on for years, long before you came here. I want it destroyed. However, William apparently signed a contract with the government that cannot be tampered with until the year 2050. Funding comes from a trust fund controlled by Congressman Brightman."

"We can't raise our children here."

"It's not that bad, Maggie. Groundbreaking treatments have been discovered here. Medications that have cured billions worldwide."

"Yet, you don't know what they are working on now?"

A long pause tested their trust for one another before Kerrington finally admitted the truth he hadn't wanted to face. "I'll take care of it, Maggie. I promise."

It had been their first argument, and it was heated, but their relationship went forward, enjoying peaceful waters – until now.

Countless questions flickered between Maggie and Benny as they exchanged glances. *Did the explosion come from the lab? Or had they experienced a rare earthquake? Most importantly, how would they keep the truth concealed from their loved ones if the explosion happened in the laboratory?*

Benny's genius swept into action. "Movie night!" he declared, with a conviction that left no room for argument. He also did not let on, not even a tiny bit, that he was worried. Delighted at the unexpected turn of events, Dorrie was granted the honor of choosing the evening's entertainment.

Benny called out to the chef. "We'll have movie night treats delivered to the media room." One by one, they filed out of the grand dining room, seeking refuge in the far reaches of the mansion. Benny dramatically waved his arm toward Dorrie, giving her the authority to ceremoniously push the button that made the heavy red velvet drapes open to conceal the grand movie screen. A temporary respite from worry had been created, a stage set for the theater of diversion.

Annella silently slipped from her room to find Glenn. Maggie hoped they could work things out. They'd always appeared so happy—or maybe Annella had simply done a great job as an actress, covering up their deeply seeded issues.

Maggie's heart was heavy and uneasy, so she skipped movie time, took the east elevator to the fourth floor, and went to her wing. There, Maggie sought solace in one of her cherished rooms, which overlooked the back of the estate. She took in the breathtaking panorama with a mix of gratitude and trepidation.

Maggie opened the windows, climbed onto her secret perch, and took a seat. She easily identified where the explosion happened. The fire was massive and near their property. Through the treetops, Maggie watched the flashing lights coming from dozens of first responder vehicles.

Maggie saw Kerrington walking back to the house from the laboratory. Her thoughts raced, wondering what he may have found beyond the heavy steel and stoned walls. The sound of a persistent doorbell echoed through the mansion, reverberating on every floor and demanding to be answered. She wondered who it was and headed downstairs to see.

Kerrington joined several men at the door and led them into his library.

Ronnie, the butler, lifted his eyebrows in astonishment as Lamar, the head of Blanchard security, closed the library's doors.

As she turned to join the others in the media room, she spotted the House Manager, Jenny Pretty, and two housekeepers at the end of the foyer, closing the heavy drapes that covered the massive wall of windows that led to the back of the estate. Maggie had never seen the drapes closed. Something was going on, and Maggie suspected it was related to the lab.

***

MAGGIE RETURNED to the fourth floor and resumed her seat outside on her favorite perch on the roof. Despite the fact that she hadn't smoked for a decade, her nerves were fried, making her crave a cigarette.

The nearby fire was out, but the smoke was thick, hanging onto the tree tops as the summer wind tried puffing it away.

Echoing sounds of heavy footsteps and muffled voices floated up from the grounds; the chatter was indecipherable, but the sense of urgency was palpable. A soft gasp escaped Maggie's lips as she saw a group of individuals clad in white biohazard suits walking toward the laboratory. It was like watching a movie scene of a plague outbreak. The impact of the grave situation hit her, causing her to inhale deeply. The smoke-laden air twisted its way into her lungs, stinging and igniting a dreadful sense of fear. Kerrington had made that same walk without wearing any protective gear.

A shuffling noise from behind startled her until she saw it was Kerrington struggling with his long-limbed body to climb out the window to be with her. She was glad to see him as it was a sign that everything was okay after his meeting. He placed his arm around her shoulders and pulled her close. Maggie cherished his comforting embrace and leaned into him, snuggling against his chest.

"They wanted to make sure the building was safe after the explosion," he said, kissing her forehead.

"Great," Maggie sighed in resignation.

"And, no, I still don't know what's in there," Kerrington admitted.

"We have to have a better plan, you know," Maggie said, looking up at him. "You can't tell me that with our brains, we can't figure a way out of this mess."

"We will. It's time we did."

"Tomorrow morning. That's our plan," Maggie demanded in a soft voice. "But, for right now, let's call it a night. That's why we have security officers. Lamar can handle the inspectors."

***

AFTER CRAWLING back through the window to the bedroom, Kerrington took Maggie's hand and pulled her onto the bed, where he wrapped his arms around her and hungrily kissed her lips. Soft. Gentle. Then, passionate—stirring Maggie's yearning for him. The harvest moon shed a warm, golden, romantic hue across the room, adding gentle reminders of the world outside.

Maggie felt as if time stood still when she laid her head on his chest and heard his heart beating, each heartbeat synchronizing with the tenderness of their love. She melted against him, surrendering to the moment, feeling how perfectly they fit together—the way their bodies aligned as if they were always meant to be. Lost in this embrace, she savored the familiarity of his scent, a blend of warmth, spice, and all the dreams they had dared to whisper in the dark.

Their lovemaking was beautiful, as always. Each move of Kerrington's hand touching her skin ignited sparks of pleasure that awakened all her senses. She marveled at the way they moved together, two bodies and souls perfectly in sync, creating an unspoken language of love. In this shared sanctuary, the outside world was dismissed and forgotten as they found solace in one another.

Maggie's heart raced with the thought of the future. She couldn't wait until they had a baby—a tiny being born from their unwavering love, a living testament to the richness of their bond. She wanted Kerrington to see the proof of how magnificent their life was together—how laughter and joy could fill a home, how the echoes of small feet would create a symphony of happiness.

Visions of a nursery painted in soft pastels danced through her mind, filled with stuffed animals and cherished stories waiting to be told. She envisioned long evenings spent cradling their child to sleep, reading fairy tales and singing lullabies, with Kerrington stationed close by, his heart full and his eyes sparkling. The thought of nurturing a life together filled her with overwhelming excitement but also a tender vulnerability—the fear of the unknown loomed, yet it only heightened the beauty of their dreams.

Each kiss felt like a symphony of beautiful moments—that would long be remembered. Moments that Maggie would later recall— and pray for their return.

As reality seeped back in, Kerrington held her tighter, sensing the wave of emotions washing over her. He looked into her eyes, those deep pools of love and longing, and in that moment, all the world's chaos faded away. "One day, my love," he whispered, "we will make those dreams a reality."

Maggie nodded, her pulse quickening not just from the heat of the moment but from the weight of his promise—a promise that anchored her heart to a future brimming with hope. She buried her face into the crook of his neck, inhaling the comfort of his presence, allowing the world outside to fade into a distant murmur.

In that beautiful cocoon of love, every kiss and touch and every sigh seemed to linger in the air, forging a connection that transcended time. They were building something eternal—two hearts intertwined, united in their shared dreams and whispered desires.

As they settled into the rhythm of their affection, a quiet contentment enveloped them, warming their hearts. While the future remained unwritten, they faced it hand in hand, ready to embrace whatever was to come.

When he kissed her goodnight, she lay her head against the pillow and closed her eyes. Little did she know how this beautiful night, filled with sacred memories, would play repeatedly through her mind like a beautiful symphony over the difficult days that lie ahead. Maggie would later recall this treasured moment and pray fervently for their return.

***

THE NEXT MORNING, Maggie and Kerrington had a private breakfast out on the veranda before work. The day already promised to be a scorcher. It was hot everywhere, and the air smelled like smoke from the still-smoldering house or the fires burning out of control across Canada. The air was stifling.

9

Sometimes, Maggie worried that climate change had indeed arrived and maybe it was too late to make things better. She was thankful temperatures weren't sizzling like they recently had been. Maggie made a mental note— no more breakfast on the veranda until the heat wave broke and the smoke disappeared.

Maggie was ready to close her IPAD when she saw the news item about the explosion last night. "Listen to this," Maggie said, reading out loud to Kerrington. *"There's nothing left of the house,"* a neighbor reported. *"My entire house shook, and my windows are shattered. Everyone came out of their houses wondering if there was a bomb. No one claims to know what happened, but it looks like a war zone. The news reporters said the explosive vibrations extended for as far away as five miles, damaging property along the way."* Maggie closed her IPAD. "We got lucky."

"We're going to destroy the lab," Kerrington said, closing his *Barron's* newspaper and sipping his orange juice. "That's the topic on the agenda today."

"Well, you have me on your side. But not so fast, there. It's not that easy to tear a biohazardous lab to pieces overnight."

"Your thoughts, then?"

"I'm not sure," Maggie said. "I want to plant a camera just to see who comes and goes and when they leave. Who are the people working there? Are they really with the CDC? I'm uncomfortable with their secrecy. I think that with our brilliant minds, we can find out what they are up to. Maybe we'll figure out what their project is all about."

"That's easy. We'll have Lamar…"

Maggie cut him off. "No. Honey. Please. I don't want him involved. Just you, me, and maybe Benny. No more. I don't know who we can trust anymore."

"Honestly, I don't know if we even need to dig that deep. I want the lab destroyed, and I'm exploring ways to carry out that plan. Then I'll let the government sue me, and it will be over."

"So. What strategic moves do you have up your sleeves?"

"I have resources in Japan. An old wise friend."

"You're going to Japan?"

"I am. I have other businesses there as well. It will be later in the week, but I have to go anyway for a meeting."

"Well, I'm glad it's later in the week. That will make room for more hanky panky," Maggie whispered back with a grin, getting up and kissing him, memories of last night's lovemaking fresh in her mind.

Benny, dressed for work, walked in, "Let's go. We don't want to be late. The car is waiting."

Chapter 2

Fahrenheit

DOCTOR SUNDAY RICHARDSON, one of Charlotte's leading neurosurgeons, leaned back with a satisfied smile as she looked over the stunning views of the city's skyline from atop Fahrenheit. The upscale dining restaurant was well known for its experience in serving creative dishes in a relaxing, breathtaking atmosphere.

Sunday had her long black hair pulled back and up in an elegant hairdo that had cost her three hundred dollars and two hours in a salon chair. The style was chosen to show off her diamond earrings and necklace. She'd gotten all dolled up just for her plastic surgeon husband, Paul. She'd planned the night as a special occasion, hoping she might get his attention.

Their daughters, Kay and May, were spending the night at a friend's birthday celebration, which made for perfect timing. It was always a joy when she was able to plan a date night and have Paul all to herself. She was hoping for an intimate night alone later when they got home. So far, their chatter consisted of anything and everything, including politics, the stock market, the upcoming Panther football season, and recent events in their friends' lives.

Paul seemed to be listening and engaged in their conversation, but Sunday also noticed he seemed distracted, almost distant. Again. She looked down and focused on the feast before her. The Hot Seafood Tower was her favorite entree, which consisted of an array of Crispy Oysters, Garlic Shrimp, Steamed Snow Crab Legs, Two Split Truffle Lobster tails, Steamed Scallops, and Salmon Moqueca.

The sunset outside the window was a delightful feature of a myriad of colors: red, orange, and pink, with hints of purple. Sunday didn't want the night to end.

When Sunday reached across the table to take Paul's hand in hers, he withdrew it almost as if it had been an instinctual move. She looked at her fair-haired husband, whose hair was so neatly groomed. She missed his smile and was reminded that she hadn't seen it in quite a while, but truth be told, they didn't often have the luxury of spending time together with their heavy surgical schedule and their children's sports events. For a split second, her stomach fell as she realized their love was not as strong as it once was after spending almost two decades together. She had to salvage this night and let him know somewhere deep down in both of them; it was still there. It simply needed rekindling.

"Sunday," Paul began, his face carrying a guarded look. Uncomfortable. Unsure, he removed his napkin from his lap and placed it on the edge of the table. Sunday knew him well. There was almost a moment where he seemed to lose the courage to continue when he picked up his glass and took a rather large sip of his brandy. He then looked her straight in the eye. "I want a divorce."

"A divorce? Why? We have a perfectly beautiful family."

"We did—but I haven't been happy for a long time. We've gone our separate ways in our marriage, and I need more than work. I want to come home to a hug and a kiss and a sit-down home-cooked meal with my family— not something the housekeeper put together for us or hot dogs sitting on bleachers watching the kids play a game I'm too tired to focus on."

"We can fix that, Paul. That's such an easy fix. I thought you were happy. I thought you loved me."

"I do love you, Sunday. I just don't want to be married to you. I found someone else."

"What are you telling me? You're having an affair? With whom? How long has it been going on?"

"A little over two years ago. I met her at a conference in New York. She's a plastic surgeon. We have a lot in common."

"I just bet you do. Who is she?"

"Ally Billingsly."

"Your partner?"

"Yes. She joined our firm not long after we became...intimate."

"Oh my God. You are such a prick."

"I've given it a lot of thought. We split all our assets fifty-fifty. Cash. Bank accounts. The house. The beach property. We each keep our individual 401K's and share custody of the children. You get a week. I get a week. That way, their lives won't be completely wrecked."

"You're insane. You know that? You fall in love with a whore and divide our lives like you're dealing out a deck of cards. Let me get this right. You plan to make this home wrecker a stepmother to my children?"

"She's going to give them a baby brother."

"She's pregnant? That's it. Take me home. I don't want to spend another minute with you. You're a monster." Sunday stood up to walk away.

Paul grabbed her arm. "Don't be this way, Sunday. You know what I'm saying is true. Yes, we do love each other, but it's not the same anymore. Let's not destroy what good memories there are."

They walked to the street together and stepped into the back seat of a private black car waiting at the curb. Sunday turned her back on Paul and stared out the window as they made their way home.

I will not cry, she said to herself. *I will not give Paul that satisfaction.*

As they approached their private drive, the air filled with the distant wailing of sirens—lots of them. They both loudly gasped simultaneously at the sight of a dozen fire trucks and other rescue vehicles surrounding their posh house.

"Is that our house?" she cried out with horror. It was a rhetorical question because, undoubtedly, it was.

"It's gone," Paul gasped, staring at the scene in disbelief.

The driver let them out when the police wouldn't let them drive any further. Sunday broke out in a run, with Paul trailing hot on her heels.

Sunday and Paul stood as solid as mannequins, suspended in time, staring at the remnants of their annihilated, once-majestic stone mansion. The thick air stung Sunday's eyes as she breathed in the stinking, acrid air.

Tears began to blur the image of the skeleton of a chimney that stood as a mere haunting silhouette against the smoky sky. The grandeur of their house was transformed into a pile of charred stone.

Lacy Brewer, a familiar news anchor from a local news channel, stood in front of bright lights and a camera. "The explosion tore through the structure with a ferocity that left little untouched," she reported with a voice filled with unbridled excitement, her eyes widened in the bright camera light. "This once stately home simply blew up, according to neighbors nearby. What I'm looking at is total devastation."

Sunday looked down at the sound of a crunching noise. Tiny fragments of her once majestic, gleaming, and stately windows lay shattered like jagged diamonds scattered around and under her feet. Unable to control herself any longer, Sunday gave in to her tears, crying silently.

Through her tears, she stared at her favorite hundred-year-old oak tree, which she had always treasured as a place where Sunday often contentedly sat as she studied and read beneath it. It was now nothing but giant, ugly, scorched limbs that were attached to black crooked fingers—contrasting wickedly against the backdrop of a full moon. Pieces of torn, charred clothing draped the long, stately branches. Fragments of an ornate chandelier, which once cast a warm glow over her happy family, hung precariously beside one of Paul's favorite T-shirts.

The pain was unbearable. She'd lost both her house and home. Her life with Paul. Even her life with her children would no longer be filled with innocent happiness. In the blink of one lovely night, which had been filled with such hope for the future, she'd lost it all. Paul put his arm around her shoulder and pulled her into his arms. She stiffened, rejecting his move to comfort her. What a lying, deceitful person he had become.

An hour later, Sunday's brain-surgeon hands, usually steady and calm, trembled as she wiped her tear-streaked face with her perfectly manicured fingers. Her black hair hung in messy tendrils across her face. With a newly found hardened voice, she demanded, "I get Missy. She's my dog, and I want her full-time."

"Yes. You get Missy," Paul replied.

Sunday nodded; glad he'd given in because she would never part with her beloved collie. She was her treasured show dog. She'd be her only comfort now.

Simultaneously, they dialed their phones.

Paul's voice became filled with increasing stress and anger as he called one hotel after another, trying to make hotel reservations. "What do you mean there are no hotel rooms available?"

Sunday dialed Maggie's cell phone.

"Hello," Maggie answered with a sleepy voice.

"Maggie," this is Sunday. "There's been a fire."

"Was that your house that exploded? I am so sorry. Are you alright?"

"It's a nightmare. We lost everything but what we were wearing. On that note, the reason I'm calling is to let you know I've had to cancel all scheduled surgical cases for tomorrow. There's no need to report to work. I know Benny lives with you. Can you tell him?"

"There are no rooms left in the city due to the *Rolling Stones* concert at the *Bank of America Stadium*," Paul announced behind her as he ended his call.

"Do you have a place to stay?" Maggie asked.

"Paul's been trying to find a hotel room. Seems uptown is sold out due to the concert."

"Come over here, then. We have plenty of room. You'll be comfortable and you are welcome to stay for however long you need. We have dozens of empty suites where the girls can have their own bedrooms and bathrooms. There are family rooms attached as well. You'll have plenty of privacy. We'd love to have you. Please."

"You don't have to do that, Maggie,"

"I insist. Where are you now?"

"At the house."

"Stay there; we'll come get you. Bye." Maggie quickly disconnected the call, giving Sunday no further opportunity to decline the offer.

***

MAGGIE, KERRINGTON, and Benny stood with their friends for over thirty minutes, watching the simmering remains in shock.

"Let's get them home and get settled," Kerrington said quietly. "They're going to need their sleep tonight."

Maggie agreed. She sensed something was amiss between Sunday and Paul, but she didn't believe it was related to the fire. Kerrington must have recognized their tension, too.

Back at the house, Maggie quickly got them settled. "I meant it when I offered you a place to stay for as long as you need. No one occupies this area."

Sunday stood looking around the bedroom, stunned by its beauty, when Maggie handed her a pair of silk pajamas. Benny joined them along with Kerrington, who gave Paul a pair of his silk pajamas and a robe.

"What time do the girls come home?"

"They are on the way. One of the parents is driving them. I didn't think it was appropriate to have them away at a spend-the-night party. I don't want them hearing it on the news or from anyone else."

The doorbell rang as they were talking, and Ronnie escorted the girls to their suite. There, everyone exchanged tears and hugs, and Dorrie offered the girls pajamas. "No, thank you, Dorrie," May replied. "We have our clothes in our overnight bag." She turned to look at her mother. "Why are we here, Mom? Has something happened?"

Paul and Sunday led the girls into the sitting room and told them about the fire. They were given privacy to get over the initial shock.

"I'm so sorry, girls," Maggie said when they emerged from the room. "Breakfast is in the family dining room at eight. Wear what you have on. All of you will need clothes, and I suppose a lot of other things. We can go shopping at South Park."

17

Sunday wiped a tear from her eye. Maggie had never seen her boss and good friend cry and was at a loss for what to say next. The reality hit her hard. They needed so much more than clothes. They needed shoes, make-up, toiletries, books, school supplies, suitcases, computers, phone chargers. The list went on and on in Maggie's head. What a tragedy for the whole family. She especially felt sorry for the children.

***

AT BREAKFAST, initially, everyone looked worn out and emotionally battered, but after eating the hearty meal, they livened up. May and Kay began bonding nicely with Dorrie. Even laughter broke out at one point.

Kerrington had one of his employees write everything on a list as the family each called out what needed to be replaced. Professional shoppers were hired to replace much of the minor needs, allowing the family to focus on replacing clothing and personal items.

By the end of the day, housekeeping personnel helped them put things away and get organized. Dinner was served, and Dorrie took her new little friends for a swim in the pool.

The following day went smoothly. The au pair got the girls off to school, and the adults headed out to work.

Chapter 3

Bruce Russell

B RUCE RUSSELL, ONE OF THE TOP medical malpractice attorneys around, drew clients from all over North and South Carolina. He sat in his home office reviewing a divorce document for the third time— only because this one was personal. He was divorcing his wife, Lila, and since he wasn't a divorce lawyer, he needed to make sure everything in the document was perfect.

Bruce knew for some time that this day would come. His wife, Lila Russell, was quite a different woman than the one he married. Ten years ago, she had a kind, free spirit and an infectious, delightful laugh that captured him when he met her. She was a volunteer, wrapping Christmas presents for the Children's Toy Drive sponsored by his company and many others.

After they married, Bruce wanted children, and so did Lila, so she claimed. Years later, they were still childless, and Lila played the traumatized victim by calling herself barren. Lila suddenly declared she'd kept the truth from him. A bad car wreck resulted in her having to undergo a hysterectomy. When Bruce asked Lila where her scar was, she'd claimed they removed her uterus vaginally. She seemed pitifully affected by the tragedy.

Soon after, Lila insisted on enrolling in college to get a Ph.D. in microbiology, claiming she'd always loved science. She contended that since she wasn't going to be a mother, she might as well do something with her life. After that, Lila just wasn't available for him. Her schooling seemingly shut the door to discussions over having children.

Lila refused the idea of adoption, claiming, "I am not raising another woman's child. Period," Lila replied. "Please don't make me do that."

Bruce offered to hire a live-in nanny.

"And have a stranger living in our house? No. I'm afraid of strangers. And what if the adoptive or surrogate mother has mental deficiencies we don't know about, and we end up with a crazy child? I'm not willing to be a part of that, Bruce. I love you, but— no, the answer is no."

The issue of being childless built a wedge as solid as a concrete wall between them. Lila spent all her time at the university, and Bruce remained alone at home at the end of the day. His brewing anger came to a head when, one afternoon, he passed a park uptown where men played softball with their children. The tear in his heart widened, growing daily until it eventually turned to burning anger—hot, like a boiling pot of liquid bubbling over onto the stove.

He hadn't meant to stray, but Lila pushed him away. He was lonely and unprepared for his feelings when Tess Larken strolled into his office seeking legal help. The emergency medicine resident was being sued along with the hospital and five other doctors. She had simply taken his breath away from the first moment he spotted her talking with his paralegal.

Tess was a stunning petite brunette who looked quite sexy in her green hospital scrubs. Her voice was gentle and kind but firm, like a woman who knew her own mind.

"I don't feel like the hospital attorneys hired to represent me are doing their job. I'm here to get a second legal opinion."

Bruce didn't wait for her to be announced. He'd been drawn to her, unwilling and unable to fight the desire to know her. It wasn't a sexual thing. Bruce instinctively knew she was the woman he should have waited for— instead of marrying in haste.

Bruce accepted her case pro bono, and by the time the lawsuit ended, Bruce had fallen in love with her. He'd learned she was anxious to find a husband and have children the minute her residency was over.

Lila had all but pushed him into Tess's arms. Before all was said and done, Bruce could no longer resist. He'd given in and kissed her. Then, Bruce asked her to marry him, promising to divorce his wife. Tess accepted his proposal, and he gave her a diamond ring. She didn't wear it, but he wanted her to have it as a promise.

Bruce placed the document in the inside pocket of his jacket. He went downstairs and waited patiently in the living room for Lila to open the door.

Guilt tugged at his heartstrings. Was he being foolish leaving his wife? Had he moved too hastily? He would be the talk of the town. Did he want that? And what of Lila? She needed him. He could feel her desperation. Her need to cling to him.

"We have to talk," he announced the minute Lila walked through the door. "Tonight. Put your things down and meet me in the dining room. I ordered pizza."

"I already ate," Lila said dismissively.

"Then sit with me because I have some issues to discuss." Bruce walked off, leaving her no chance to respond.

Lila filled her wine glass and took a seat at the dining table. "I have a headache, so can we make this brief?"

When the pizza delivery man arrived at the door, Bruce's wallet was upstairs, so he reached into Lila's pocketbook to get cash. He stood frozen like a statue, staring hard at the evidence of her betrayal. Sticking out the edge of a side pocket, barely visible, was a packet of birth control pills prescribed in her name. According to the number of pills missing and the prescription date, Lila was actively taking them and had even taken one that morning. *Nothing is real,* he said to himself. *I'm married to a pathological liar. A game player who has played me like a fiddle.*

Whatever pity he'd had for divorcing her evaporated. Bruce could see Lila clearly now. She was a cold-hearted bitch who cared for no one but herself. She cherished her life at the top of the social ladder, being married to him, the most successful malpractice lawyer throughout the Southeast. Lila had a lot to learn.

Bruce removed the packet of birth control pills and stuck them in his pocket. Calmly, he joined her in the dining room and took a seat, prepared for war, determined to manage the conversation like he might interrogate a witness on the stand. He licked his lips in eager anticipation, ready for the final battle.

"I heard some interesting news today," Bruce started in. "My secretary offered me her sympathy for our loss. The whole office is talking about you losing our baby boy. Are we pregnant? Refreshen my memory. Have we had sex lately?"

Bruce watched her face fall and delighted in the awestruck moment. When the doorbell rang, he smiled. "You ought to get that."

Lila quickly got up to answer it–glad to escape the trap she'd been caught up in.

"Are you Mrs. Lila Russell?"

"I am."

"You've been served," the man said before hustling away.

Lila turned towards Bruce; her face flushed a deep red. "You're divorcing me?"

"I am. I'm going downstairs to get a bottle of wine. Make sure you read the papers thoroughly while I'm gone. Oh. And also, you'll need to think of a reason why I found these in your pocketbook." Bruce tossed the birth control pills across the table.

Bruce escaped to give her time alone and went to the basement, deliciously taking in the aroma of the wine cellar. He couldn't wait to return and hear what Lila had to say about the pills.

Like a bolt of lightning, a sudden flash pierced his brain, bringing painful light that traveled in regular rhythms through his eyes, electrifying his body. His limbs went rigid, making him incapable of controlling his body. Shaking violently, he sent the bottle of wine crashing to the floor before losing consciousness and falling forward down the stairs.

***

LILA GRIPPED the legal notice in her fist and ran towards the cellar when she heard Bruce fall. She found him in the midst of a frightening, violent seizure with blood pouring from his head. For a second, Lila contemplated not doing anything, thinking there was a significant probability he would die if Lila left him alone. According to the papers she'd just read, Bruce was leaving her penniless. No alimony. Nothing. She'd signed a prenup.

If she let him die, she'd get it all—but what if they found out about the pending divorce? They could accuse her of pushing him down the stairs.

Lila grabbed a bar towel, wrapped his head in it, and called 911. It would be the last good deed Lila would do for anyone. Something inside of her snapped as she explained the events to the paramedics.

Chapter 4

Emergency Department

A LTHOUGH MAGGIE and Benny worked in the OR, they were off duty when they got an urgent staffing crisis call from the ER. Dorrie was spending the night with friends, so they decided to respond and work an overtime shift.

Maggie took the opportunity to take Glenn aside privately in one of the ER areas that didn't open until later in the day. "What's going on with you?"

Glenn looked away, unable to look her in the eye. He seemed to be caught by the question. Maggie wasn't about to let him avoid her question. "You're not yourself. You haven't been for a bit. You're drinking is over the top, and I think you're developing a problem handling your alcohol. The way you spoke to Annella—it's not you. You were very hurtful at dinner, and we're all worried. There. I've said what's on my mind."

Glenn continued to look away before finally letting out a deep sigh as if Maggie had just released him from a private nightmare. When he looked at her, there was a trace of tears welling in his eyes.

"How do you live with it? The horror of that night. It changed me. Like they always say, life flashes before you when someone aims a gun your way. Split seconds of horror hit me hard before the bullet tore through my head. Every single day, out of nowhere, I see the image again, right there," Glenn pointed to the area in the ER where they were both standing when it happened. "You with a gun to your head while thieves forced Willow to grab all the narcotics and put them in a bag. How do you get past that? I watched them drag Willow out the door. All that splashes through my mind in seconds, and bam, I'm back there again, watching it happen in a place I love. How do you do it?"

"I don't, Glenn. I have the same memories. Well, not the same. I didn't get shot, but I held you on the floor, right there, watching the clock tick by until enough time had safely passed to call for help. I try never to look at the clock. I won't allow myself to look at the spot where you were shot. Or where I was standing when they held the gun to my head.

The sounds of a gun being fired on television brings it all back to me instantly. It's not that I don't suffer the same thing. I've researched PTSD and found my way the same way you will. Alcohol is not the answer. Try practicing Mindfulness. I'll get you some of the reading material that helped me. I will help you, Glenn, but please stop drinking before it destroys you. I love you. You are family."

"It's not as easy for me, Maggie. It's hard after you've been shot through the head. I've had to restore my thought process even to make my way back here. I'm not going to let it take me over," Glenn lowered his voice to a whisper. "I'm frankly scared everywhere I go. Sometimes, I feel like I'm losing my mind. Having a drink now and then eases my thoughts." Glenn pinched the bridge of his nose to keep tears at bay.

"Have you sought counseling?"

"No. I haven't. It's something I don't want to talk about, Maggie. If you hadn't brought it up, I wouldn't be talking about it now. It's my private hell."

"It's not just your private hell, now, Glenn. It's in our lives. All of us. It's affecting everyone in your life. Our family. Our household."

Glenn leaned against the counter, held his head back, and looked at the ceiling. Maggie knew she was making him uncomfortable, and she was hurting for him as well, but it had to be done- this confrontation. Glenn was spiraling out of control. "Fix it, Glenn. See a counselor and make the call today. If you don't know who to call, ask the chaplain. Talk to Sister Marguerite. She sees staff in crisis."

Glenn disappeared from the ER shortly after their talk. He returned an hour later with a more relaxed look on his face. "I talked with her. The Sister. I'll be seeing her often – for help."

Maggie smiled and placed a comforting hand on her friend and brother-in-law's shoulder.

Not an hour later, the helicopter nurse's voice blasted over the radio. Maggie turned up the volume.

"We're five minutes out with an open head injury. GCS 8. Vitals within normal range. Fell down a flight of stairs during a seizure."

Maggie and Benny headed to the trauma room as the secretary called out, "Trauma Code One. ETA five minutes out by air."

Glenn stepped to the head of the bed, gowned, gloved, and wearing his face shield mask. He was back in complete control again, as if he had permission not to be afraid anymore.

Doctor Sunday Richardson, a well-known, beautiful brunette and in-demand neurosurgeon, arrived. The two close friends acknowledged each other.

Bruce Russell's stretcher blasted through the ER entrance, with medics yelling out the report along the way into the room. Maggie pushed the red button on the trauma room wall to start the timer and transcribed the medic report onto the paper trauma chart.

A minute later, Bruce's blood loss was controlled by the physician stapling his skull laceration closed. Bruce was waking up which was a good sign. He was quickly transferred to the CT scanner.

Richardson stood beside Maggie in the scanner's control room while Bruce's body slid through the humming scanner. Within minutes, they knew the problem.

"It's an anaplastic oligodendroglioma," Sunday said, her voice low and filled with a level of sadness. "We'll need to confirm it with biopsy tissue, but I'd place a hundred dollars on my diagnosis."

Maggie caught the seriousness. Russell, a brilliant lawyer, had a brain tumor that carried with it an extremely high possibility of death.

"The location of the tumor will make it difficult to achieve complete removal without damaging critical structures within the brain," Sunday explained to Maggie before they entered Bruce's room.

SUNDAY BRIEFLY examined Bruce as Maggie stood by, wondering how they would take the news. Sunday evaluated Bruce's ability to receive the diagnosis and make sure the head injury wouldn't interfere with his ability to understand what she was about to say. Convinced he was coherent and able to process the complexity of his diagnosis, Sunday plunged ahead. She chose her words carefully and delivered the tragic news about the deadly tumor as gently as possible.

Bruce asked about treatment options.

"We need to get you into the OR as soon as the oncologist, a cancer specialist, clears you. They may want radiation or chemotherapy delivered before surgery. We've consulted them. They're on their way."

Lila delivered the perfect performance on receipt of the news. She cried hard yet leaped for joy inside. She'd been saved from the poor house. There was no way Bruce would go ahead with his divorce plans now. He was too sick to do anything anytime soon.

Moments later, Sunday's words lingered in Lila's mind. She could hardly bear to be in the room that was laced with the sterile scent of the hospital. Her casual response to the devastating news morphed into a tide of frightening and conflicting emotions. The doctor had carefully woven silver threads of hope through the fabric of tragic news, but Lila focused on what the doctor hadn't said. Death was a strong possibility.

She could see the despair on Bruce's face as the reality of the news took hold. Bruce's hazel eyes, once filled with light, appeared clouded as he processed the unraveling reality—a tumor was living and growing in his brain. It was big enough to impair his ability to fight the mightiest battle of his life.

Lila's gaze flickered to Bruce, and in that moment, her heart wrestled with a wild storm. Tears spilled down her cheeks again, tracing paths of sorrow alongside glimmers of relief. She was freed from financial ruin but wasn't entirely sure she could repair the damage in their relationship. Lila reached for his hand—a hand that felt so solid yet frail—and she realized that this setback could be her lifeline.

"Bruce," she whispered, her voice trembling like a leaf caught in an autumn breeze.

"We'll get through this together." Her words felt both hollow and profound. She could hear the desperation in her voice, yet deep inside, her private thoughts played a secret melody of relief that their marriage might be repaired. Bruce, with all his fears and uncertainties, would come to realize he needed her—now more than ever.

The irony was bittersweet. Lila had prepared herself for the worst—his plans for divorce had loomed over her like a massive thunderstorm—following her wherever she went. But now, amidst the cacophony of beeping monitors, IV pumps, and whispered medical consultations in a nearby room, Lila felt a strange sense of power.

"I-I can't believe this is happening," Bruce stammered, still trying to reconcile the news rumbling through his mind. "What if... what if I don't make it?" His voice cracked, revealing his vulnerability and his most intimate fear of his diagnosis. He felt exposed to the world—naked and afraid. Bruce rolled over and pulled at his hospital gown that felt like a prison uniform, visible proof of his frailty.

She wasn't going to let him hide. Lila came around to his side of the bed, leaned down, and firmly looked into his eyes. During the exchanged glance, an unexpected flicker of understanding passed between them—the kind that overshadowed earlier arguments and discontent. She was hoping it was a bridge in their relationship.

"We're in this together, Bruce," she reassured—her heart racing, caught in a tangle of uncertainty and redemption. "You have to believe that. The surgeons, the treatments—everything can turn this around. We will face it side by side, and I'll be right here no matter what."

***

THE FOLLOWING MORNING, Lila Russell fidgeted with her bracelet while patiently waiting for Bruce to talk to her again. He was due to be taken to surgery at any moment. Bruce awakened that morning a changed man, filled with a fury she had never seen before.

All morning, his hateful words and cruelty sliced through the air like a razor, each one shredding the fragile trust that had been built the night before. The warmth of their previous night was gone like it never happened. She shivered as she looked into his blazing eyes.

"Traitor." The word hung in the air, erasing every beautiful moment they'd ever shared. Lila flinched at the harshness, feeling each syllable of his tirade. She sat rooted in her shame, desperately looking for an excuse for all the wrong she'd done. The room felt smaller. Lila's heart raced as she listened, unable to move.

His cruelty was unbearable, but she deserved all of it. Shamefully, she recalled him pulling out a packet of birth control pills. She was driven to escape his room, his wrath.

In the hallway, she stopped Doctor Richardson's nurse, Maggie. "Does a brain tumor change people?"

"It can happen," Maggie replied. "Depending on where the tumor is. However, other things can come into play, like medications and such. Sometimes, patients complain that they don't feel like themselves. Don't forget he's most likely angry about the diagnosis, and he's trying to cope with the changes the illness might cause in his life."

Lila returned to her chair, back straight, with perfect posture, as always. People constantly watched her because she was Bruce Russell's wife—and he was powerful and obnoxiously wealthy. Whatever Bruce wanted, he got.

She thought about their property scattered throughout the South: a vast, beautiful historic house on Queen's Road in Charlotte, a Charleston oceanfront beach house, a Lake Norman house on the water, and a luxury yacht. Bruce enjoyed the good life and liked displaying his wealth. He said it showed he was successful and thereby brought him more business.

Nervously, she opened her pocketbook, pulled out her lipstick, and freshened her lips—thinking, after all, Bruce could return to his former self any minute. After recapping her lipstick, she looked down and slipped the tube back into her fine-leathered Gucci pocketbook. Lila's eyes froze on the blue divorce papers, and her stomach plummeted so hard she felt it might reach her feet. An awful feeling of angst and worry settled in as she drew her hands into tight fists. She was losing control over everything.

Lila's life had gone to hell in a hand-basket in one night. Truth be told, trouble had invisibly reared its ugly head in their marriage about six months earlier when he shoved her against the wall during a fight. She suspected that was when the tumor apparently began growing viciously in his brain, not making its presence known until tonight. It had been the first and only time he'd ever laid hands on her. She was sure that had to be when it started.

Bruce turned over in his bed and said, "Once the surgery is over, so are we."

"You're still divorcing me?" Lila retorted, shocked by the news. "Are you serious?"

"I am."

"Why? You need me now more than ever, Bruce."

"You lied to me, and you've become a boring and stuck-up snob. You've let money go to your head."

"You don't have grounds for divorce," she responded, working hard to keep her voice in control and fear-free. "I've been a dutiful, faithful wife, Bruce. I've fulfilled my wifely duties and never denied you once."

"Try to recall, if you might, Lila, with that thimble-sized brain of yours— when, exactly, was the last time I asked you to fulfill my manly duties, as you put it?" Bruce asked, rubbing his head like he was in pain.

Lila searched her mind for an answer but couldn't think of how to respond. If anyone had changed since they married, it was him.

"I have pharmacy receipts for birth control pills," Bruce continued. "And I can always subpoena your physician. Let's do this while it is not complicated, Lila," Bruce said, lowering his voice. "We don't have children. We have a prenup, which makes things so nice and tidy. I simply don't want to be married to you anymore. I found someone else who wants a family and children and someone who loves me the way you used to."

"My love for you hasn't changed, Bruce. Not at all. I'll sue you for adultery, you know."

"Not a chance," Bruce said. "Just sign the papers. I'll give you decent alimony for one year to help you get adjusted. But I want all the jewelry I gave you during the marriage back as per the prenup."

Lila cried back angrily. "Then—I'll sue her for **Alienation of Affection**. The courts will be behind me. You can't have affairs and ruin marriages in the state of North Carolina and not pay for it."

"Won't do you any good. Tess doesn't have any money,"

"Not yet. But once you marry, she will, and you'll have to pay her debt." Lila spat back.

Lila stood in shock, shaking all over. Indeed, all this wasn't over the birth control pills and not having children. Briefly, she wondered if the new woman in his life was the real reason he'd turned against her. Maybe it wasn't the tumor at all. Had he been such a mean man all along? If his whore friend won, Lila would get revenge if it was the last thing she did. Revenge on them both. Bruce and Tess. She'd rather die or go to prison for murder than give Bruce to her.

At that moment, Lila entered an unstable and enraged state, determined to get even. She'd be damned if she'd ever let Bruce see her cry. She was too proud to let Bruce know how much he had hurt her.

Lila had been foolish when she allowed herself to love Bruce so much. What was there to love about him now? He was a fierce fighter, and without a doubt, he fully intended to knock Lila right off the golden social ladder, where he'd placed her as his trophy wife. Lila sighed. She'd be left living in a small house, living off the salary of working in a laboratory. She ached inside at the thought of such a dismal life without Bruce.

According to Lila's prenuptial agreement, Bruce kept everything he had when he entered the marriage. She would leave with what she'd brought into it—two thousand dollars. He'd paid for her Doctorate, so that was hers. Plus, alimony. She would get that only because he committed adultery. That was in the prenup as well.

The divorce papers had come as a shock. The pain burned a deep hole in Lila's soul. She needed him to talk with her, but he wasn't open to negotiations. Bruce remained sullen and mute all the way up until they rolled him out the door to surgery.

As soon as his bed cleared the doorway, Lila called her attorney to see what advice she could give her about her lousy predicament.

"The news isn't good," her lawyer reported. "The prenup is locked solid. You didn't have children, so there's no custody or child support to dispute."

Chapter 5

Operating Room Neurosurgery

T HE SURGICAL SUITE was abuzz with activity, preparing for Bruce's arrival. Complex surgical instruments were placed with perfection on sterile tables to be used to remove Bruce's intricate tumor. The staff chatted amongst themselves as they always did. Except this time, their voices were laced with tension as a surgical technician reminded all to double-check their work. "Our next patient has doctors all over the place shivering in their shoes. He's a malpractice lawyer who has made hundreds of millions suing doctors and hospitals all over the South. I Googled him. It's true."

Maggie shushed the gossip as soon as she came through the door, holding her wet, scrubbed hands in the air, careful to keep them from touching anything. She quietly reminded them that although the patient was sedated, he might still be able to hear.

Sunday trailed directly behind Maggie, following suit, hands up, avoiding contamination. Two techs dressed them per sterile surgical protocol, each placing a sterile surgical towel on their wet hands. After being fully gowned and gloved, Sunday held her hands clasped in front of her, staring hard at the CT films one last time.

Maggie watched Sunday's piercing brown eyes darting quickly around the image, memorizing every single part of the tumor once more—as if the more she stared—the more it would change the outcome. Maggie sensed her nervousness. It was definitely an extremely challenging operative case. "Damn," Sunday muttered under her breath—and she was not known for cursing.

Maggie was glad she wasn't a surgeon standing in her good friend's shoes. They were both nervous. The odds were definitely stacked against Sunday—and if she failed at the task before her—a malpractice suit would follow them both out the door. Every licensed professional feared Bruce because of his reputation. Anyone caring for him knew they were putting their reputation on the line if anything went wrong.

The minute Benny, the circulating nurse, placed the headlamp on Doctor Richardson's head, tension escaped from her and trotted across the OR like a contagious plague, infecting everyone present and making them as tense as she was. Maggie sensed a feeling of doom–like an intuitive warning telling her she should take heed. She looked around the room.

"Let's go. The patient is under," Bob, the anesthesiologist announced.

As a well-seasoned neurosurgeon, Sunday's hands moved with precision. The tense atmosphere faded as her sharp, steady fingers displayed her well-honed surgical skills. The only sounds in the room came from the grinding saw, surgical instruments hitting against stainless steel, and the hissing of the anesthesia bellows.

Richardson used her headlight with precision, its beam brightly illuminating the intricate landscape of the surgical field. Within an extraordinarily brief time, Sunday had the skull flap open and had a clear view of Russell's brain. The tedious work began. Benny, the circulating nurse, moved the high-powered surgical microscope into place after ensuring the sterile draping was appropriately in place.

Glancing at the monitor, Maggie raised her eyebrows. Bruce's heart rate was rising. With questioning eyes, Maggie caught the anesthesiologist's attention. With a warning look, she nodded toward the monitor.

Bob responded, his eyes hunting information on the monitor screen. His voice was intentionally loud and urgent. "Heart rate's getting fast—blood pressure is dropping, too."

Maggie's eyes tore from the monitor to the complex anesthesia equipment. Her apprehension climbed. "There's an increase in CO_2, doctor. Looks like we have Malignant Hypertension, Sunday." Maggie was careful to keep her tone calm yet still colored her message with urgency. "Call a **Code 37**, Benny."

Maggie heard another "*Damn*" escape Sunday's lips for a good reason. A Code 37 was always a dreadful thing. Always. Sunday spoke with equal urgency without taking her attention away from the surgical field. "Maggie, drop out and help Bob get the situation under control," she ordered.

Maggie hastily removed her scrub gear while Sunday skillfully moved the microscope and covered the surgical site to keep it protected until surgery could resume.

"*Code 37, Suite 3. Code 37, Suite 3,*" Benny's voice blared across the OR speakers. He repeated the call once more. "*Code 37, Suite 3.*"

The doors burst open with OR staff shoving the life-saving **Malignant Hyperthermia Response Cart** into place. A Code 37, aka Malignant Hyperthermia, was a significant life-threatening event and was due to a severe and potentially deadly reaction to anesthesia agents. Severe muscle rigidity and a rapid rise in temperature presented a destructive effect on body organs.

Although the event was rare, all OR staff had to attend practice drills once every six months to ensure everyone was adequately prepared for the *all-hands-on-deck* event that was lethal if not brought under control immediately. Time was of the essence to keep the malpractice attorney alive.

"What's the temperature?" Maggie called out.

"103 degrees," Bob responded. "I've discontinued anesthesia and connected a new ventilation circuit."

Benny documented all the incoming information in the unique Code 37 document as the procedural information was rapidly shouted out for everyone to hear.

"Cooling blanket is active," a nurse announced, flipping the switch on the hypothermia blanket to help combat the rapid rise in temperature, which would climb dangerously high very fast.

"I'm inserting the arterial line in the left radial," the assisting anesthesiologist announced.

"I'm giving Dantrolene," Maggie confirmed. Dantrolene was the specific antidote for the reaction to anesthesia agents.

"Temp is 105.6. Heart rate 145. Blood pressure is 80 systolic," the updates echoed through the room.

"Dantrolene is in. The second dose is ready," Maggie reported, her eyes locked on the clock. Without missing a beat, she prepared a bicarbonate injection, administering it with practiced precision and reporting, "Bicarb is going in. Do we have ice packs in place?"

"Affirmative," Benny responded. "I've also notified the ICU to expect the earlier than-scheduled arrival. They said they need to know your plan, Doctor Richardson," Benny said in an urgent voice, looking directly at the surgeon, seeking guidance.

Sunday held her head up, looked away from the field for a moment, and evaluated the situation. "How are the blood gases?" she asked, her voice reserved and calm.

"Metabolic acidosis," Maggie called out, posting the lab results on the big computer screen for all to see.

As a result, Bob adjusted the ventilator settings.

"Surgery is canceled," Sunday announced. "Note the time on the code clock. Tell the ICU we're closing, and we'll be on our way at once," Sunday ordered.

In the locker room, Sunday added refreshing drops to her weary brown eyes. She was thoroughly pissed that Bruce's surgery was delayed. His tumor was vicious and growing bigger by the day. Time was not on her side in this case.

***

AN HOUR LATER, the battle still raged on with Bruce now in the Neurosurgical Intensive Care Unit. Maggie was happy to see her friend Nurse Bonnie was in charge.

"It's nice to see you again. It looks like our patient is stabilizing. If you have another operative case, you can go back to surgery. We got this," Bonnie whispered reassuringly.

"We do need to get back. The ER is transporting a kid with a post-ATV brain injury."

"See you later. I'll keep you updated."

"Holy Toledo," Benny exclaimed as he and Maggie made their way back to the operating room. "That dude barely made it through all that."

"Let's hope he survives the night."

***

NONE OF THEM made it back to Blanchard House in time for dinner. After ditching their hospital clothes, the three of them ate sandwiches in the Gilded Bar at Blanchard House. The alcohol didn't take long to lift their moods.

"I'm worried about our patient," Benny said. "You know, he's Tess's love."

"Our Doctor Tess Larken, as in ER doc?" Sunday asked, raising her eyebrows in surprise.

"I don't like the idea, and I flat out told her so. She shouldn't be involved with a married man. It brings nothing but trouble," Benny touted, taking another giant bite out of his turkey and Swiss sandwich.

"Well. At least he's a lawyer. He should be able to get a divorce in a heartbeat," Maggie added.

"Talking of heartbeats. I'm not so sure I can buy that many for him," Sunday said, her voice low. "Don't repeat that. I probably shouldn't have said that."

"We've seen his films. It's not like you're spilling the beans about something we don't already know. What a mess Tess got herself into. She thinks that man walks on water. I guess she doesn't know."

"It's going to break her heart," Benny said with resolve. "There's nothing we can do but stand back and watch. Poor girl."

"Well…" Sunday spoke, her voice uncertain. "Paul left me tonight. He's divorcing me–against my will, I might add. He's rented an apartment at the Residence at South Park. His girlfriend, one of his partners, is moving in with him. They're having a baby. I just wanted you to know because I expect it will become a hot topic of gossip in the hospital."

"Are you okay," Maggie asked, astonished.

"No. Reflecting on it, I feel like I barely know Paul anymore. He delivered the news like we were nothing but business partners renegotiating a deal. Unemotional and cold. I felt like I was meeting with my banker to discuss interest rates. Only I didn't do any of the talking. It will take me a long time to get over his attitude towards me. It took him less than five minutes. Then poof. Everything was over. He gets the girls every other week. I haven't even had a chance to find an attorney."

"What can we do for you?"

"Help me find the right divorce lawyer," Sunday said, her lips quivering as tears forced themselves from her eyes and trailed down her cheeks. Her voice broke as she spoke. "Just be my friend."

Benny got up and hugged her hard. "You got that. We're your family forever."

Maggie joined Benny in giving her friend a long, sweet, comforting embrace. "Yes. We love you, and we will always be a family. Don't you worry about that girl."

They didn't linger in the Gilded Bar for long after eating. All were exhausted from the long stormy day and turned in, ready to face another big day come morning.

Chapter 6

Neurosurgical Intensive Care

TWO HOURS LATER, Lila sat bored to death watching Bruce lying helpless in bed, listening to negative thoughts racing through her head. *How did I not notice anything? Was I really so wrapped up in myself as he claimed that I didn't see the signs of Tess— another woman taking over my life? How did I miss the giant tumor eating his brain? Was I too wrapped up in getting my Doctorate so that I could prove to him and his snotty social circle that I was a woman of value?*

Lila had to admit she never intended to get a job and go to work. All she wanted was a degree. The delightful piece of paper proved her importance. Lila looked over at Bruce and frowned, shaking her head with disgust, thinking. *Well, at least now I can get a decent job if I have to. What a dirtbag. I deserve more, and he owes me. I hope the bastard dies!*

Lila had no idea what was in Bruce's will or if he had altered it to include his new tramp as his beneficiary. Malpractice <u>was</u> a practical choice for her if he died. She was still legally his wife. Her mind raced through future possibilities.

Doctor Richardson planned to take him back to the OR as soon as he was stable and safe enough. Lila's mind was glued to the doctor's latest news that things could still go wrong. Bruce's diagnosis was a complicated one, and his future depended on whether Dr. Richardson could remove all of the tumor. If Lila could come up with a reason to file a hefty malpractice suit, it would solve her money problems for life.

***

FIVE HOURS LATER, Lila was continuing to fight her demons as anxiety raged through her body. She was angry beyond description. Angry with Bruce. Enraged with the surgeon for not getting the tumor out. A deeper part of her was even more furious with the doctor for having saved Bruce's life earlier in the day.

Lila struggled to get her emotions under control by practicing mindful thinking. But no matter how hard she tried to stop her ruminating behavior, it didn't work. The dreadful feeling of being trapped brought a sinking feeling in her stomach and a heavy pounding in her heart. Lila fought to get her breathing to slow down. As her head began to spin, Lila grew terrified of her thoughts, fearing she might spin out of control again and end up in the ER in restraints, as she had done so many times in the past.

On evening rounds, Maggie and Sunday chose the wrong moment to enter the room to speak with Bruce's wife. Maggie had called the woman arm candy earlier in a conversation with Sunday, implying Lila was a sexy blond bombshell and trophy wife with a nasty and rude attitude that belied her beauty. Maggie relayed an earlier instance where the bombshell raised a wagging finger at her in the ER.

"Nice of you to finally show up while my husband is here fighting for his life," Lila started the minute they walked into the room. "What kind of doctor are you waiting so late to talk to me?"

"A brain surgeon," Sunday responded wryly. "I've been in the OR saving a child's life."

Maggie noted that for a brief moment, Blondie seemed caught for words.

"How did this happen? I told them he'd done this before. Getting fever during surgery. You should have been prepared. And you didn't even get the tumor out. My God! Now, he's dying," she said, pointing to the monitor. "Someone should revoke your license because you clearly are inept at your job!"

Sunday quietly began her assessment, determined not to argue with the woman. With a hand motion, she showed she wanted Maggie to intervene on her behalf.

Maggie was quick to oblige and made a considerable effort to keep her voice calm, kind, and under control, as she recognized that Lila had an explosive personality. "Your husband is not dying. His vital signs have stabilized, and his latest laboratory results show that he is out of the woods.

He's making good urine, meaning his kidneys are okay. That's all good news."

"Well, he might be okay now, but I'm not. Not by a long shot. I've been sitting here waiting and worrying with no one telling me anything."

"Nurse Bonnie reported she's updated you on his condition every hour."

"She's not the doctor. I'm talking with our lawyer. He had this condition, and no precautions were taken. That's negligence. You should have asked me about his history."

Sunday glanced annoyed at Maggie and said, "I'm finishing rounds if you'd like to handle this."

Maggie's longstanding ER supervising skills came into play as she addressed Lila's rude behavior.

Lila's jaw dropped when Maggie calmly wrote down the number of the legal department on her business card and handed it to her. "Feel free to call our legal department about your grievances. The way you spoke to Doctor Richardson was abusive and not acceptable behavior. Our facility has Standards for Patient and Visitor Behavior posted at the entrance to every floor, and you may need to familiarize yourself with it. I'm sure you wouldn't want to have your visitation privileges suspended." Maggie then quietly left the room to end the confrontation as it only promised to escalate further if she remained.

Rage raced across Lila's face. *How dare the nurse speak to me in such a way?* Lila wanted to slap Maggie across the face. More than that, she visualized giving the nurse a sharp, brutal blow, making her pretty face not so beautiful for the rest of her life. Lila shook her head, trying to shake the image out of her mind.

Lila reached into her pocketbook with shaking hands and removed her elegant, jeweled pill case. With trembling fingers, she took out an anxiety pill and popped it into her mouth, swallowing instantly without water. Gradually, Lila began to experience a sweet relaxation as the wonder pill metabolized and floated its way through her body. As her muscles calmed, the trembling feeling lifted, freeing her from the sense of spiraling down the drain of no return. With her perfectly manicured hand, Lila wiped the tiny beads of sweat from her forehead as she recalled bits and pieces of her long history of anger management issues and the results they brought once she exploded.

As if watching a movie, intrusive thoughts swept through her mind. Memories flashed the results of her violent behavior towards others. Blood erupting from faces. Noses being broken. Eye orbits crushing under her fists. It was a magnificent feeling at the time, but along with the good sense of getting revenge, it also brought her great grief. She was placed into therapy at an early age and eventually gained control of her anger management issues.

Stop. Stop thinking about it. Lila said in her head. Things were better now. Bruce's love had brought her healing and built her confidence by making her feel welcome in his world of high society, a world she'd always wanted to be a part of. From the first moment he'd wrapped her tightly in his arms, she sensed she'd landed in a heaven-like atmosphere of safety and security. And now, it was gone. It had to be the tumor. If they got it out, maybe he'd love her again.

Lila knew time wasn't on her side. Bruce's latest attack on her self-esteem brought old behaviors to the surface. She was afraid, no, she was terrified of what she might do next. It was time to call her therapist.

Chapter 7

The Au Pair

WHEN WILLOW DIED, Kerrington had hired a German au pair to take care of Dorrie's every need. The au pair's duties were to escort Dorrie to school and any after-school functions. She also helped with homework (per Kerrington—only as needed), and she was to teach Dorrie how to speak German five days a week. The most important duty of the au pair was to keep Dorrie's life organized and make sure Dorrie learned how to keep up with her calendar of events and punctuality. Kerrington wanted Dorrie to be kept busy, so she didn't have time to dwell on her mother's death.

The au pair became permanent household staff, and now it was the end of the current au pair's contract, and per the hiring agency, she had to return to Germany.

When it came to Dorrie learning the refined lifestyle, Maggie stepped aside, understanding that Kerrington wanted her raised in the same manner he was raised. He made every effort to spend a lot of time with Dorrie and teach her. Kerrington wanted her to go to an Ivy League college, and the rest would be up to her, but Kerrington definitely wanted Dorrie to become a classy lady people would admire and respect. He'd taken her to work with him on many occasions and liked for her to attend board meetings. Kerrington even had her last name changed to Blanchard.

Kerrington insisted on the au pair because neither Maggie, Benny, nor he had the time in their schedules to get Dorrie to every event on time. Not to mention, it was how Kerrington was raised.

***

LATER THAT EVENING, after the debacle in the OR, Benny, and Maggie enjoyed after-work cocktails in the lanai while Kerrington took

Dorrie to the movies to see *Barbie*. Maggie chuckled at the thought that Kerrington had agreed to see *Barbie*.

"We have another interview tomorrow for Dorrie's new au pair."

"How long is she willing to stay?" Benny asked.

"She said she can stay up to a year."

"Where's she from?"

"Paris."

"Well, that's good. We can learn French. Or at least Dorrie can."

"Want to join the interview? Kerrington has a meeting."

"Sure. Why not?"

***

THE NEXT MORNING, Maggie and Benny met with Amelia Petit from Paris, France. To say she was beautiful would be an understatement. The slim brunette was dressed to the nines, and her makeup was not overdone but perfect. Benny seemed to become another person when he focused on Amelia. He actually stuttered before he held out his hand.

"Very nice to meet you, Amelia."

Amelia smiled and blushed, tilting her head down for a moment. The light from the window glazed against her hair, instantly highlighting the deep colors of her healthy mane, long and flowing as if she had just stepped out of the beauty shop.

Benny became tongue-tied while staring at Amelia. And it worried Maggie. Instantly, Maggie began to size Amelia up, wondering how she would fit in with the family.

Amelia flew through the interview with flying colors. She wanted to live in America to experience a new culture and learn more about the language. She was planning on enrolling in an American History college course at Queens University. Amelia far outshined the other applicants, and Maggie found her to be refreshing with a beautiful, relaxed sense of humor.

After getting Benny's approval late that afternoon, Maggie signed the

44

six-month contract with Amelia, as stipulated by the hiring agency. Maggie would extend it by another six months, provided Amelia's performance was satisfactory.

Maggie took her on a tour of the house, and it became clear Amelia had never stepped foot in a mansion before. Maggie laid out the rules. She would work eight hours a day, and the rest of the time was hers. Maggie showed Amelia her bedroom, which was next to Dorrie's.

"This is my room?" Amelia gasped, clearly astounded by the size.

"Yes. The rules are laid out in the handbook on your nightstand. The most important rule is you are not to bring guests of any kind into the house or onto the property. Ever. My husband values our privacy. You have free use of the pool, bowling alley, and other fun things, but you have to make sure the house manager knows in advance—in case a family member may be using it. Other than the exception of Dorrie, you are not to spend time in any area of the house where a family member is working, relaxing, or resting. The house manager, Missus Pretty, will give you a tour of the rest of the property. She will go over that with you. Also, the second floor is off-limits at all times. The floor belongs to Kerrington's sister, Annella Wryn. And the fourth floor belongs to my husband and me. Any questions?"

"The entire floor is Annella's? The movie star. Oh, my. I'll be living with a star. She's all over the magazines. May I talk to her?"

"Only during family meals. Please make your conversations brief and don't ask about her personal life unless she brings it up. Also, please don't stare at her."

"I got it. Wow. The house is so enormous. It's beautiful. I will love living here. I can't wait to tell my mother."

"That is okay, but no photographs or films are to be taken of the family for security purposes, including Dorrie and especially Annella, or any part of the property. Posting on social media about Blanchard House and anyone who lives or works here is grounds for immediate termination. Are we good?"

"Yes. Oh yes. I promise."

Maggie introduced Amelia to the Chief Housekeeper, Jenny Pretty. Ms. Pretty took Amelia on the rest of the tour.

***

AMELIA FIT RIGHT IN like a new pair of gloves. After Kerrington met Amelia, he approved of her attending family meals.

At dinner, she seemed momentarily uncomfortable about the silverware. "There are so many to choose from," Amelia said with a light laugh.

Dorrie giggled, stepped in, and showed her how to pick which utensil to eat with, depending on what was being served. "If you get stuck, watch Maggie and follow her."

Dorrie stunned the table with a litany of French and Maggie laughed, delighted at the sound. Dorrie quickly warmed up to Amelia. She sounded like a different child, and she was genuinely happy, as she had been before her mother died.

Benny chimed right in, laughing and trying to speak French. And, of course, Annella Wryn was all over it, too, speaking French. It was a beautiful start for Amelia.

***

AFTER DINNER, Maggie, Kerrington, and Benny had drinks on the lanai. All the large fans and the cooling system were stirring above to beat the oppressive outdoor heat wave, which was slowly crawling its way through Charlotte once again.

Maggie was quick to jump into the discussion of the lab and planting a hidden camera. "We should focus on who is entering and exiting the lab. Until at least you've solved your other plan. I want to know what they're doing."

"I still think Lamar Floyd should be involved," Kerrington stated.

"I still say no," Maggie replied.

"Why? He's the head of security, Honey. It's not like you don't know him," Kerrington calmly replied.

"Yes. That's true, but Lamar is too tight with his former partner, Detective Hanes, from homicide. When those two longstanding cop partners get together over drinks, no secrets are lost between them, and Lamar gets loose lips. I've given it deep thought since the explosion. I want to keep our private investigation to ourselves, that is if you—Benny—are willing to help. What do you think?"

"Well…" Benny stammered, looking back and forth between Kerrington and Maggie. "I don't want to get in between you two."

"For crying out loud, Benny," Maggie said, agitation clearly in her voice. "This is your house too, and we <u>know</u> the secret back there could very well be deadly. I think a leak to Lamar's homicide friend could hurt us."

"Okay. Lamar is out," Kerrington said. "What do you say, Benny?"

"Well. I could use another adventure," Benny said, laughing. "It's been a while since we tracked down the serial killer. I'll do research and find out what equipment can give us a better bang for the buck."

"So, that solves that," Kerrington said, leaning back in his chair and sighing. "It's clear the two of you lack exciting activity. I'm officially out of it for a bit, which is good for you thrill seekers. I'm leaving for Japan."

"I can't wait to see what you bring me," Maggie declared, clapping her hands in anticipation. She knew Kerrington's gifts were always top-notch and thoughtfully chosen.

As the conversation turned to other things, Maggie scrutinized Kerrington with a curious eye. He looked tired, which was unusual for him. His face was flushed. She placed her fingers against his forehead, feeling his skin, noting it was a little warm but not hot.

"See what happens when you marry a nurse?" Kerrington said, laughing at her, pulling away. "They're always poking at you and examining you, looking for problems."

The table went silent, and Kerrington instantly regretted his words. Benny's deceased wife, Willow, had been a nurse.

"I'm sorry, Benny," Kerrington said.

"No, man—don't be sorry. Don't. We all have to move along. Life goes on. It has to," Benny paused for a brief moment, reflecting. "For me, it has to. I could use an adventure."

"Cheers," Maggie said. "I'm so excited."

Kerrington laughed and got up. "The heat is catching up to me. I'm packing it in."

They all soon followed.

Chapter 8

Kerrington Blanchard

ERRINGTON WAS ON his way to the hospital board meeting when he experienced a scratchy feeling in the back of his throat. He recalled feeling weak and not like his usual energetic self during his morning workout at the house but didn't give it much concern because he never got really sick. Even with all his worldwide travels during COVID-19, he'd never caught it, and it had been years since he'd even seen a simple cold. Never the flu. Plus, he had been vaccinated for both. What was happening?

When Kerrington exited the car, his muscles hurt so severely he could barely walk. He also noticed a peculiar burning sensation in his hands. A prickly red rash dotted his fingertips, and within the quick walk to the ER entrance, some of the rash turned purple and spread over the entire palms of both hands. Kerrington's mind quickly backpedaled, trying to recall if he'd touched anything unusual. Just the ordinary things. And he'd foamed his hands prior to leaving the house. It was a Maggie rule.

Dizziness and weakness came fast. So did the blinding headache and sore throat. Kerrington tried to shake off the symptoms by telling himself he was probably dehydrated, but that didn't vibe with the fact that he always drank plenty of water and had done so all morning. He was cold and started shivering so hard he began having rigors—despite the outside temperature of a hundred degrees. When his chest began to burn, Kerrington bent over, gasped, and recognized he was seriously ill. His lungs and abdomen were burning hot like fire. Even through the severe dizziness, one thought came through loud and clear. For the first time in his life, he was actually acutely ill.

***

DOCTOR SUNDAY RICHARDSON hummed to herself, happily anticipating tonight's plans with her daughters. Since moving in with Maggie, Kerrington, and Benny, she seldom saw them. She was ready for some fun.

Sunday spent most of her free time holed up in their living quarters, looking for a house and trying to restore pieces of their former life. Her girls amused themselves playing with Dorrie, either in the pool or the movie room. She longed for order. Sunday needed sleep so last night she'd made sure to turn in by nine p.m., so she'd be ready bright and early to present herself to surgery.

***

SUNDAY sighed in relief as she pulled her surgical gown off and doffed her gloves, throwing them into the red-lined bin of biohazardous waste. Before leaving the room, she checked the level of the ICP line, which monitored the pressure inside the young boy's brain. He'd been in a car crash on his way to work at the hospital across town where he was an ICU nurse. Sunday knew the fellow, and he was a good nurse. She'd placed burr holes into his skull to prevent brain damage. She smiled briefly, thinking to herself he'd be all right. Sunday waved goodbye and made her way to the main ER corridor. When she popped her hand against the automatic door opener, both doors flew open wide. Her jaw dropped when she spotted Kerrington staggering in the hallway – near death.

Kerrington barely made his way over the threshold of the ER entry when he spotted Sunday. "Doctor Rii…," was all he could get out of his mouth before he collapsed to the floor. Sunday pressed the intercom button and paged overhead, "Cora and David to the ER Main Corridor STAT – with a crash cart." Cora was the Triage Nurse, and David was the Clinical Supervisor.

"Kerrington, what happened?" Sunday asked, hoping to get the underlying story out of him before he lost consciousness.

Kerrington didn't answer.

"Guys, we need a temp," Sunday ordered. "He feels ridiculously hot. Get him on a non-rebreather with high-flow oxygen, and let's get two large-bore I.V. lines going with Normal Saline wide open. Draw a rainbow of blood tubes and get cultures, if you can."

"Doctor Richardson, take a look at this," David, the black, heavily muscled nurse, said, motioning to the rash on Kerrington's arms as he scanned Kerrington's forehead with a thermometer. He announced to the group. "Temp 105.6 degrees."

Sunday took one look at the rash and vividly remembered seeing similar rashes on Ebola victims when she spent a summer in Kenya before starting her surgical residency. She whispered to herself, "My God."

"I… can't… breathe… ," Kerrington struggled to talk—his voice was a husky whisper. "I'm on fire," he said.

"We've got you. I've got you," Sunday replied, speaking in the most soothing voice she could find as she watched blood trickle from Kerrington's nose and mouth. "David, call overhead for Doctor Sloan to respond using BSL 4 protocol."

David called for a response overhead using his cell phone. He repeated the announcement. His request served two purposes. One was to make sure Glenn arrived, protected from whatever virus they were dealing with. Secondly, all the ER doctors and nurses were made aware that there was a highly infectious person in the ER. In response, they would close all patient doors and stop all incoming and outgoing visitors. Triage and all other personnel would review all patients with a different eye and look for fever, rashes, or other concerning symptoms. Security would stop all entry into the ER. Employees and visitors would be diverted to use the main entrance of the hospital. ER staff would enter only by the ER employee entrance.

"David, have security close the hallway at both ends."

The conversation took place within a blink of an eye as all hands moved quickly over Kerrington's body, assessing and working to save his life.

"We'll be giving you a dose of Propofol. You might feel a little stinging sensation on your scalp," Sunday warned Kerrington as soon as she confirmed Cora had obtained IV placement. She nodded to Cora as she began gathering the equipment for intubation. "Give him the loading dose of Propofol and give Rapid Sequence Intubation drugs."

"I'll call respiratory for a ventilator," David offered.

"No!" Sunday warned. "No one else can come near. We'll ventilate him with the ambu bag – after I get the tube in."

As soon as Kerrington's head relaxed and bobbed to the side, Sunday slipped the laryngoscope in place and quickly followed it with the endotracheal tube. David automatically connected the ambu bag and began to press in together, filling Kerrington's lungs with oxygen. Sunday, listened to both sides of the chest for air movement and announced, "Placement is confirmed. We'll get a portable chest x-ray upstairs."

Glenn entered the hallway, fully dressed in protective gear, and joined them on the floor beside Kerrington. When his eyes caught the rash, his eyes met Sunday's. "We can't bring him into the ER. Whatever he's got looks like it's severely infectious, and it's better not to take chances."

"Is it Ebola?" Cora quietly asked, her bright eyes widening with fear.

"I believe that might very well be our working diagnosis until it's proven otherwise," Glenn replied, his face grim.

"Jesus," Cora responded. Quickly, she donned a pair of goggles, wishing she had time to put on a gown. She double-gloved and passed more gloves and goggles out to everyone.

"Our entire household may have been exposed. Kerrington attended breakfast this morning," Glenn replied, disposing of his syringes in the red box. "That was two hours ago, and he was perfectly fine."

Sunday and Glenn exchanged glances that communicated their unspoken agreement that their hospital needed emergency high-level protection from the deadly infectious agent, lying before them inside Kerrington. They knew they needed a well-thought-out plan before moving him through the hospital to the ICU. "Any thoughts?" Glenn asked.

"Level 4 isolation for sure until we know what we're dealing with," Sunday said, easily sliding the breathing tube into Kerrington's lungs. "I've never seen a presentation like this."

"David," Glenn ordered. "We will move him to the exterior hospital isolation room now. Call Respiratory and have them set up a ventilator. Then, have them leave. We can run the ventilator without their involvement."

David activated his radio with the orders as all hands flew through the air—applying monitor leads and preparing for immediate transport. Cora brought the stretcher from the isolation room, which was found right around the corner from outside the ER. After they carefully loaded Kerrington on the gurney, they pushed him carefully and quickly the short distance to the hospital's exterior isolation room. The room was specially designed for the containment of radiation in case of a nuclear plant accident or as a containment area for highly infectious patients that needed BSL4 or lower-level isolation.

"David, limit the nurses to you and Cora. As soon as he's transferred to ICU, please report to the quarantine area. Make sure no one gets contaminated by you two."

Within fifteen minutes, the ICU managed to pull its act together. This involved finding the most proper room for the patient and finding staff to care for the infectious patient. They usually looked for nurses to volunteer for the assignment, as some nurses had children or sickly family members at home.

Sunday placed a central line as David arranged for the move.

Glenn made many emergency phone calls to different governmental agencies, which mandated the immediate reporting of highly infected persons. Then he quickly flipped through all the medical apps he had stored on his phone, flipping through picture after picture of rashes, trying to identify the cause of the infection positively.

Kerrington's rash was now body-wide–appearing to be one big, massive eruption. He dialed the Health Department hotline. "I think we may have a case of Ebola," Glenn reported. "The patient is extremely critical, and he came from quite a large household, indicating there may be many more victims. The CDC has been notified, and they are on the way."

"David," Glenn said quietly. "Please get the 9-1-1 supervisor on the phone and ask for total diversion of all ambulances except for Level One Trauma. Has the OB patient been diverted to the main entrance?"

"Got it. I'll also move triage outdoors."

"Good idea."

Cora rolled the see-through isolation tent over Kerrington's bed. It encapsulated the entire bed, ensuring no spread of infection would occur during his transport to the ICU. When security notified them that all corridors were secured and empty, they moved in synchrony, slowly and carefully, to the Medical Intensive Care Unit.

When the transfer was complete, Glenn and Sunday dreaded their new tasks.

***

UPSTAIRS IN THE OR lounge, Maggie and Benny were on a brief break, waiting for Sunday to arrive. Someone from the ER had called to say she was detained in an emergency. During their wait, they searched the Internet for spy cameras to plant behind the lab. Maggie's private cell phone rang.

Then, Sybil Good, the OR supervisor, called Maggie to let her know all of Doctor Richardson's cases had been canceled. Right on the tail of that notification, Glenn called. His voice was urgent, which set Maggie's fear off. *What the hell was going on?*

"Maggie. Kerrington is in the hospital. He's been admitted to MICU," Glenn said. "His condition is critical. He has a severe, life-threatening infection," Glenn announced.

Maggie gasped. "What type of infection?"

"I'm not sure. The Health Department is working the details out with the CDC."

"I'll be right there," Maggie said, getting up and putting on a disposable surgical gown over her scrubs.

"You can't," Glenn warned. "We believe he has a deadly infection that's highly contagious. We had to place him on a ventilator, and he's currently in a medically induced coma."

"Oh, my God, Glenn. This is so bad. What does all this mean? Is he dying?"

"He's very critical, Maggie."

"I'm coming. I have to see him."

"He can't have visitors," Glenn said, but Maggie had already disconnected the call and was out the door to MICU.

54

"What happened?" Benny questioned, hurrying to keep up with Maggie's pace.

"I don't know. Kerrington may be dying. He's got some weird infection. Glenn said the CDC is involved," Maggie announced as she swiped her ID badge to call the staff-restricted elevator.

"Oh God. If the CDC is in charge, that's unwelcome news."

***

THE STAFF-ONLY ELEVATOR opened into the Medical Intensive Care Unit. Sister Marguerite, having been notified by Glenn of the situation, was waiting for them. She guided them down a long corridor to a big, heavy door. **ISOLATION UNIT. No visitors. Employees only.** They did not enter the doors. Instead, Sister Marquerite led them to a viewing window to the left of the door. Glenn, dressed in full biosafety gear, pulled the curtain open wider so Maggie could see her husband.

Maggie's finger flew to her lips as she gasped. Glenn called her on her phone.

"Jeez," Benny whispered. "Lord, have mercy."

"You have to go home at once. I'm concerned both you and Benny may have been exposed. Kerrington travels a lot. I couldn't get travel information from him."

Glenn came to the edge of the large transparent glass window and spoke in a muffled voice. "Has he traveled outside the country lately?"

"Yes. Sometimes, Kerrington goes to two countries on a single trip. He owns hotels and businesses worldwide. I would have no way of knowing."

"Do you know where he keeps his passport?"

"I'm not sure."

"We need it," Glenn informed her. "The Health Department will want to see it. We've sent multiple types of smears and specimens to the CDC. Ebola is a working diagnosis for now, but I feel like we're dealing with something a lot more sinister here. We're lowering his fever, but it's still relatively high right now. Seems like every time we get the fever down and think we're gaining some semblance of control, it shoots back up in no time. Of course, we are aggressively treating his other symptoms as well, which are tachycardia and hypotension."

"I don't get it. Kerrington was fine this morning, Glenn. You saw him at breakfast–he was fine. He felt warm but not hot. How could he have gotten so sick so fast? It's so hard to fathom how he could have gotten such a crazy virus–and it must be really rare if you're having trouble identifying it."

"We're all thinking the same thing. Every member of the Infectious Diseases Think Tank is scratching their head in wonderment. He's under the Sepsis Protocol. And we're starting antivirals as we speak. The rest, well, we simply don't know, Maggie."

Maggie collapsed, leaning against the window sill in shocked disbelief. "It looks to me like he's dying, Glenn," Maggie whispered. "Tell me the truth. You may be his doctor, but you are also family—my brother-in-law and Annella's husband. She needs to be told about how sick her brother is."

"She's next on my list to call. To answer your question—yes, Kerrington is extremely sick, Maggie, and yes—he may very well be dying, but we're doing everything we can. I don't believe he has reached the extremely toxic phase yet, but remember, we're dealing with an unknown virus at this time. That makes it hard to predict which way he'll go clinically. He's a strong man–that's greatly in his favor. You do know we must place all of Blanchard House under quarantine until this is figured out."

"Are you serious?" Benny fired off in disbelief.

"I am–per orders from the CDC," Glenn responded. "I've notified Lamar. No one comes or goes from the house. And you two need to head directly home. Do not re-enter the hospital for any reason. You should also tell the housekeeper to have all groceries and other supplies delivered. No one leaves. Not even to go shopping. Don't be surprised if agents are posted outside your door. That's how serious they're treating this."

And so, they left. It was hard for Maggie to walk away from Kerrington's window, knowing it may be days before she'd be released from quarantine to visit again. The reality of the moment hit both Maggie and Benny hard as they snapped their NIOSH masks tightly against their faces and headed to the closest exit.

"It had to have come from the back of the estate, Maggie," Benny spat out, his voice filled with rage. "I know it did. I'm sure of it, but the question I want answered is what the hell is it—and how the hell did it get there? Just think, for one minute—if Kerrington got sick while traveling in a foreign country, through crowded airports and buildings —the likelihood of him being the only infected candidate is an oddity. How is it that **NO ONE** else has gotten it? Meaning, he had to have gotten it on our property."

Chapter 9

Ming Fu

MING FU STARED at himself in the mirror with pride. It was his twenty-fifth birthday, and he had to admit he looked as handsome as ever. Not one wrinkle yet. No more pimples. His skin was flawless. Ming turned his face from side to side. Yes, it was true. According to his sister, Ling Nui, Ming was the identical twin of **Yang Yang,** the highest-paid, most handsome Chinese movie star ever. A curvy, satisfying smile overtook his face at the thought. For sure, then, he could attract a beautiful upscale Chinese woman to be his wife.

He was proud of his Chinese heritage, and his highest goal was to be successful and impress his parents. They were constantly on the lookout for the perfect bride for him. Most importantly, Ming wanted to make it big and make lots of money. H wanted to pay his parents back for the expensive costs they endured to send him to America to attend college and become a scientist. He smiled again at the memory of his sweet, kind mother, remembering her voice, calling him *my beautiful boy.* She often verified his high intelligence by also calling him her *genius son.* He was a genius, according to tests administered to him in school. It wasn't just his mother bragging.

Ming ran his fingers through his short, jet-black, neatly combed hair. For the umpteenth time, he wished it were long again. Ming liked it longer and wanted to look like the popular American boys, but the last time he'd grown it out, when his father saw it, he instantly demanded Ming cut it. "My boy is not a girl. You will follow our culture." They hadn't understood how much it meant to Ming to twirl his index finger through his locks when he was perplexed by something related to his work. He hoped one day, his parents would bend on the issue. Ming grinned again at his reflection. His teeth were perfect. He flossed and brushed every day as he was taught. It was his job to avoid expensive dental bills. His mother taught him that good teeth make for a healthy body.

He took a satisfied breath. Ming had big dreams of becoming a worthy scientist. He wanted to add good to the world so his family would be proud. He wanted to save the world in some way. It would make him worthy of a fine bride. Having a wife was also on his goal list. Hopefully, he would find a beautiful Asian girl to marry. Someone from a high-quality family. A smart girl. One with high intelligence. He wanted a life partner with whom he could talk and share his science. Hopefully, she would bear him one boy-child who was as bright as he was, and then, of course, he wanted a girl-child that could sing to him like his little sister used to. He missed his family so much.

Ming picked up the stale cupcake his brother Tron had given him two days ago. His non-stop work had distracted him from eating it. Studying and working at his part-time job consumed his every moment, but it brought him immense joy. Ming was in his final year at *Holden College Institute of Science,* where he studied Genetics and Laboratory Science. After graduation, Ming would have his Doctorate, and he was sure he'd get an impressive job working as a research scientist at one of America's top private biological research institutions. He could work circles around all the scientists he'd worked with. It came naturally to him. It was his gift.

His face beamed with happiness when Ming thought about his future life, enjoying a career working in research as a true scientist. Ming revered genetic engineering, but his current job at the private lab left him stifled and bored as his talent was far advanced for what he was doing for a living. Ming was brilliant at manipulating genes, developing gene therapies, and conducting advanced research in various genetic engineering applications. Genetics talked to him, revealing their deeply hidden secrets.

Ming had a clandestine side hustle, unknown to anyone but his distant friend Mario. His friend had secured a vicious rare virus through the black market, for Ming to work with in secrecy. Not even his brother Tron, who was his boss, knew about it. If Ming succeeded at developing a vaccine cure, it would prove his value to the world. Visions of his dream coming true were so clear in his mind. The reality was almost within easy reach. He was so close to the end of his journey. Soon, he would finally experience the joy of success–the payoff he'd patiently worked for would finally come his way.

Ming swept the washcloth across his face and walked away from the mirror.

***

WHEN THE CLOCK hit five p.m., Ming filed out of the lab on his way home, trailing behind the other workers. His brother, Tron, joined him.

"I feel like having a big American burger tonight," Tron said. "Want to come to **Five Guys** with me?"

"No. Thanks. I think I'll eat my sandwich by the river. You know, unwind."

"See you later, then. I'll be late getting home."

Ming waved goodbye. As soon as Tron was out of sight, Ming circled back and made his way to the lab, looking back from time to time to ensure he was alone. His pace quickened with excitement at the thought of spending the next many hours in solitude, working on his secret project buried deep in the bowels of the lab.

Ming headed to the third-floor level and made his way to the secret entrance that led to a fourth-floor lab that apparently no one else knew about. He had accidentally discovered the hidden floor quite by accident when he went searching for a chemical kept in the closet on the third level. He had stumbled, making his way around the unfamiliar, unused area. When he'd reached his hand out to protect his fall, his hand hit the edge of a moving picture frame on the far wall. Concealed behind the picture was an elevator door that led to the glistening, large lab that no one else knew about. It gave the appearance of having never been used. The laboratory's owner, Mr. Blanchard, never came to the lab, so Ming was secure from the threat of accidental discovery.

Ming made a habit of constantly repositioning the picture after getting into the elevator and closing the door to ensure no one else spotted the secret elevator door. Ming pressed the button to the fourth floor. In less than thirty seconds, he was in his glory, headed to work on the life-threatening tasks of the night.

When he opened the massive, heavy steel **(BSL-4)** door, a giddy sensation erupted inside. The bright lights came on and bounced off the sparkling, clean, stainless-steel tables.

In the world of science and medicine, scientific words were used to describe the level of safety when working with hazardous infectious substances.

Biosafety Level 1 (BSL-1) Personnel work with microbes with little or no threat of infection. Workers wear basic personal protective equipment (PPE) such as goggles, masks, and gowns.

Biosafety Level 2 (BSL-2) poses only a moderate health risk. Staff wear (BSL-1) essential gear plus face shields when required.

Biosafety Level 3 (BSL-3) deals with microbes that can cause severe or lethal diseases that are airborne, meaning they spread through the air, like tuberculosis and West Nile virus. Respirators and coveralls may be required in addition to BSL-2 PPE.

Biosafety Level 4 (BSL-4) is the strictest. It deals with fatal viruses, such as Ebola and Marburg. Only a handful of this level of lab exists worldwide. Level 4 viruses have no treatment available.

Ming exhaled a tightly held breath. Yes. It was his lab, and his project frightened him most days because the virus he was working with, **Veridian XV**, was very deadly indeed.

The day Ming discovered the discreetly hidden lab years ago, he'd immediately purchased Veridian XV off the deep, dark black market Internet. The top-secret virus was considered to be a weapon of mass destruction, a virus so potent it could easily and quickly wipe out a country—even the world. Veridian XV was deliberately created for use as a biological weapon due to its potential for severe disease and substantial risk of transmission. The virus required containment in a (BSL-4) laboratory. Thus, Ming was ever so anxious to develop a vaccination cure to secure the world from such horror.

The Veridian XV virus moved with lethal, deadly force through the bodies of animals in foreign testing labs, therefore developing a reputation as a toxic virus that promised to deliver an extremely high mortality rate in humans. One scientist in Spain died eighteen hours after contracting the virus in an accidental exposure in a private lab. Great fear soon erupted throughout the scientific community. Veridian XV, indeed, was a perfect war weapon.

Veridian XV symptoms began within hours of exposure, resulting in high fever, respiratory distress, hemorrhaging, blistering rashes, and organ failure.

Several scientists worldwide were discreetly racing to find a cure before Veridian XV got into the wrong hands and caused a worldwide pandemic far worse than COVID-19.

Finding a cure would make Ming a science star and extremely rich.

Ming looked past the large window at his little monkey friends. They were all nearly dead. It was time.

He quivered with the most intense fear he'd ever experienced as he stepped into his BSL 4 suit and crossed through the automatic doors into the room. Ming's heart picked up its pace, hammering hard against his chest wall. He sucked in a deep breath from his respirator and clumsily made his way over to the refrigerator. Ming stared at the cure he'd made. He'd already drawn the yellow vaccine cure up into pre-prepared syringes with great apprehension before removing them. Carefully and gently, Ming injected each treasured monkey with what he hoped was the cure. He couldn't bear the thought of any of them dying. It was a feeling that didn't exactly go hand in hand with being a research scientist. But Ming wasn't a cold person. He stood in place for almost an hour before finally having the courage to exit the chamber.

Before drifting off into a worried sleep state, Ming repeatedly prayed for a miracle cure for his monkey friends.

***

THE NEXT MORNING, Ming awakened on his cot. His early morning dreams had been filled with significant worry about the explosion near the lab the other night. Ming was home with his brother, a few blocks from the lab when it happened. The nightmare began with a massive cloud escaping from the lab, which looked much like an atomic bomb explosion. Running through the city, he watched thousands of people die, choking to death on the streets. His parents exited the cloud, crying out to him; their eyes filled with great disappointment in him. As their bodies melted, he screamed out with shame. Realizing it was a dream, he forced himself to wake up.

Ming bolted from the cot as if it were on fire. Realizing all was okay, he wiped the sweat from his face and turned to face the monkeys. With great trepidation, he scanned each of his animal friends. His heart surged with joy.

Every single monkey was alive and moving! One was even making light chatter noises. Ming did a victory dance all around the anteroom. He held the cure. Only him! He'd done it. He'd pulled off a miracle. He must make more. Now!

***

MING'S JOY WAS short-lived, as he had to return to his real job upstairs. It brought him back to the real world of having to make money, which was a necessity. He was extremely far from being able to pay off the private loan he'd taken out to buy the virus. His college professor encouraged him to take on the project, and when Ming complained that he didn't have the money to pay for the virus, the professor offered to connect him with a powerful moneyman.

Congressman Brightman met with Ming privately, listened carefully to Ming's plan, read through Ming's notes, and agreed to fund the project as long as the loan remained anonymous. That money was due to be paid next month. As he made his way down the stairs, Ming wondered if Brightman would extend the deadline. Since he no longer had to pay for college tuition, he could save faster. Still, it would take much time. The loan was for half a million dollars. Ming took a seat at his usual workspace, his face still grim and worried.

"Stop what you're doing. The CDC is shutting us down. Mr. Blanchard, the property owner, developed a severe and rare infection. The land and every building on it is under quarantine. They say your risk is small because we're so far from the main house, but they've ordered everyone from the lab to go home and self-isolate for five days. Once the CDC clears us for return to work, I will call you. You will be paid for your time, and you are free once we take your temperature and make sure you don't have a fever. Thermometers will be distributed. Each of you will take your temperature every four hours, even during the night, and call me with the results. I'll be in touch. So, go now. Do not stop anywhere on the way home. You should stay in an area of your home where you can be alone until further notice. Keep your family safe, even if that means sending them to stay with friends or family. If you need a hotel room, please let me know. Thank you."

Ming wanted to vomit. His desperation swept over him, filling him with overwhelming dread. Now what?

Chapter 10

Blanchard House

MAGGIE WAS PLEASED to discover that Jenny Pretty, the head housekeeper, had calmly taken care of the quarantine needs. Maggie and Benny skipped dinner and headed straight to Kerrington's office to search for the passport.

Thirty minutes later, Maggie found the passport locked in the small safe in Kerrington's closet. Relieved to have that significant task out of the way, they grabbed a snack and went to the Blanchard House Gilded Bar.

Built during the Gilded Age, the elegant bar was round with shiny mahogany chestnut brown wood encircled by black leather-backed stools. It was fashioned after the **Round Robin Bar** in Washington, DC, which was famous for lobbying. Kerrington's grandfather was known for holding southern political meetings with high-powered, strictly male guests after dinner in the bar. Wives held their social gatherings in the rather large parlor, well away from the smell of cigar smoke.

In the back and to the right side of the bar were elegant booths with marble tables and lush black leather seating. Benny always chose a seat that overlooked the entrance, not that he was expecting anyone tonight—but it was a fascinating place to sit when Kerrington held political gatherings after a big dinner. During these events, Benny and Maggie learned much about governing the nation. Kerrington always encouraged Benny and Maggie to attend, but neither took part in general conversations as both recognized they were too ill-equipped to chime in.

"I don't remember Kerrington traveling to an Ebola-stricken area," Benny remarked as he sat.

"He would not have willingly gone to an infected area. Quite frankly, I'm hesitant to give his passport to anyone. It seems they should have their way of getting that information, and the first thing I'd like to know—does he even have Ebola? I heard we don't have a definitive diagnosis yet."

"Who knows what it could be since the National Institute of Health lifted the moratorium allowing scientists to engineer viruses to be more deadly and easier to spread? Talk about opening Pandora's box."

"Oh, my heavens," Maggie sputtered as she suddenly looked up at the television, grabbed the remote, and turned up the volume.

"You're right about that," Benny responded, spilling his beer as he set his heavy mug down with a thud, diverting his full attention to the broadcast.

A Bright red **BREAKING NEWS ALERT** flashed on the Charlotte local news.

"That's us, Benny," Maggie announced. "The CDC is pulling into our drive." They watched, stunned, as a caravan of official-looking CDC trucks pulled into Blanchard House driveway.

"I'll make sure Dorrie is asleep, so she doesn't see what's happening," Benny snapped as he shot up and rushed out the door.

Maggie took off behind him and ran headlong into Lamar, who was in full response mode with a security team hot on his heels.

"Do NOT let them into the main drive," Lamar ordered, "Direct them to the service drive. I'll meet them out back."

Officers rushed out the front door and down the drive to greet the invaders.

When Benny returned to the entrance hall, he was out of breath. "Dorrie's asleep. Sunday, and the girls are upstairs. They can't see this part of the house. Sunday can't know about the lab. She has enough to worry about right now without us throwing a curveball her way. What the hell is happening, Maggie?"

"Beats me. Whatever it is, it's big," Maggie replied, eyes widened with curiosity. "I can tell you one thing. They're not here for Kerrington's passport; surely, they're not here to swab the house at this time of night. I'm guessing they're here for the lab?"

Benny and Maggie took their drinks and retreated to the back lanai, where they secretly watched the commotion going on by the lab on the far side of the estate. It was hard to tell what the CDC team was doing because gardens surrounded the building, and it was dark. Lamar stood to the far side, watching the operation far enough away from the lab that he didn't need protective gear.

Unable to bear it, Maggie and Benny marched across the five-acre expansive lawn to where Lamar stood. "Can you see what they are doing?" Maggie quietly asked as they lowered themselves, hiding behind the tall hedges. They edged closer to the workers in Hazmat gear.

"They're carrying boxes," Benny whispered back.

"Congressman Brightman ordered it shut down and scrubbed," Lamar explained in a deep voice as they sidled up beside him. "The CDC declared they're taking possession of every item in the lab to ensure the virus that attacked Kerrington didn't originate here. I told them in no uncertain terms that the lab team here is working on a new Alzheimer's drug that has shown great promise. It was kept top secret because they didn't want the formula stolen. They not up for listening."

"I'll say," Benny piped up. "They mean business."

"Kerrington does not have Ebola," Lamar announced. "I just got off the phone with Glenn. Kerrington caught a virus that is believed to be some form of new biological weapon. Veridian XV. It's similar to Ebola but much more lethal. It's a hemorrhagic fever type. Let me manage these people," Lamar said. "This will be an all-night event. Congressman Brightman wants to get out of hot water and make sure he has proof that their project is not related to what made Kerrington sick. He's setting up a special committee to investigate the events surrounding Kerrington's exposure."

Maggie looked at her watch. It was almost midnight. "Let's go, Benny. He's right. It's getting late," she said in resignation.

When Maggie returned to her room, she saw her cell phone blinking, showing she had a new message timed two hours earlier. It was from Glenn. He was on night duty and needed to talk to her urgently.

Maggie speed-dialed him, and he was quick to pick up. His voice sounded troubled and tired. Glenn, to Maggie's dismay, confirmed Kerrington's diagnosis. It was Veridian XV.

"I'm not familiar with it," Maggie admitted.

"Not many people are. It is considered a biological weapon of mass destruction. All the infectious disease gurus are spinning their brains, holding intense think tank sessions, even now, in the middle of the night, trying to get a pin on how Kerrington got it. Currently, there are no other cases anywhere else in the world that we know of—at least for now," Glenn said with a final sigh. "We should pray it stays that way because if it spreads, it will cause such a massive pandemic, that carries with it the promise it will make COVID look like a tea party."

Maggie placed her cell phone on the bedside table and stared straight ahead for the longest time before finally burying her face in her hands, rolling back on the bed, and sobbing. Terrifying fear laced together with the thoughts that Kerrington might very well die was more than she could take.

Dover jumped up on the bed and whined. He laid his face between his front paws and watched Maggie, rubbing his nose gently against her hair.

***

THE NEXT MORNING, Lamar met with her when she exited the Master suite door and entered the foyer. "I just met with the house staff," Lamar said, clearing his throat. "I was soothing their ruffled feathers and fear, which is justified. They're calmer. I've hired more security staff."

"So, what was the CDC outcome?" Maggie asked.

"They stripped the lab—all of it. I didn't go down personally to see for myself, even though they said it had been scrubbed and was safe— but I did fly a drone down into the lab, and it looks empty. Everything is gone."

"Well, that's a relief – but I still don't trust them."

"One more thing," Lamar reiterated. "The CDC said they'll oversee the media. No talking to anyone. Period."

***

GLENN CALLED often with updates on Kerrington's condition. "We are waiting for the CDC to give us more information. They are being very close-lipped about everything. Kerrington is still in critical condition. We're treating him aggressively with broad-spectrum antibiotics to cover the possibility of any bacterial involvement, although the cultures are clean so far. And we're giving antivirals."

"How is his fever?" Maggie asked.

"Not giving in very much to antipyretics. It's a problem." Maggie became quiet. She was exhausted, and there didn't seem to be anything else to ask. It was all unwelcome news anyway.

Glenn reminded her to watch all the house staff closely, and Maggie confirmed she was making frequent health rounds. "So far, everyone here is well."

***

LATE IN THE EVENING, Benny caught Maggie resting in the Solarium. He grabbed two cold beers, popped the tops, and sat down beside her.

"I don't trust them," Benny said, his voice low and worried. "The CDC. Look at what all they hid from us during Covid. I want to go down there and see for myself if they took everything. Lamar could very well be in cahoots with them all."

"That would not surprise me. Not one bit."

"I planted a video camera," Benny whispered, leaning in.

"Where?"

"Outside the lab door. I want to see if they're lying. Let's just see if anyone comes or goes. Then we'll know for sure. If everything is gone, there should be absolutely no reason for anyone to enter the place."

"As soon as we clear quarantine, I'm going down there," Maggie insisted.

69

"Not without me, you're not," Benny shot back.

"Whatever. You know, there's one thing I can't figure out. Supposedly, this Veridian XV virus is a BSL Level 4 virus, requiring the highest level of safety suits to work around it or take care of anyone infected with that level of virus. Yet, we were in the lab and went through every level. Not one of the floors was equipped to handle Level 4 BSL."

"So why is the CDC all freaked out about it being here? It's not their project. Or, maybe, they know more than they're letting on."

"Good point, Benny."

"We've got a lot of investigating to do."

***

IN SILENCE, they watched the news build minute by minute. The locals expressed their anxiousness about the new Veridian XV virus being in their city. They demanded that the city government answer questions—which they hadn't been able to do up to this point.

As much as the mayor tried to keep panic at bay, by the end of the day, it made a mighty presence that enveloped the entire metropolitan area. People stayed inside their homes, didn't answer their doors, didn't send their children to school, and double-masked if they had to go out. It was as if the Covid 19 pandemic was back, terrifying people. Hospital staff called out, afraid to go to work. People stopped coming to the ER unless they were near death and were forced to come.

Despite announcements that there were no other victims of the virus, many people fled town, causing massive traffic jams that led out of the city. The interstates leading to the heavily populated city were barren. Emergency Response Coordinators brushed off their Pandemic Plans, and community leaders conducted their parts of the plan. All involved persons carried out pressing tasks. County responders counted the stockpiles of medical supplies located in various hidden warehouses scattered throughout the county. Hospitals did an inventory of all masks, gowns, gloves, and high-level protective gear. Patient ventilators were counted. Urgent calls were made to find extra supplies, if needed. Fear stretched all the way to the state level, getting the Governor's attention. Getting ahead of the game and documenting precise inventory amounts was crucial. Heads would certainly roll if anyone found themselves lacking supplies.

Unnecessary surgeries were canceled just in case surgical staff needed to report to the ER and ICU for the expected surge of infectious cases.

Chapter 11

Quarantine

MAGGIE BURIED HERSELF deep in the trenches of Veridian XV research. The more she learned, the more frightening it became. Information was sparse, but it seemed it became alarmingly clear it was pretty similar to Ebola and other hemorrhagic fevers. One fact was inevitable – it was a very deadly and vicious virus. Unlike Ebola, the symptoms appear anywhere from one to five days after exposure. The signs and symptoms range from high fever, severe headache, fatigue, muscle pain, abdominal pain, gastrointestinal issues, difficulty breathing, profound weakness, and severe rash. Kidney and liver complications were shared, along with bleeding.

The only good news was the quarantine time after exposure was five days, meaning her time in confinement would be over soon, as long as she didn't have a fever.

Maggie received frequent reports from Glenn over the phone. Glenn was in hospital quarantine but still attended all meetings with the CDC, the health department, and Kerrington's physicians via Zoom conference. Therefore, he kept Maggie up-to-date with the latest information regarding Kerrington's condition—which was like riding a roller coaster with many severe downhill sharp curves and turns.

Without being allowed to see him, Maggie could only use her vivid imagination and experience, as a critical care nurse, to paint pictures in her mind of how Kerrington might look. And with each day, she became more insistent about receiving numbers. – all of them. Glenn caved as Maggie's persistence grew. Finally, he sent her faxes of lab results and vital signs. Maggie understood more. Kerrington was dying.

MAGGIE STOOD BEFORE the vast wall of windows overlooking the estate. The overcast, misty day mirrored the dark, miserable emotions brewing within her.

Her carefully crafted defenses against angst, worry, and sorrow, which she had built over the years, were deteriorating. Her nursing diagnosis was Ineffective Coping Disorder. Maggie sensed her world had once again become an unstable house of cards, ready to collapse any minute.

Without Kerrington, every day required heroic effort to move forward and perform even the simplest tasks. There was nothing to look forward to. Time brought terror and alarm. Every hour, Maggie pondered over her circumstances. Her anxiety increased two-fold as her vivid imagination swept her into places she didn't want to go. Eventually, the choking anxiety forming inside seemed like an expanding volcanic mountain, ready to erupt and spill her quivering nervous guts everywhere.

Maggie turned away from the window and crawled back into bed, burying herself beneath her luxurious bedding. Dover quickly joined her, snuggling close like always, knowing and sensing she needed comfort.

Moments later, Benny pounded on Maggie's door. "Maggie! Open up."

"Come in," Maggie called back, leaning up.

Benny threw the door open. He was standing beside Sunday in the doorway. "Glenn called. The quarantine has been lifted. We can rejoin the world."

"I can't," Maggie replied. "Not today."

"Really? If you can't do that, Maggie, it's time you sought counseling. Your mood is affecting the entire household. You've got everyone tiptoeing around like they're on eggshells, in mourning, and I can't take it anymore. Neither can Dorrie. Or Sunday. Kerrington isn't dead. Get up, get dressed, put your best foot forward, and hug our daughter. Then, we're going to the hospital. We'll visit Kerrington and be as close to him as we can get. He needs you."

"Our first case starts in two hours," Sunday added, using her voice of authority. "We have a lot of cases today. So, move fast."

"Shut the door, then. I have to get ready."

AFTER MANY DAYS of no further outbreak, people began to return to their everyday lives again—eager to feel all was well again.

Maggie was eager to see Glenn again but was shocked at how pale he looked, having no exposure to sunlight during his confinement, which had been strict because he'd had known intimate exposure to Veridian XV during Kerrington's resuscitation.

"Unfortunately, Kerrington isn't showing improvement," Glenn said, his voice low and gentle. "You'll be able to view him through the window of his new room. They moved him into a specially designed unit. He's the only patient."

A heavy pressure spread across Maggie's chest, bringing with it a brief wave of nausea when she saw Kerrington critically ill on a hospital bed. She placed her fingers up to the thick, cold glass window and let out a light gasp of terror. His beautiful, healthy, tanned body was severely bloated and covered with a wicked purplish rash. Although she knew he was on a ventilator, the sight of Kerrington with a tube coming from his mouth gave her a light shiver. Like most critical patients, he was covered with IV lines and tubes going in every direction that freakishly reminded her of how dead kudzu vines looked like in winter. She counted seven IV bags. Big ones. Little ones. Tears formed in the edges of her eyes as her lips began to tremble. Maggie knew enough from what she saw that everything she'd feared was accurate. His condition was moribund, and he was dangerously near the point of organ failure.

***

LATE IN THE AFTERNOON, several lawyers arrived at Blanchard House along with Kerrington's Chief Financial Officer and Chief Executive Officer. Maggie and Annella were pulled into the meeting.

The meeting was brief, and Maggie was left with a stack of papers to review. It was Kerrington's wish that Maggie be included in all business decisions and that she would step into his place if he died. He had talked with her about his wishes, and at the time, Maggie dismissed the possibility of that ever happening anytime soon because he was such a magnificent picture of health. Tanned. The kind of gorgeous man that belonged on the cover of

GQ magazine. He cared for his body by working out religiously. His skin was impeccable, thanks to his religious use of expensive body products. Kerrington was also a financial genius. *How the hell am I supposed to replace him?* Maggie wondered, feeling inept and helpless. *It's like a horrible joke.*

Annella was to control her portion of the company, and she elected not to get involved, which was her choice because her part of the business already had people in place to run things.

Maggie was overwhelmed with significant worry. Facing his corporate people and the stacks of papers and binders brought home the reality that Kerrington may never come home.

But the one strange thing—the thing that mattered the most to Maggie—wasn't here in the piles upon piles of papers. The lab contract was missing. She'd plundered through all the files, cabinets, and desk drawers in his office while looking for his passport, but the contract was nowhere to be found.

Maggie's heart burned inside with warm, deep hunger—a craving filled with severe loneliness that only Kerrington could fix if she could just hold his hand one more time.

She searched the house, calling out to Dover, her best friend, to follow her. She was on a serious hunt, determined to find the needed paperwork.

***

BY DINNER TIME, Maggie's mind was exhausted. She'd did not find what she was seeking.

Maggie glanced over at Amelia to thank her when she was caught by surprise. Amelia's eyes were glued to Benny's, and he was enjoying her glances. She couldn't help but wonder what the hell was going on between them. Whatever it was – it definitely was not a good thing. It was pretty inappropriate.

After Willow's kidnapping and tragic death, Benny had netted forty million dollars for Willow's wrongful death. The hospital paid it for not providing proper security. Dorrie received forty million as well. Her money went into a trust fund, not to be touched until she was twenty-five. And Maggie got thirty million for pain and suffering. She had set up a charity fund, put all the money in it, and built a battered women's shelter, calling it **Willow Haven**. Money always spelled trouble.

"Benny. Will you join me for a drink after dinner? I have some hospital stuff to discuss."

***

AFTER DORRIE WENT TO BED, Maggie met Benny in the Gilded Bar for cocktails, knowing it was his favorite room in the house. The dark mahogany usually provided Maggie with comfort—but not tonight. Maggie was nervous about talking with Benny about Amelia.

"So. What's the latest?" Maggie asked, tweaking Benny, hoping he'd confess about Amelia.

"I have the camera recording set up and checking it throughout the day. It's a good piece of surveillance equipment. Great visibility. So far, nothing has happened—but you never know. I've got a feeling all is not well."

"Do you ever think about the night of the explosion?" Maggie asked.

"I do, as a matter of fact—I think about it a lot."

"What do you think?"

"You don't want to know," Benny replied. "I'm as bad as you are when it comes to having an overactive imagination."

"Spill it, Benny. Come on," Maggie replied dramatically.

Benny paused for a moment, looking hard at Maggie, his eyes filled with concern. He took another sip of his drink. "I do wonder if what made Kerrington sick came from our lab. On the night of the explosion, he went in there without protection. There could have been a leak. Maybe there was another secret project going on. A possible secret level BSL 4 area we don't know about. Okay. There. I said it. That's what I think."

"Amen. I needed to hear you say that because it's been my biggest fear."

"The question is, what do we do now?"

"We follow anyone who enters or exits the building, and then we question them about why they're here if the lab is closed. Is anyone lying to us? There are too many unanswered questions. I'm convinced Kerrington got the virus here. It's eerie, and I can't shake the feeling," Maggie admitted.

"I agree." Benny shook his head aggressively in acknowledgment. "I'll call Landon Sykes, the drone guy we used for Willow. I bet he has great spyware."

"That's a great idea," Maggie agreed. She paused an uncomfortable moment before changing the subject. "There's something else," Maggie said, her voice stuttering.

"What's … um… what's going on between you and Amelia? I saw you making serious eyes over each other at dinner."

"That is flat-out not true, Maggie."

"Well, maybe you aren't aware of it then, but I know what I saw, and you can't make goo-goo eyes at Amelia in front of Dorrie. She's your daughter, and that makes you Amelia's employer. If things go bad, she could sue you for inappropriate conduct. Don't risk putting your newly found wealth at risk, Benny. It's easy to handle," Maggie went on. "Except for dinner, stay away from her. Stay downstairs."

"I got it. Say no more. I won't look her way again."

Chapter 12

Neurosurgery Operating Room

THE DIMMED OR suite held an unusually tight silence except for the occasional tinkling of instruments against each other or the sound of suction. Sunday had asked for the music to be turned off, a sign she was tense and worried. With the exception of essentially required surgical dialog, no one spoke throughout the surgery, and it had been almost twelve hours.

Maggie shifted from one foot to another, praying for Bruce Russell's life and his brain. As far as she knew, his wicked wife hadn't contacted the legal department. Otherwise, she would have been notified. Maybe Lila Russell was just a neurotic, aggressive woman who liked being abusive because it made her feel powerful.

Sunday worked diligently at removing the tumor, and they were almost done. They had maybe an hour or two to go.

Maggie was annoyed by having to wear a diaper. Not that she'd needed it. So far, she'd managed to hold her urine without having to relieve herself and briefly wondered if Sunday had been forced to go in her diaper. She didn't smell anything.

When she heard a Code Blue announcement, Maggie's mind at once shot to thoughts of Kerrington. She couldn't figure out where the code was being held. As she blinked hard to keep her eyes free of tears, she shot off a prayer for him. *Please don't let him die, Lord. Please.* His situation was becoming increasingly difficult for Maggie to handle as each day ticked by. Life had become similar to a Spinning Tea Cup ride of unwelcome news, then good news, as Kerrington went from near death to being stable, then back at death's door, all within days of each other. She wondered if all the stress would continue to stack upon her each day until it eventually forced her to take medication to keep herself in control. All she did was worry all day, hour after hour, to the point her stomach was twisted in knots that wouldn't calm.

It was taking a toll on Maggie. She'd never had a nervous breakdown, but that's where she feared she was headed.

The latest symptom to arrive was tremors. They started three nights ago. Maggie could feel them trekking, building, and running rampant throughout her body when she tried to go to sleep. Usually, a Tylenol eased it—and so far, the tremors hadn't appeared in the OR, but if they did, she realized she wouldn't be able to scrub in anymore. Maggie glanced over at Benny. He, too, was full of sadness.

All Benny really wanted in life was a wife and maybe a son. Maggie had been too hard on him about Amelia. Clearly, he was pretty taken with the woman. Maggie dwelt on the romance building between the couple. Suppose Amelia got another Au Pair job. Then, Benny wouldn't be at risk of a lawsuit and could date her openly. *Suppose he married her?* Maggie wondered. She actually liked Amelia a lot, and so did Dorrie. Amelia got along well with Kerrington, Annella, and Glenn. Maybe she might actually fit in quite well with the blended family. Perhaps she should back off and let them fall in love. Possibly it was the right thing.

The sounds of surgery snapped Maggie back to the task at hand. She'd worry about that later.

***

IN THE ICU, LILA FIDDLED with her watch, eager for Bruce to return to his room. The feeling of helplessness was brutal, spinning her around and around like a Ferris Wheel, dumping her stomach with every drop.

Do you really have to go to such to such lengths? Are you that desperate? Lila knew the answer. She was, indeed, that desperate. Lila reached into her pocketbook, opened her pill bottle, and popped a happy pill. Something to ease her fear and anxiety. Again.

She was convinced the world had it in for her—plotting against her every day, and the answer was clear. She had to protect herself. It wouldn't be easy, but then again, it never was, not when it came to being loved. And especially when it came to men. Cheating men would just as soon toss a wife to the side of the road for a hot new fling.

It wasn't fair. If she didn't even the score for herself—no one else would. So that was that. Lila spent the next several hours dwelling on thoughts of Bruce being with Tess. Revenge options wrangled about in her mind, such as poisoning or drugging him, but none of them were proper for a hospital setting. She could never get away with it. Lila was tired of thinking about it when suddenly, an idea that could work in a hospital came to mind. Something that would appear to be the hospital's fault. Lila would give him an infection. And she had the resources to pull it off. But she had to hurry. Time was of the essence.

Lila checked in with the nurse and asked when Bruce would return to his room. He assured Lila it would be well into the night shift. "Not until after midnight was my latest update, but things are going well, so try not to worry."

"That's hard to do. I think I'll take a walk for a bit, then, to ease my nerves."

"I understand," the nurse said before checking his watch and heading into another patient's room.

Lila made a beeline dash for the lab where she worked while getting her PhD. By the time she arrived, she was hot, with a prickling sweat breaking out all over. If she got caught, her life would be ruined. Breaking would most likely be the charge, plus robbery, but she couldn't back out.

Bruce was well known in the city, and once divorced, Lila could count on her former friends to instantly start gibber-jabbing about her and besmirching her reputation, laughing about her instant poverty. She had no choice but to do what she planned. Bruce asked for it for being such a lying two-timing piece of shit, and Lila was not giving up the lifestyle she deserved. She was definitely not going to live an impoverished life in a small house while he moved Tess into her bed.

The plan was simple, and she promised herself she wouldn't get caught. Lila would obtain Streptococcus pyogenes or, hopefully, a polymicrobial type of bacteria that would cause a lethal, fast-moving, flesh-eating bacterium infection. Then, she would transfer the specimen to Bruce and thus give him a wicked necrotizing fasciitis. It would be difficult for him to fight because he was immune suppressed from chemotherapy. Plus, he was on steroids to decrease the swelling in his brain, which in turn would reduce his ability to fight off the infection. It would make for the perfect infection storm. Once it grabbed hold, the bacteria could spread rapidly and easily eat Bruce's brain tissue at a rate of an inch a minute.

Then, she would sue the hospital and Doctor Sunday Richardson for hundreds of millions. She didn't need Bruce's will changed. So, what if he left everything to his new whore. Screw him. He'd be dead, and Lila would be rewarded for wrongful death. *Revenge is sweet, my boy.*

***

LILA HAD FIFTEEN MINUTES to make it into the lab, get what she came for, and escape without anyone seeing her. Having previously worked here when she was in college, Lila knew the ins and outs as well as she did the back of her hand. Still, she was feeling jittery. She hoped that things hadn't changed in the lab since she'd graduated and finished her clinical hours.

Before entering, Lila scanned the dimly lit doorway. Lila had her old key, so she quickly entered through the back door, which was unobserved at this time of the night.

On the night shift, the back part of the laboratory was typically unmanned until one a.m. or until they got caught up with all their night shift stat labs. Her window of opportunity was tight.

Lila searched the storeroom beside the lab to make sure no one was taking a nap in the hidden area, which staff were known to do on their break. She tip-toed around the boxes that lined the wall, occasionally watching to ensure no one was nearby.

Lila knew precisely where to go to find the perfect specimen, and she headed directly for it. Quickly, she saw what she was looking for—a live specimen from a contaminated wound. Lila slipped on her gloves, and using safe precautions, she loaded the specimen onto a Q-Tip and placed it back in its protective vial.

The phone next to her pierced the area with a loud ring that caught Lila by surprise, causing her to jerk so violently that she almost dropped the specimen. Bright lights suddenly illuminated the entire lab, filling her with instant terror. She quickly sank to her knees and skirted under the closest desk.

A woman's heels clicked loudly nearby and then stopped as she answered the phone. Lila's heart pounded so hard in her chest that she could hardly hear anything else, much less the conversation. The little bits and pieces of whispered words she could decipher led her to believe the conversation was personal, like possibly a clandestine call with a lover. She prayed the woman wouldn't take a seat and drag the chat on endlessly. Nervously, Lila checked her lab coat's edges to ensure they weren't sticking out. The woman was so close to Lila that she could easily reach out and touch the toes of her shiny black shoes. Beads of sweat dotted Lila's forehead as she struggled to move deeper under the desk. Lila began to shake as she imagined how it all might go down. Police. Handcuffs. Fingerprinting. Jail. The news.

Lila was saved by another phone ringing in the front office. The woman whispered a brief *I love you* before hanging up and racing off to catch the call before they hung up. As soon as she was clear, she made a mad dash to the corridor's safety without being noticed.

***

LILA SLIPPED back into Bruce's room to find him back from surgery. Still sweating from her furiously fast trip, Lila stood at the door watching the nurses gathering in the conference room for the change-of-shift report. Bruce was sound asleep, and based on appearances, the surgery seemed successful.

Her stomach churned with a loud gurgle as she stared down at him and thought about what she was about to do. Her hands shook, knowing there was no going back once it was done. Bruce appeared to be in a profoundly deep sleep, still recovering from anesthesia. She was counting on him not waking up. If he did, her plans were over.

She edged her chair close to his bed and carefully scrutinized the tidy white surgical dressing covering his head. It smelled fresh, like an OR. Lila knew from his earlier surgeries exactly where the surgical incision was underneath the dressing, so she knew exactly where to aim the Q-tip.

It was fifteen minutes before Lila summoned up enough courage to act. Quickly, she pulled the lethal bacteria-laden swab from her purse, careful not to contaminate herself. With one fast move, Lila leaned in, stuck the Q-tip under Bruce's dressing, and gave it a good hard and wide rub. When she removed the swab, it had blood on it, meaning she'd been successful in her efforts to inoculate him with the deadly germ.

"What are you doing, Ma'am? You're not supposed to touch his dressing," the nursing technician said as she entered the room to empty the soiled laundry bin and line it with a fresh bag.

"Oh, I'm not," Lila quickly lied, jerking her hand back along with the swab. The tech startled Lila so severely that she dropped the swab on the floor. "I was stroking his neck," Lila explained. "He likes it when I do that. And I'm wearing gloves. See?" Lila lifted her free hand to show the nurse.

"That's thoughtful," the tech replied, shooting her a sly look. "But please don't get near the dressing. And make sure you wash your hands after removing the gloves."

The clinical technician moved slowly as she exited the room, clearly ready for the shift to end.

Lila was about to recover the specimen from the floor when the registered nurse entered and checked the monitor, reviewing Bruce's vital signs.

"Are you new?" Lila asked, trying to build a relationship. "You don't look familiar."

"I'm a traveler from the city. New York, that is." The nurse was about to come over to Lila's side of the bed, where it would be easy for her to see the swab. Lila's mind raced. *What do I say if she sees it? Tell her it was there when I came in. Did I know about it? No. Act surprised.*

An earlier laundry tech popped into the doorway. "Doctor Knox needs to see you in room three. He's in a hurry."

The traveling nurse turned on her heels and hurried out of the room. Quickly, Lila leaned over, picked up the swab, placed it back into its container, and safely tucked it back into her pocketbook. She re-gloved, grabbed cleaning wipes, scrubbed the floor, and then washed her hands thoroughly.

The VIP ICU suite was excellent, and Lila caught a fresh night's sleep that came quickly when her head hit the pillow.

THE NEXT MORNING, Maggie and Sunday made rounds on Bruce and remarked about how well he'd done with surgery. Maggie clicked the computer mouse several times and reviewed the data gathered overnight. "Everything looks good," she told Lila. "He has a low-grade fever, but that happens sometimes right after surgery. We'll keep an eye on it."

"Thank you, both, for everything you've done for Bruce. I'm very appreciative."

"You're quite welcome," Sunday replied. "We'll round again after our next surgery."

Lila smiled as sweetly as possible. She was delighted to have heard about the low-grade fever. Maybe that meant the bacteria was hard at work already.

Chapter 13

The Kiss

L ATE IN THE AFTERNOON, Tess left the ER and stopped in the restroom to brush her teeth and apply fresh makeup before hurrying to the Neurosurgical ICU to check on Bruce. It had been a long, exhausting night and the last of three twelve-hour shifts.

Lila was lying on the sofa in the VIP area of Bruce's room when Tess quietly entered, unaware of Lila's presence. Bruce had awakened during the night, and Lila was relieved. She watched with hidden curiosity as Tess approached Bruce's bed and kissed him on his lips.

"Stop!" Bruce cried out, his voice furious. "What are you doing?"

"I wanted to kiss you before I head home. I worked the night shift and couldn't get up here to see you sooner." Tess took Bruce's hand. "You look so good."

Bruce snatched his hand away from Tess. "Who are you? Get out of my room."

Tess backed up, offended and shocked. "Do you not recognize me? I'm Tess, your fiancé."

"I'm married. I have a wife named Lila. Get out of here."

"What's going on, Mr. Russell?" Maggie asked as she entered the room on rounds.

"This... woman... assaulted me. She kissed me...on the lips," Bruce cried out, his face flushed red with alarm.

"Ma'am. I'm going to have to ask you to leave," Maggie ordered as she stepped between Tess and Bruce. Secretly, she raised her eyebrows in warning to her old friend from the ER, making sure that neither Bruce nor Lila caught her expression.

"I'm his fiancé, Maggie," Tess defended, whispering at Maggie and holding up her ring to show proof.

Lila stepped out from behind the curtain, feeling smug and delighted at the turn of events. "I'm Lila, Bruce's wife, and I saw everything," Lila declared, giving Tess the evil eye. "The ring on her finger is a joke."

"They're in the middle of a divorce," Tess replied, trying to still be professional. "Tell them, Bruce."

"She's out of her mind, nurse. Lila is my wife, and I don't know what she's talking about. A divorce? My head hurts," Bruce cried, reaching for Lila's hand. Lila, delighted at his show of affection, picked up the phone and dialed. "I need a security officer in my husband's room. He's been assaulted by a staff member. We're in the Neurosurgical Intensive Care Unit. VIP suite one,"

Maggie looked wide-eyed at Tess and whispered. "You need to leave—this can't be undone. Go. Quick."

"She's crazy, Maggie. I didn't assault him," Tess responded, turning her back on Lila, who was shooting darts of hate towards Tess.

Two no-nonsense security officers urgently entered the room, and Lila quickly took charge, pointing at Tess. "This woman, a doctor, sexually assaulted my husband. I saw her kissing him on the lips. He asked her to leave."

The chief officer stepped close to Bruce. "The lipstick on his face matches hers," he noted, pointing at Tess and looking at her ID badge. "Are you a doctor from our ER?"

"I am. I'm a third-year resident."

"Dr. Larken, are you assigned to this case?"

"No. I'm not. I'm his fiancée."

"That's a bald-faced lie," Lila retorted. "Get her out of here. This chaos is not good for my husband. Please."

"Dr. Larken, we'll need you to come with us."

Tess pulled away. "I haven't done anything wrong here, officer."

"Take her out of here. She sexually assaulted me," Bruce cried out.

The second guard stepped forward and said in a low, calm voice, "Come with us now, Doctor Larken, on your own, or we'll have to do this the hard way. The police are on the way. They'll meet us in Dr. Sloan's office. We'll sort this out downstairs."

"Oh, my God," Tess spewed. "You people are crazy."

One of the guards remained behind to question Bruce, taking great care not to upset him. The second security officer escorted Tess away.

Lila's heart leaped with joy as she realized the moment's beauty. *Bruce genuinely doesn't know Tess. And he seems to have forgotten about our divorce. It's like a dream come true.* Then, her stomach flopped as she visualized placing the flesh-eating bacteria specimen under his dressing. She'd poisoned him, and it was too late to take it back.

***

Maggie checked Bruce as soon as the officer finished questioning him. She reviewed the recent computer data. He was on prophylactic antibiotic treatment yet his temperature was higher than acceptable. Maggie called Sunday to let her know.

On Maggie's exit, she found Lila outside Bruce Russell's room, near hysteria, rambling on to security about Bruce's memory loss. She tried calming Lila down to get an intelligent story out of her.

"I'm sorry for the other day," Lila said, "I've been such a mess since Bruce became sick. I'm so afraid he might die. He's all I have. And this woman…"

"It's over now, Mrs. Russell," Maggie said soothingly. "I'm concerned about a developing fever, and I'll be back after I talk with Doctor Richardson."

Nurse Bonnie approached Maggie. "This a brewing teapot, and it's already the talk of the hospital. We know Tess. She's not the bad person here. She loves Bruce. And now… what a bag of worms. It could destroy Tess's career."

"Well, if it's true, we've got a tricky situation on our hands," Maggie declared. "We can't get involved. That man is a powerful powder keg. We can all get fired at a whim with one word from him, whether he's in his right mind or not. He clearly does not remember Tess at all."

Doctor Richardson arrived in response to Maggie's urgent text. After thoroughly examining Bruce, she became less concerned. Bruce made solid eye contact with her and seemed entirely appropriate during the exam, except for the fever and post-surgical amnesia. "Do you remember the woman from this morning?" Sunday asked.

"The kisser? No. I don't know her. I've never seen her before today."

"Do you know the woman standing at the foot of the bed?" Sunday asked, pointing to Lila.

"No. I don't," Bruce said, then paused when Lila gasped. He looked hard at her. "Oh. Yes. That's my wife. Yes. She's Lila. My wife."

"Don't be alarmed, Mrs. Russell," Doctor Richardson said to Lila, pulling her aside. "Occasionally, short-term memory loss occurs after extensive brain surgery, and usually, it's temporary. In some cases, however, it can be permanent. The longer it lasts, generally, the more of a chance it's permanent. We'll keep an eye on him. Have you noticed any other unusual behavior?"

Lila wanted to tell the doctor how Bruce had his old personality back. She noticed it immediately after he woke up. He treated her differently— kind and gentle—the way he did when they got married. He seemed to have forgotten entirely about the discussion of divorce. She held the information back from the doctor. Lila didn't want it to end and prayed the memory loss was permanent. "Is he going to be, okay?" Lila asked. "Maggie said he had a fever."

"I am concerned he may be developing an infection, but he's covered with antibiotics, and we'll watch him closely. Don't worry."

***

MEANWHILE, DOWNSTAIRS, Glenn Sloan, prepared himself for the upcoming meeting with Tess. He felt edgy. Not himself. He chastised himself for not telling his counselor, Sister Marguerite, about his drinking. When she'd asked him if he had a drinking problem, he'd flat-out lied. Pride got in his way. As a doctor, he would never admit to that weakness. Since then, he'd struggled to get a grip on it, yet failed despite his best efforts. It wasn't like he was a drunk, falling all over the place. He just drank enough to take the edge off of the bad memories he suffered when working in the ER. No matter how he tried to make the sound of the gun firing and hitting him in the head, it wouldn't go away. Instead, it intruded on his thoughts at the worst times. And this was one of them. He adored Tess, and the upcoming confrontation with her would be painful. He took the key from his pocket, unlocked the right bottom drawer, and pulled out a bottle of **Kettle One** vodka. After taking a couple of gulps, he put the bottle back, locked the drawer, and leaned back in his chair, mellowing instantly as the warm feeling settled across his body. He closed his eyes just as the knock came on the door.

Tess entered. The security guard hovered behind her until Glenn dismissed him by explaining. "The doctor isn't a threat. I'll be fine. You can leave."

The officer nodded and stepped into the hall. "I'll be right outside should you need assistance," he said before pulling the door closed behind him.

Glenn turned to face Tess, whose eyes were bloodshot from crying. "Are you okay?"

"No. I don't understand any of this. Bruce loves me. I wouldn't have kissed him otherwise. I wouldn't have even entered his room. What's going to happen to me?"

"What were you thinking, Tess? Where was your judgment? You kissed a male patient in front of his wife. That little kiss is now a significant issue. The patient told security that he intends to press sexual assault charges against you and possibly even sue the hospital to boot."

"He's my fiancé, Glenn. You know that."

"I do—and what was my response when you blessed me with the news? *He's a married man.* That is precisely what I said. What normal, upstanding man gives another woman a ring and officially asks her to marry him when he has a wife? My God, Tess."

"You know he loves me. He's planning on divorcing Lila."

89

"At this current time, Tess, the man does not know you. That may change in the future, but for now, the situation has placed me in an extremely uncomfortable position."

"You're my friend, Glenn. Please."

"Yes. You are my friend, but you are also under my supervision," Glenn said before looking away long enough to recover his professional self. He cleared his voice. "I've notified the North Carolina licensing board of the charges made against you. Unfortunately, Tess, you will not be allowed to see patients until this is resolved. As far as your residency goes, you are officially suspended from the program. I'll need to take your hospital ID. All your accesses to hospital computer databases have been removed."

Tess sat in the closest chair and hung her head, burying her face in her hands, and sobbing so loud and hard her shoulders shook. Glenn got up, walked over to her, and gently placed his hand on her head. "I'm so sorry, Tess. I have no other choices at my disposal. I think you might want to consider hiring a lawyer."

"Bruce is my lawyer. Who will take me on now after all this."

"I'll help you find one. In the meantime, keep an extremely low profile. Do not, under any circumstances, discuss this with anyone. Hospital people talk – and if you confide in the wrong person, your words will be twisted, making things even more difficult for you. Hospital gossip is brutal, and even if this all resolves itself, the grapevine will keep on talking about it, adding untruths to it – and there you go. Be wise."

"Do you think Bruce will ever know me again?"

"I honestly can't say, Tess. I hope he regains his memory and straightens all this out, but it's a little too late for that. Stand up. Recover yourself. Hold your head high. Human Resources is waiting in the conference room to officially guide you in what you can and cannot do under these circumstances. The police are there as well. I want you to know I am still your friend, and I am here for you to help you in any way I can. I'll be visiting Bruce later today to see if things have changed. Otherwise, Doctor Richardson will keep me apprised of developments."

Tess stood, and Glenn gave her a sad nod, noting it was time for her to go.

Tess paused at the door, looking back at Glenn. "I might as well tell you because you need to know. People are talking about you, Glenn. They claim you're drinking on the job. I believe you've had a little today– not long ago." She lingered, waiting for a response. "I consider you a friend, Glenn. You can call me if you need to talk with someone. I want to help."

"It's under control, Tess."

"You're wrong, and until you acknowledge that, you are in for a rude awakening. Your fingers tremble sometimes. You've got to get rid of the monkey on your back because if you don't, the people talking about you will become too noisy. Higher-ups will hear them. Just saying."

Tess closed the door and left, leaving him alone with his private thoughts of hell that had entered his life when he wasn't looking.

After a deep sigh, Glenn picked up the phone and called Sister Marguerite. "Can you see me? I'm in crisis, Sister."

***

TESS'S NIGHTMARE became a living beast. One loving kiss ended her career in an instant. She was officially charged with sexual assault. True to his word, Glenn posted her bond to keep her out of jail. Tess went home and stared at the wall in shock as the whole reality of the day profoundly sank in. *I don't have the money to pay for this huge apartment. Bruce paid the rent. How will I survive? How could I have been so stupid?*

Chapter 14

Amateur Sleuths

A FTER EVERYONE had gone to bed, Maggie met Benny in the bar, drinking wine and eating a late-night snack of tuna and salmon sushi.

"So, what's up?" Benny asked.

"I've been thinking and I want to talk about Amelia," Maggie replied. "If things are developing romantically between you two, I thought maybe we could have her transferred to another post. I was too harsh in my earlier assessment of the situation. I want you to be happy."

"I am happy with things just like they are. I like having Amelia here, and I think Dorrie would be crushed if Amelia had to leave on account of my selfish feelings. Dorrie's so excited about learning French, and she's so good at it. I can control myself for Dorrie. There are other women in this world. I just have to wait until the right one comes along."

"Very well," Maggie replied. "If you're sure."

Benny's phone alarm went off. "Holy shit. There's activity. Someone's in the lab!"

In unison, they jumped up and ran for the yard. No sooner had their feet left the deck than the alarm went off again. "Damn," Benny said, stopping to look at the phone. "They're already gone. What the heck is going on?"

"Why so fast?" Maggie queried, looking towards the lab with a more than curious glance.

When they returned to their late post-hospital meal, Benny connected his phone to the television at the bar. They watched as a small, framed man entered the property from behind the lab. Benny rewound the tape to see where the man had gained access to the property. "There," Benny pointed.

"Is there a hole in the hedge, or is it a doorway opening? Did you ever notice it?"

"No. I didn't," Maggie replied, looking closer at the screen as she took another bite of sushi. "But we'll never find it this late, not as dark as it is."

"So, what's the plan?"

"We'll check out the hedge in daylight, for sure, and then, I'm going down into the lab."

"Not without me, you're not," Benny touted with widened and determined eyes. "We are working for the next two days, anyway."

"Then we'll check out the hedge first thing before work and take a trip into the lab the first day we're off. Until then, we will watch and see if we can discover a pattern in his visits."

***

THE NEXT MORNING, Maggie and Benny scouted the area behind the lab and with great difficulty they finally discovered a fake hedge constructed to open like a door.

They exited the property through the hedgerow to find a service-type private road leading to a small neighborhood that included half a dozen modest, older concrete houses. A couple of old cars were parked in each gravel driveway.

"What do you make of it?" Maggie asked in a whisper.

"It's odd—very peculiar to find houses this small on this side of town. It's unheard of, to say the least." Benny replied.

***

BACK AT THE HOUSE, they plotted and planned their next move. "We have to be ready to go at a moment's notice. Provided we're home," Benny suggested. "And we get out there and try to stop them."

"And, then what?"

"I guess that depends on what we find."

Ding. Ding. The camera alert sounded. Benny's eyes widened.

Maggie's brows furrowed as she took in the recording. "Who is that?"

"I can't quite tell. It's a man, for sure. He looks awfully familiar."

"Oh, my God, Benny. It's Glenn. What the hell is he doing out there?"

"He looks like he's searching for something."

"Glenn? Why?"

"I'm going to go find out," Maggie said, heading out the door.

Glenn was walking back to the house when Benny and Maggie caught up with him.

"Well, speak of the devil," Benny said, trying to look innocent and keep a bit of humor in what was clearly not an amusing situation. "I hope he's not suspicious about where we found Kerrington."

"What are you doing out here, Glenn?" Maggie asked.

"I went for a breath of fresh air. It has been tough at work lately. Long days. Stressful. I guess you heard about Tess," Glenn offered.

"Yeah. That was a real bummer," Benny replied.

"Anything interesting going on out here," Maggie kept at the topic, noting how slick Glenn had been in diverting the reason for his presence.

"The air feels good. Makes a tired soul feel stronger."

Maggie became even more nervous when she spotted Sunday crossing the lawn and coming towards them. She motioned with her eyes, warning Benny of further complications.

"What are you guys talking about? You're all gathered around in a circle like you've got some dreadful secret you don't want to share. What's happening that is so important out here in the middle of the lawn?"

Benny shot Maggie a look of desperation.

"I saw Glenn out here and thought maybe he'd want to share a beer in the bar," Maggie said, trying to guide everyone back to the house. "How about it, guys?"

"Thanks, but no thanks. I've stopped drinking. I need to spend alone time with Annella before she shoots off to Rome," Glenn replied, heading towards the house.

None of them spoke as they walked the expanse of the lawn back to the mansion. Maggie noted Glenn looked worried—distressed would be a better description. Whatever was bugging him, he wasn't going to talk about it. Maybe he was more upset over Annella going away than he had let on. He'd been going to counseling, that much he had told her.

Maggie dismissed her worry as he had genuine reason to be upset and out of sorts due to the harrowing situation with Tess. They all loved her and cared about her. *Let it be,* she told herself, but Maggie couldn't just let it go. Hopefully, he hadn't spotted the lab—she prayed not.

Chapter 15

The Au Pair

THE AROMA OF freshly popped popcorn tantalized Benny's senses as the family settled into lush leather chairs in the Media Room. It was family movie night, and they all quickly settled in to watch *The Summer I Turned Pretty* while eating their snacks and downing fizzling sodas.

Dorrie was mesmerized right from the start, but Benny could not concentrate. Instead, he found himself captivated by Amelia—unable to tear his eyes away from her. Tonight, he saw her in a different light. He was held captive by a sexual tension that was new to him. She was developing a real connection with Dorrie. He found himself attracted by her light laughter, angel-like beauty, and ability to reach down to an adolescent level. They were bonding significantly.

When Amelia caught Benny looking at her, she acknowledged his gaze with a smile. Her last glance pierced right through him, igniting a fire of emotions he thought he had long forgotten. The feelings were primal, awakening a sense of masculinity within him that had been dormant for too long.

Benny had to admit his relationship with Amelia had taken off faster than a race car at a NASCAR race, stirring deep feelings inside—good feelings, a warm kind of happiness. Finally, all it took was for him to hear her laughter again to send him off on a rush of sweet emotion. Maybe it was time he had a heart-to-heart conversation with Dorrie about her thoughts about him dating again.

After the movie ended, Dorrie left the room. Benny wasn't prepared when Amelia came over, sat beside him on the sofa, and took his hand in hers. Benny froze. The skin-to-skin contact stirred his insides with a sizzling hot feeling. She kissed him on the cheek, got up, and walked away.

***

BENNY'S DREAMS THAT night were invaded by hot, passionate, naked moments with Amelia in his bed. Then, out of nowhere, Willow appeared at the bedside in a long, flowing gown. She whispered his name. Benny sat bolt upright in bed, horrified, trying to cover Amelia from Willow's eyes with covers.

"It's okay, Benny," Willow whispered. "It's time for you to live and love again." Willow gave him her precious smile and disappeared as fast as she appeared. Benny awakened and looked madly around the room, searching for Willow, only to realize it had only been a dream. His heart sank. His beautiful sacred Willow had been breathtaking. She'd always been so kind. Her thoughts about life reflected a deep caring for people. She held strong ethics.

Willow had been the most caring woman he'd ever met. He'd once seen her take the last five dollars she had for her hospital dinner and give it to a homeless woman with two children, who needed to return to the shelter before supper so the children could eat.

Later in the same day, Benny had caught sight of Willow drinking water and eating saltine crackers as her meal. And that had been the moment he'd fallen in love with her. It didn't matter that she was married to a no-good jerk who beat her. He loved Willow, and that kind of love simply had no boundaries.

Benny sat quietly, thinking about his life. Before Amelia, he'd been much happier. Contented with his hospital life. Dorrie. His place in the Blanchard family. But did he want more than simple contentment? He wasn't getting younger, and he did yearn for a son. He'd even contemplated adopting one. But wouldn't it be better if he married and had a wife to help him raise the child—or better yet, birth his child? It was something that had been on his mind a lot over the past six months, yet the memories of Willow plagued him and made him feel horribly guilty like he was betraying her. Was it time he made himself move forward? Truth be told, Willow was gone from him forever. He should start thinking about his future. What did he want?

UPSTAIRS, AMELIA SAT in the dimly lit, oversized, and elegantly decorated bedroom suite, thinking about Benny and questioning whether or not she was ready for love. She was gun-shy. Her love life had been one disaster after another. The last romantic interest called her selfish and even declared she couldn't love.

There was the triumphant, financially independent chef, Jon Paul, who was drop-dead gorgeous, kind, generous, and thoughtful, with a brilliant career ahead. But after a year's engagement, Amelia broke up with him a week before the wedding. He couldn't get the night off to go to her friend's birthday party. After deep thought into their relationship, she decided she didn't want to be married to a man who worked evenings and nights. So, she broke it off, knowing it crushed him.

Then, there was Louis, a resident physician in emergency medicine. Their relationship was happy, and they planned to marry after his residency was up, when he made more money. But when he completed his residency, she discovered his incessant studying was far from over. Plus, his new job had him working night shifts on a rotating schedule. She wanted a man who would make time for her, so she gave him back his ring and said goodbye.

The last love was Jimmy Dawson, an American she met in Paris on vacation. He was a cop, and she fell head over heels with him. She would have done anything for him, but he dragged things out and became very hesitant when she brought up getting married or even engaged. That's when she found out he was an undercover cop and leading a secret life most of the time. The last time she heard from him, he told her he had an opportunity to go completely undercover, which meant he would totally give up his identity. When she asked him about marriage, he simply replied, "We wouldn't last. You're too self-seeking for marriage, girl. You're a taker. So, why would I want to marry you?" She'd cried for a week. He'd been so mean. Hurtful. When she tried to find him to talk, she discovered he'd definitely gone deep undercover. There was no trace of him. It was like he'd disappeared from the planet. What kind of person does undercover? A lying and deceiving person who turns on friends. He'd made a fool of her and enjoyed it. After all, he made a career out of betraying people.

After failing at romance, Amelia adopted the que sera, sera attitude. She decided to become an au pair and travel the world. Romance and marriage were no longer on her agenda.

Benny had changed all that from the moment she met him. The spark was there. Best of all, he was a lovely man who made time to be around her. And, according to Dorrie, he was filthy rich too; he worked days and was smitten with her. Amelia would not have to work to travel the world. They could live a life of luxury and travel the world in grand style. He could give her a mansion, and she'd never have to worry about money again. She would be rich.

Chapter 16

The Alert

IN THE BACK of the estate, Benny rechecked the camera near the lab and straightened it to give a better view of the entrance. It was perfectly aimed. He reset the settings on the phone app to make sure it was set to record each event.

Maggie joined him, carrying a box. "Delivery."

Benny excitedly took the small box, set it on the picnic table, and opened it. "You. Look at this man. It's tiny."

They both stared at the small black drone that looked like a ball. Benny quickly read the instructions. "It's not as powerful as the ones we used last summer, but it'll get the job done."

"Exactly what are we going to do with it?" Maggie wondered.

"Look in places where the fixed camera can't see."

***

IT WAS MIDNIGHT when Maggie and Benny went out to the lab. Maggie opened the lab door, and Benny set the drone off. Benny gasped with enjoyment. "It looks like something out of a spaceship."

They watched in awe as it floated almost invisibly down the dark stairwell, turning corners with ease. Thirty minutes later, they had not spotted anything of interest until the elevator door opened, and a person stepped out. Benny and Maggie quickly exited the drone from the building, grabbed it, and fled into the brush.

When the door opened, Ming stepped out, looked around, left the property, and disappeared.

The two of them took off to catch him, found his house, and watched it, holding their positions momentarily. The lights were on, and behind the curtained windows, they saw the man walking around inside.

"I want to go see if it's the same man," Maggie whispered.

"No. Not now, Maggie. We know where the house is, and I want to look at the camera footage. I don't think we saw him well enough to identify him, even if he is in the house."

The two of them returned to Blanchard House and retired for the night.

Chapter 17

Fever

B RUCE RUSSEL BECAME seriously ill overnight. The first symptom was a spike in his heart rate to one hundred twenty-four beats per minute. Previously, it had been a rock-solid rate of ninety beats a minute since admission.

At the nurse's monitoring station, Nurse Bonnie noticed the climbing heart rate on Bruce's screen and quickly responded to his room, where she found him violently shivering. His temperature was one hundred and four degrees, indicating the onset of a severe complication in a fresh post-op patient.

Lila watched Bonnie calmly, knowing the flesh-eating bacteria she'd planted was taking effect. She watched Nurse Bonnie perform a thorough but quick examination before grabbing her cell phone and making a call.

"Call the Rapid Response Team for Bruce Russell."

Within less than three minutes, Doctor Richardson and Maggie came charging down the hall. Richardson did a rapid but thorough assessment. Without a doubt, her experience told her Bruce was infected. His mouth was parched, and his lips were red, both a result of his fever. Maggie checked the computerized information on Bruce, tracking his vital signs. The symptoms had hit less than thirty minutes ago. She checked his labs. They hadn't been drawn yet so she phoned the lab and changed the blood draw to STAT.

Lila watched as Maggie and Sunday held their heads together, chatting about medical topics that were too low for her to hear.

"Is Bruce, okay?" Lila asked, using an innocent voice.

"He's developed a significant fever," Doctor Richardson replied. "So, we'll be treating him for infection immediately."

An hour later, Bruce's eyes suddenly rolled back into his head as his body became stiff. His arms and legs flailed about violently. She knew it was a seizure, and it terrified her. Lila reached up, flipped the cover-up on the Code Blue button, and pressed it hard.

Immediately, the operator called out overhead, "Code Blue. Room eight. Neurosurgical Intensive Care 8." She repeated it two more times, but by the time she got to the third announcement, the room was filled with a response team.

"He's not breathing," Lila cried out hysterically. Don't you need to start CPR? Don't just stand there like a bunch of idiots. Do something!!!"

"It's okay, Lila," Maggie soothed. "It's normal for patients to stop breathing briefly after a seizure. He's okay. He'll start breathing again very soon."

"No, he's not okay," Lila snapped. "Did you see him? He was jerking all over."

"We're giving him medications to quiet the seizure activity and get his fever down. He'll be okay," Maggie said as Doctor Richardson left the room to answer a phone call.

Lila nodded. She internally congratulated herself for such a fabulous acting job. They would never suspect her of anything. Quietly, she stepped over to the sofa and sat, forcing herself to cry.

Maggie removed the dressing and was happy with the wound—there was no draining, redness, or swelling. She carefully redressed it using a sterile technique.

"His blood pressure is ninety-two over sixty-four, a lot lower than usual," Bonnie declared, pressing a button on the monitor to print out a rhythm strip. She showed it to Maggie. "His heart rate went back up to one hundred and forty a minute. He's septic."

"Let's get a set of blood cultures and continue antibiotics as ordered until I talk with Doctor Richardson. Also, let's give him a liter of IV fluid, wide open, then back the rate to one hundred an hour. Call me with vital signs when the IV fluid challenge has been completed. Did you give him acetaminophen?"

"I did. Right after I called you, the patient's temperature began coming down."

"Great job, Bonnie. I'll be back to check on him. I ordered a stat head CT, so be prepared to transport when they call for him."

"Sure thing, Maggie. I'll keep you posted."

***

LILA WANTED TO VOMIT. A change of heart took over. What had she done? All for his money. The seriousness of her actions hadn't hit her until Bruce had the seizure. No matter what had passed between them, she still loved him. His seizure made her take hold of her mind again. It reminded her of the night they found Bruce's cancer when she'd found him lost and confused in the wine cellar. That was the night he had his first seizure. The same type of seizure he'd had today. She couldn't take it anymore. Her hands trembled as she dug in her bag to find her anxiety pill. Quickly, she popped one, and soon, she was under control again.

With that thought, Lila got up and went home. She desperately needed sleep and to be alone. And she wanted to pray for forgiveness.

***

WHEN LILA GOT HOME, she took a long, soothing hot shower, washed her hair, slipped into her pajamas, and slept for hours.

After she got dressed, she ate a peanut butter and jelly sandwich. Her grandmother always made her one when she thought Lila was unsettled, and it always made her feel better—comforted.

Her mind slipped back to the years she spent at **Hanford Hall**—a center for adolescent mental health as a result of what her grandmother had termed as a nervous breakdown.

Lila was diagnosed with Impulsive Borderline Personality Disorder. Her psychiatrist pointed out the signs and symptoms he based his diagnosis on.

"You can be very charismatic, Lila. You're energetic, engaging, motivated, and even flirtatious at times. On the downside, however, you act impulsively and engage in dangerous behaviors without considering the consequences. We need to work on that. Your behavior is often entirely inappropriate, as evidenced by your wide mood swings. You show intense anger and lose your temper frequently. When you do—people around you become afraid you may harm them."

Over the years of therapy, Lila learned the root of her behavior was an intense fear of abandonment. She admitted to having taken extreme measures to avoid real or imagined separation or rejection. She also admitted to often feeling shamed.

Lila had been in therapy for years. She took medications when she was afraid. She had stopped cutting herself, which was good. Her cutting behavior was how Lila ended up seeing the psychiatrist in the first place.

She stopped therapy after marrying Bruce because she was terrified, he might think she was defective. In truth, she'd fallen into her old ways. She acted impulsively, without thinking it through or even calling her doctor; she'd done the unthinkable in response to Bruce's rejection. All she could do now was hope she didn't get caught. She needed to check her behavior and get it under control. No more sarcastic or bitter remarks to the doctors. She would take a pill the minute she entered Bruce's room to stay chilled.

Lila settled in and opened the mail to find bills and more bills that Bruce always took care of. "Boring," she quipped to herself. Briefly, she wondered if they would get paid. That caused her to worry. "As if I don't have enough to think about."

The last bill was from a luxury apartment building uptown. A big red PAST DUE notice was stamped on the front. Lila checked through the other envelopes and found another bill from the same company. She studied it briefly before a ding-dong went off in her mind. It was from the same building where Tess lived. Bruce was paying her rent and owed over ten thousand dollars for two months. No wonder Tess was desperate. She was living a high life on Bruce's money and was about to lose it. *Not anymore,* Lila said to herself, smiling broadly. *Let her get evicted. I'm not lifting one finger to help her.*

She went through the rest of the mail, specifically looking for signs of divorce notifications, and breathed a sigh of relief when they weren't there.

Lila then searched for more documentation by going through Bruce's briefcase and any other place she thought she might find divorce-related material. She found none.

When she got to Bruce's office, she scored big. The divorce decree was in his top desk drawer. Lila sat back in his bold leather chair and cried. It was a nightmare. She found a new will, leaving everything to Tess. He hadn't signed it yet. After studying the papers thoroughly, she discovered that both the **Power of Attorney and Medical Power of Attorney** were still in her name. Could she make the divorce filings null and void? Also, he had not signed the divorce papers yet. That problem, Lila would eradicate.

Chapter 18

Mario

I T WAS WELL AFTER NINE o'clock when Maggie and Benny returned home from the hospital. The surgical cases had taken much longer than expected, and both were exhausted from the longer-than-normal shift.

When Maggie stepped out of the car, a wave of sweltering, humid, oppressive air hit her in the face, making her feel like she'd just opened an oven door. The heat dome settling around the Charlotte area was overwhelming, making their adventure less appealing.

Benny checked the camera to ensure no one had entered the lab. "It's empty. Hurry, Maggie. Let's go."

They ran as fast as they could across the thick, green, luscious, wet lawn, which was slippery in places as the sprinklers had been on for quite a while.

When they got to the lab, Benny rechecked the camera footage to ensure it was still empty. Noting all was clear, the two carefully descended the flight of stairs. Maggie could tell at once upon entering that the air had been shut off as the air smelled musty and stank. The room was barren scientific testing equipment, giving it an eerie type of feeling. "Looks like Lamar was right," Benny said." The CDC took everything."

"So, what's the plan now?" Maggie whispered.

"Head to the elevator," Benny said before suddenly placing a finger of warning against his lips. The laboratory door echoed from above. He pulled Maggie back, and they quickly tucked themselves deep into a corner that was not visible from the elevator.

"Shhh!" Benny whispered.

They listened as the humming elevator continued. The bell rang as it passed each floor before finally stopping.

Maggie and Benny ducked behind a wall and stood lifeless like statues, unsure what to do next. They caught each other's eyes through the darkness.

"Did you hear that?" Maggie asked in a lowered voice.

"The elevator? Of course, I did."

"No. The bell. It went off four times. Not three."

"You misheard."

"I heard four. I swear. Why would it ding four times if there are only three floors."

The sound of the elevator returning silenced them as four more bells echoed through the corridor. Maggie elbowed him to make her point. The elevator door slid open. Neither of them got a good look at the man because they were trying to hide in the small space.

"Follow him," Benny whispered when the man headed up to the exit stairs.

Maggie trailed behind Benny as they fled, hurrying to keep pace with the slender man without being spotted. He exited the property through the lush, tall back hedge. She wiped the sweat from her forehead as more perspiration prickled from her armpits. The muggy humidity significantly added to her discomfort. Maggie swatted at a mosquito biting her forearm, making her even more annoyed by their adventure.

Maggie and Benny slid behind the man through the hedge opening, which was well hidden from view. They followed him to a small, aging yellow cinderblock house. Benny led them to a partially cracked open window. He motioned to Maggie to listen. They had to lean well into the bushes to hear.

"Welcome home, Ming," a loud man's voice called out.

"Mario! What are you doing here?" Ming asked, his speech sounding surprised and laced with fear.

Maggie tried to see the faces but could only see Ming's.

"You betrayed me," Mario angrily shouted as he got up from his chair. "How? What did I do?"

"You didn't keep it safe. That was the agreement. I am not going to jail," Mario raged, placing his hand on Ming's throat and backing him against the wall. "Did you squeal on me? Did you tell them I sold you the virus?"

"Who? The government? No. No! I haven't talked to anyone."

"I don't trust you, Ming. Not anymore," Mario exclaimed, releasing his hand grip. "Do you have the cure?"

"Yes. I do."

"Is it here?"

"No. It's safe. Locked in the lab. It works. I gave the monkeys the virus—and they got really sick. Then, I administered the cure—and twelve hours later," Ming announced, snapping his fingers for effect, "They're alive. Jumping around in their cage—not sick anymore. We're going to save the world! We'll be famous and rich. Maybe we'll even win the Nobel Prize. We'll get any job we want!"

"I sold you the virus in good faith, Ming Boy, and you let it loose. Now, everyone is looking for where it came from. All that money and fame, shit, it ain't going to do me any good if I'm locked in prison for the rest of my life. You didn't protect me. When they get through with you… you'll turn on me."

"It won't go like that, I promise, Ming cried back."

"I know it won't because you won't live long enough to tell anyone anything."

Ming cried out and backed up hard against the window. Maggie and Benny ducked and crawled away to the edge of the woods, no more than twenty feet away.

"No. No. Don't," Ming cried out.

Those were the last words Maggie and Benny heard as they escaped into the woods.

FEELING ITCHY ALL OVER, from the bushes, Maggie ran straight into the pool shower. Benny jumped into the pool, unable to wait.

"Okay," Benny said, getting out of the pool. Maggie joined him, her clothes dripping wet. Both dried off with a towel. "Here's what we know. Ming apparently purchased the virus from Mario. The virus somehow escaped the lab during the explosion. Supposedly. Do you think Mario killed Ming?"

"How do I know?" Maggie questioned, raising her eyebrows dramatically. "Do I think he did? It's very possible. Quite probable."

"What do we do?" Benny asked, scratching his arm where welts had popped up in a small area on his skin.

"We certainly can't go back there to find out. Maybe we should call the police."

"And tell them what? We're peeping Toms that might have witnessed a murder. What then? They get there, there's no dead body, and they come back to us and ask what we saw, how we saw it, and we're arrested for peeping. They'll ask how we know Ming and question us as to what we were doing at his house. To be sure we both will get our licenses revoked for peeping and breaking the law. I say we keep our mouths shut, get our butts into the lab, and secure the cure. That's our immediate top priority," Benny said with finality.

"So, let's retrace our steps. What are the facts?" Maggie replied.

"It's starting to make sense. The explosion hit so hard that it literally rocked all the buildings within a mile radius. Kerrington walked around the lab. Then, he gets some funky virus. Those two clowns, Ming and Mario, were in cahoots, working on a biological weapon. Granted, they wanted to cure the world, but damn." Maggie added, looking hard at Benny.

"On that note, I wouldn't exactly call them clowns, Maggie. They're pure genius. I just wonder why no one else, including us, has gotten sick. We've been all around the outside of the lab. So has Ming." Benny added, raising his eyebrows.

"It stormed later that night after the explosion."

"Could it have washed away?"

"Who knows? Could it even <u>wash</u> away?" Maggie began to mumble her words as thoughts rolled through her head. "Worse yet—maybe Kerrington didn't get it walking around the lab that night. Maybe he knew about the project and was exposed to it by being in the lab itself. My God. Did he know?"

"Suppose," Benny added, with a curious look overtaking his face. "Just think about it. The virus surely isn't just sitting around the lab unprotected. It has to be in a temperature-controlled environment. Fully protected. Even with an explosion as big as the one we experienced, it would be difficult, if not impossible, for it to leak out of the building without contaminating everything in its path. The more I think about it, the more I'm convinced that Kerrington, at one point in time, went into the lab and handled the virus. It's the only explanation. The <u>only</u> one."

They stared at each other before Benny finally got the courage to speak. "We'll never know unless he lives. The point is that the cure is in the lab, and Kerrington needs it. We've got to get our hands on it before someone else does."

"The second big hurdle facing us is getting the cure to Kerrington. Gaining access to his Isolation Unit is as complicated as trying to break into the White House." Maggie said with a sigh. Heavy curiosity laced her tone as she continued. "Our list of tasks sucks. We have to enter the lab—find the cure—steal it—sneak into a quarantined area, and give Kerrington the vaccine without being caught. That's a tall, complex, and dangerous set of orders. I'm convinced we're nuts, my friend."

"That's an accurate assessment," Benny agreed with a light laugh. "We both have to work tomorrow, and Sunday has a heavy surgical schedule. What about after work tomorrow?"

"In the dark?"

"In the dark. We have no choice. Time is running out."

When Benny stuck his hand in the air, Maggie hesitated, then finally high-fived him. With hung and worried heads, they headed inside to get changed for dinner.

MAGGIE WENT STRAIGHT TO her room after eating, where she slipped into her sleeping shorts and a tee shirt.

Over the next hour, she surfed the Internet, searching for ways to kill Veridian XV. A freezing environment only slowed the virus down. According to **WHO**—the World Health Organization, temperatures above one hundred and fifty degrees Fahrenheit would kill most viruses. But would it be effective against killing Veridian XV? She pondered the idea until she fell sound asleep.

Chapter 19

River's Edge

I T WAS A BEAUTIFUL early Saturday, with the air holding a bold new crispness of fall due to the cold front moving through the area. Ming, wearing his N-95 mask snugly against his face, raced down the river's edge sidewalk to the emergency room. Time was running out, and he desperately needed medical attention. Ming knew the rapid rise and fall of his chest was a sure sign he had Veridian XV.

Mario injected him with the virus during their altercation. After rolling on the floor, Mario managed to get the needle into Ming's neck before Ming removed it, turned it on Mario, and stuck the needle straight into his jugular vein. Ming got up, grabbed his mask, and ran out the door.

He escaped into the woods behind his house to hide from Mario and desperately tried to find his way through the thick bush to the lab. It was like a maze—the thick brush left him lost and bewildered, unable to figure out which way to go. He retraced his steps, hoping Mario was gone so he could take his regular path to the lab. Ming wondered if Mario was still alive. Had he killed him?

The virus surged through his body, violently owning him. The first symptom that hit him was a tightness in his chest, followed by profuse sweating pouring out from all his pores. His skin burned fiercely, and it rapidly turned red with a firey rash that overtook his arms and legs. Ming sadly realized that he would never make it to the lab to get the cure. Having spent most of the day, every day, in the lab or classroom, Ming wasn't the fittest of souls. He was well on the thin side after having skipped too many meals over the years. He was an easy target for the virus. Weakly, he laughed at himself. He hadn't even finished eating his birthday cupcake.

Ming headed for the hospital, doubting he could make the trip. He formed a solid plan in his mind. Ming would promptly tell them that he had Veridian so no one would suffer. He'd tell them about the cure and where they could find it. Then, he would tell them about Mario.

Thoughts circled his brain all the way to the hospital. How would the virus reign down upon him, and what atrocities and suffering would it bring his way? Would he make it to the hospital or die a failure without one person on the planet ever knowing about his life's work? Maybe, by some stroke of good luck, he would make it and be remembered as the man who tried to save the world. Or perhaps they would claim he attempted to destroy America. God. It was so not him. Ming's heart flip-flopped when he realized there would be no wife. No children. His family would be forever dishonored. His chin trembled as tears of shame dripped from his eyes.

Briefly, he stopped and sat on a bench by the river's edge to catch his breath. With finality, he stared down at the water rushing by below, as he did every Saturday morning as he practiced mindfulness meditation and centered himself. Ming tried to reassure himself.

Those were his last thoughts before he fell off the bench. Raindrops tapped against his cheek, forcing him to open his eyes. Ming searched the skies for rain clouds. They were beautiful, fierce, and like him. He would survive.

Ming pulled his mask down, opened his mouth, and caught several raindrops to quench the dry desert feeling invading his mouth from the building fever. His hand shook with rigors as he placed his mask back in place. Ming promised himself if he lived, he would write about his experience of how Veridian had so rapidly consumed his body. That was an important fact he'd failed to predict.

***

TWO RIVER WALKERS spotted Ming's body on the sidewalk and called EMS, who immediately asked if he was breathing. They confirmed he was and added, "He's got a bad rash that looks like a bad allergy."

Glenn was sitting in his office on the hospital campus, where he was caught up in his duties as the medical director of 911. The medic radio caught his attention, and his heart began to race as adrenaline surged into his body. Jumping out of his chair, he ran out of the office and down the street to the scene, which was only one block away. He yelled orders over the phone to the ER. "Get isolation ready for BSL 4 and call a Medical Resuscitation Code three minutes out. We might be looking at a CPR that is in progress upon arrival." Glenn arrived, the first on the scene, followed by two ambulance vehicles with blaring sirens. A bevy of police cars accompanied them, coming to a screeching stop at the edge of the park.

Glenn looked at the patient from a distance. "It's confirmed. Possibly Veridian. Have the police and medic go to a publicly closed radio channel." Glenn approached the river walkers. "Did anyone go near him?"

"No, sir. We thought it might be that bad virus everyone's talking about."

"Did you see anyone else go near him?"

"No, sir. The park's quiet today. There are not many people here because it looks like rain will pour down any minute."

"I'll need you to hang out here to talk to some folks. Can you do that?"

"Yes, sir. Are we in trouble?"

"Not at all. You did great."

Glenn quickly shot out calls to the infectious disease team at the hospital, the health department, and the CDC.

Ming regained consciousness long enough to whisper to Glenn between gasping breaths. "I have Veridian. I'm a scientist. I have a cure." Before he could give out more details, he lapsed into unconsciousness.

Glenn rapidly secured his airway via endotracheal tube placement, and Ming's bed was enveloped in a clear, heavy transport isolation case that would prevent the virus from escaping during transport.

He stood relieved but shaking in shock during the aftermath of resuscitation, as he watched EMS hustle Ming down the sidewalk to the ER. "Finally!" Glenn said to himself, plunging his celebratory fist high in the air. "Thank you, God. We have the link."

Chapter 20

Doctor Sunday Richardson

DOCTOR SUNDAY RICHARDSON was anxious to get Julie Snipes, a thirty-three-year-old mother of twins, on the operating room table as soon as possible to repair her brain aneurysm, fearing it might rupture. Snipes was currently stable and booked for surgery at eight a.m. sharp.

At 7:30 a.m., Maggie and Sunday walked into the OR, dressed and ready to go.

"Doctor Richardson!" The OR scheduler called out. "They need you downstairs in Trauma to evaluate a multiple trauma patient! Your eight o'clock aneurysm repair was bumped for a traumatic brain injury."

The ER was wildly overflowing. The air was filled with loud moaning and crying coming from the Trauma Bay curtains. Blending in were the screaming voices of senseless psychotic patients lying on stretchers that lined the walls.

A trauma patient was being evaluated in the hall behind hanging bed sheets clipped to IV poles that served as privacy shields. It was undoubtedly the worst day Sunday had ever experienced in the E.R. She overheard the attending physician begging the Charge Nurse to put the ER on diversion.

Sunday entered Bobby Smith's cubicle and got a quick report from the senior resident. The bright-eyed and spirited seventeen-year-old high school football player sustained a severe traumatic injury to the brain when a tow truck ran a stop sign and plowed into the side of the school bus. After looking at his head CT, Sunday examined him and ordered him to be sent straight to the OR.

The operative case was chaotic from the moment the teenager was pushed into the operating theater. Smith had a fractured femur that was temporarily stabilized in the ER, and the necessity for neurosurgery trumped the need for surgical intervention for the femur fracture.

Lex Turner, the middle-aged, highly experienced anesthesiologist, hurried to secure the patient's airway, his professional hands dancing through the air. He was always so particular with his tray of tools. All his carefully prepared medication-filled syringes looked like a rainbow with brightly colored labels. They were always placed in the exact same order to prevent mistakes.

He grunted as he always did when things didn't go smoothly. A light grunt. Not disruptive. Those who worked frequently with him were familiar with the sound.

Sunday was quick to respond to the sound and spoke loudly, not giving him the chance to speak. "What up there, Bob?"

"We have a challenging blood pressure issue. I'm giving the patient a fluid challenge." Lex's hands rolled the IV control clamp upwards, releasing fluids to flow rapidly into the patient's veins. "We may need to consider giving blood."

"Do we have consent?" Sunday asked.

"We do," Lex confirmed.

"I spoke with him in the ER," Maggie said. "He was adamant about being willing to accept blood products despite being a Jehovah's Witness. He said for us to give it to him if his life was threatened. I couldn't reach the mother. He's a minor but turns eighteen this week."

"Damn," Sunday said. "He could be bleeding inside from the femur fracture. Can someone check his foot for a pulse?"

Benny, the circulating OR nurse, quickly reached under the drape at the patient's foot. "Present. Not strong, but it's there. Capillary bed refill is a little slow but present as well."

Sunday sighed as Lex let out another small grunt. "Let's get the blood up here, Benny," she ordered. "We'll make a final decision when it's time."

"The decision is made," Sunday said boldly. "I'm not letting this kid die. It's his wish. If it were a week from now, we wouldn't be needing this conversation. His mother should have answered her phone. Was the call made from an official hospital line? Please tell me it wasn't from a personal cell phone."

"It was a recorded line identified as coming from the Emergency Department. I left a message. We didn't hear back."

"The blood is on the way," Benny announced, hanging up the wall phone. "The front desk is bringing it straight to the room."

Maggie kept a firm eye on Smith's pressure as Sunday worked rapidly, trying to complete the surgery and get the patient off the table before he crashed.

"His blood pressure isn't responding to the fluid challenge. Systolic is eighty with a heart rate of one twenty," Lex announced.

Maggie looked Sunday's way. Tension had carved small wrinkles of intense worry on her forehead. "Where is the blood?" Sunday's voice was filled with loud frustration.

Benny picked up the phone just as the door opened. "Blood is here," he announced as an OR nurse's hand shot across the partially opened doorway, holding two units of blood that were carefully rubber banded together. He rushed the valuable, life-saving crimson bags over to Lex, where they both rapidly double-checked the labels against the patient's ID wristband, ensuring the proper identity and the blood group match.

Lex, having already properly primed the blood tubing, punctured the unit of blood and hung it high on the IV pole. "Blood is up and going."

Everyone in the room let out a collective gasp of relief, and surgery went forward.

***

ONE HOUR LATER, Sunday and Maggie left the OR, their scrubs soaked in sweat beneath their surgical gowns. The operative procedure went smoothly after the blood transfusion stabilized the patient. Sunday expected an excellent outcome for the boy.

They both dreaded the moment when it was time to speak with the family. The waiting room was filled to the brim with the entire football team present. They loudly cheered when they learned that their team member, Smith, had survived his brain operation.

"May we speak with you privately," Sunday asked, holding her hand out towards the closed door of a small private counseling room.

"Please don't close the door. The room is too claustrophobic," the small, thin-framed woman requested.

Leaving the door open, Sunday plunged forward to deliver the details of the surgery. "We had a struggle with Bobby's blood pressure related to his femur fracture. He was unstable and didn't respond to IV fluids, which we had hoped would raise his blood pressure back to normal limits. Per his pre-op request, we gave him blood, and he is doing well now. They are repairing his femur fracture as we speak. I think he'll recover nicely."

Mrs. Mary Smith's jaw dropped wide as she gasped with a look of horror, placing her hands against her cheeks. "You gave my son blood? Bobby is a Jehovah's Witness. You have condemned him to hell! It's against the teachings and beliefs of our faith."

Sunday looked frantically at Maggie for an answer, certain that this moment would lead to a malpractice lawsuit.

"He signed the transfusion consent," Maggie said.

"He's a minor! With a brain injury!"

Mary Smith collapsed into a nearby chair and howled repeatedly. "My boy! My boy! You destroyed him."

The students, overhearing the mother's cries, looked at Sunday like she had just committed a heinous crime.

"Go! Both of you! Leave me be. Please. Just go," Mary cried out.

Sunday was rescued by the sound of her pager going off, requesting she return to the OR stat.

THE THIRTY-THREE-year-old mother was urgently taken to the OR. Her brain aneurysm ruptured during her delay for surgery after having been bumped to make room for the actively dying Smith boy. Thankfully, someone had seen to it that she was prepped and ready for Sunday when she walked into the room.

The atmosphere in the OR was stressful for the first hour, but the surgery had been successful. Sunday shot Maggie a grim look as they popped off their gloves. "The patient needs to be closely monitored. I fear she may have suffered a brain insult from the delay and rupture." It was hard to face the husband and two teenage girls that it would be a wait-and-see situation. "We won't know her brain function until she wakes up, but I'm optimistic because the surgery went well," Sunday said before they left the room.

***

DURING A BRIEF break, Maggie got a page from CT and called them ASAP, as requested. "This is Maggie."

"The film is up on Bruce Russell," the technician confirmed. "You and Doctor Richardson need to take a look at it like—super-duper STAT."

Maggie and Sunday raced to the closest imaging stand and pulled Bruce's CT films for viewing. In unison, they both moved their heads closer and stared in disbelief.

"Are those gas bubbles?" Maggie asked.

"In his brain? How?" Sunday asked. It wasn't really a question but more of a rhetorical statement. "Flesh-eating bacteria?"

"That's impossible," Maggie said, staring in disbelief at the films.

"It's apparently quite possible because definitely it's what we're looking at. Get the ICU on the horn and have him placed in isolation," Sunday ordered. "And order a septic workup. Let's go."

The two of them headed for the ICU and were greeted by a large **Contact Precautions** sign already posted on the door. They both quickly gowned and gloved and entered the room. "I can smell it from here," Sunday observed. She completed a thorough exam while Maggie helped. "Let's check the wound."

"I checked it last night. It looked good," Maggie confirmed. "I don't understand. According to his data, he's already getting septic. How the hell did he get necrotizing fasciitis?"

"I'll bet you a hundred bucks his incision doesn't look good now," Sunday said, furrowing her brow as she removed the dressing. "Flesh-eating bacteria notoriously blossoms and spreads rapidly, especially in a fresh surgical wound. Not to mention he has cancer, and he's on steroids."

The more they unraveled the dressing, the greater the foul stink of infection presented itself.

Maggie gasped when she saw the wound. "It <u>definitely</u> didn't look like this yesterday."

"Like I said. It moves fast," Sunday replied, her voice filled with disappointment.

Maggie automatically handed Sunday a culture swab, so Sunday could obtain a specimen for them to send to the lab.

"Get him booked for the OR for wound debridement immediately," Sunday ordered, removing her gloves and gown. After a thorough hand scrubbing, they exited the isolation anteroom and headed back to the OR, exhausted and hungry.

"I still don't see how this could have happened," Maggie repeated her earlier thought.

"Me either. I scrubbed Bruce's surgical site thoroughly. I'm always diligent when doing surgical scrubs because I'm so mindful about stopping infection before it starts. That's why I do the scrubs myself. You saw me. You were there. Please do me a favor. Let's keep this under wraps until I can talk to the lab. Infectious Diseases are likely all over this case as we speak, and you know things travel and get blown out of proportion."

***

BY THREE O'CLOCK, Bruce was safely back in his room and full of the required antibiotics to cover the infection.

"I'm on call, so I'll spend the night in the on-call room. I'll keep close tabs on him," Sunday said, just before heading off to see a few patients in the clinic. "Do rounds for me. Let me know if I need to do anything.

"Will do."

Chapter 21

Isolation Room

FTER ROUNDS, MAGGIE dropped by to see Kerrington. Nurse Bonnie Holliday, who was on duty, said visiting was okay, but only briefly. "We're expecting an admission."

Maggie stepped up to the viewing window of Kerrington's room and instinctively pressed her trembling hand against the cold, heavy glass window—her heart ached with a profound longing that was so deep it quickly shattered her every sense of well-being. She yearned to reach through the glass barrier and touch her husband's face, to caress his skin with her fingertips, to hold his hand and let him know she was with him and not alone. Maggie's eyes, filled with unshed fresh tears as she stared fixated on the love of her life—her heart crumbled with each passing moment. Kerrington, viewed by the world as a giant, was so frail and vulnerable. As a nurse, a feeling of paralyzing powerlessness twisted in her chest. Kerrington's condition was dire, more so than ever before, and the weight of that reality pressed down on her like a suffocating cold fog.

The rhythmic hiss of his ventilator served as a cruel reminder of the battle he was fighting and losing—each breath a reminder of his struggle. Maggie's eyes hovered over the IV bags, a nursing ritual she performed with each visit. She scrutinized the drug labels, looking for new medications that might offer a glimmer of hope or proof of him losing his struggle with life. Her gaze moved to the infusion pumps, noting with a sinking feeling that the pressor dosages had been increased. Pressors were used as a desperate measure to stabilize blood pressure, but it was clear Kerrington was becoming more unstable by the hour. She became overcome with the feeling she'd experienced so many times before—death's shadow was lingering over his body, inching forward each day with relentless determination.

Maggie's shoulders sagged in defeat as she wiped her eyes. She looked down, trying to hide her tears from the familiar faces of nurses and doctors bustling about in the corridor behind her.

Kerrington's eyes, once a piercing bright blue that earned him the nickname "Hawk" on Wall Street, were taped shut as a precaution to prevent them from drying out.

Maggie wasn't the only one wondering what the future held. The financial world was abuzz with roaring and frightening speculation as markets reacted wildly to the uncertainty of Kerrington's fate. His illness was veiled in mystery and had become a global sensation. His connection to the Veridian XV virus became a relentless viral sensation on social media, capturing everyone's attention. News anchors were desperate to get information about him. Panic rippled through every place he'd visited before his illness, yet no other cases had emerged, leaving only questions without answers and heightening fear in its wake.

Maggie's heart clenched as slices of Kerrington's former image captured her heart. The sunlight streaming through the hospital window glistened through the magnificent locks of his prematurely silver hair, a poignant reminder. He'd been such a strong man. So handsome and tall. Her powerful hero. Kerrington had always carried a certain elegant air about him. His hair and stature had given him the edge in the boardroom—and when he spoke, people clung to his every word because he was not a man to waste words. Would she ever see that beautiful part of him again? Or hear his laughter as he shared riddles with Dorrie? Maggie clenched her eyes together. It was hard being a nurse— having the ability to read the signs and sum things up. Truth stared her in the face. Her beautiful warrior was fighting the mightiest battle of his life—and he was losing it. She understood the grim reality of his condition, and it terrified her.

"Hi again," Bonnie said softly, pulling Maggie into a comforting embrace. "I got a free minute and just wanted to talk to you. I'm so sorry, girl."

Maggie returned her hug and deliberately held her close, seeking to absorb some of her friend's strength. "I'm so glad you are his nurse, Bonnie. Please. Please. Be careful."

When Bonnie released her, she sought Maggie's eyes, reading them as only a nurse can. "Are you okay? Can I do anything for you?"

Maggie sighed. "Pull off a miracle," Maggie replied respectfully, her smile a fragile attempt at hope.

The two stood silent, staring at Kerrington, their friendship providing comfort without needing to speak.

Bonnie's phone went off. Maggie couldn't hear what was being said but knew immediately, from Bonnie's look, that it was horrible and urgent. She hung up.

"You have to leave. Now. We have two cases on the way up. They're entering the unit now. I have to get dressed to help."

"Veridian cases?"

"None other. Call me later."

Maggie exited the isolation area just in time to see one of the new patients roll out of the elevator inside. She couldn't help but look back through the door. Beneath the plastic bed tent, she could make out the patient's face. It was Ming. The second patient was Mario.

***

JUST AS MAGGIE reached the entrance to the OR, Benny appeared practically out of nowhere.

"Maggie," he called out, forcefully grabbing Maggie's arm and pulling her back out of the automatic door the minute she entered. "Ming is nearly dead, and his house is crawling with CDC peeps. It's all over the news."

"I know. God, help us, Benny. When does the bad luck stop?"

"Guess what Ming's last words were before he passed out?

"Tell me?"

"He told Glenn he had a cure."

"A cure? For Kerrington. He might be cured?"

They both immediately notified the OR they had a family emergency and left the hospital immediately.

Chapter 22

Ming ICU Isolation

MING AWAKENED to the purring sounds of the ventilator and beeping infusion pumps. There was a person dressed in an encapsulated white BSL 4 personal protective suit. They were changing a glass medication bottle filled with a milky white fluid. Ming assumed it was propofol, the Michael Jackson juice. They were keeping him sedated with it to keep him calm while on the ventilator. When the person turned to face him, he smiled despite his mouth being filled with a thick tube that went to his lungs to allow air to reach his lungs. A warm, fuzzy feeling came over him. The Chinese woman smiled back. She was the woman from his dreams. The woman who would become his wife. His eyes trailed to her white suit. The name written in black magic marker read Sheng, M.D. Ming couldn't tear his eyes away from her angelic porcelain skin.

A Chinese face with lips the color of persimmons and eyes like obsidian pools of black shining glass, filled with wisdom and intelligence, yet full of kindness. Her short-cut ink-black hair shined like a midnight river of silk. Every movement of her hand was graceful despite the bulky gloves. Her name told of family success and abundance. But her spirit, a mixture of vulnerability and resilience, was what captured his heart. He wanted to tell her all about himself and brag about his success as a scientist. He was hopeful that she would love him if she knew him. He wanted to remove her gloves, hold her hands, and take her into his arms forever. Yes. She would be his wife.

Ming's eyelids became too heavy to keep open. His heart filled with happiness and contentment as he listened to her humming to herself as she worked. It was a sweet, familiar folk song from his childhood. **Yue Liang Dai Biao Wo de Xin**, meaning the moon, represents my heart. Yes, they were alike—kindred spirits. He drifted off to sleep, hoping he would live to hold her in his arms.

***

THE NEXT TIME MING opened his eyes, it was dark outside the hospital window. Several boats floated in the river. He searched for Doctor Sheng but found a Black man with broad shoulders at his bedside. The name on his suit was Lucas, RN, NP. His strong hands were changing the dressings on Mings's arms, applying a thick white paste to blisters that wept yellowish blood-tinged fluids. He was filled with horror and longed to cry out with confession and ask how many people he'd killed. Had the virus gotten out and spread, killing thousands, maybe millions? Shame hovered over his soul. His mind rapidly summed up his critical condition. So many new IV drips with medications. Big bags, little bags, and medium-sized bags. IV poles that held three pumps a piece. When the nurse suctioned his endotracheal tube, the secretions were yellow instead of clear. Ming tightened his eyelids together, wanting to cry yet unable to. He wanted to live. *I have so much more I want to do. I have the cure. I can't let the world die. I have to get well to tell them where the cure is kept. I can't die in vain. I have children to make.*

***

AFTER THAT DAY, there were no more meaningful periods in Ming's life. His mind, no longer a sponge for knowledge, hovered in a deep state of unconsciousness, floating from one day into the next.

Chapter 23

BSL 4 Laboratory

IT TOOK MAGGIE and Benny quite a bit of time to find the fourth level because the entrance to the elevator leading to the fourth floor was hidden behind a sliding wall across from the main elevator.

"This place is way too creepy," Benny said. "It's giving me the heebie-geebies."

Maggie agreed. She wanted to send Benny back out of the lab, but she knew she needed him as a lookout and to help her don the heavy-duty safety equipment.

When the door opened to the fourth level, automatic lights brightly illuminated the entire floor. Most of the entry-level housed a simple utilitarian-type office area. There were old-appearing steel desks topped with green antique bank lamps. It seemed to Maggie not much work was done in the area anymore. Only one desk had papers and files on it. The rest didn't appear to be in active use.

They quickly perused through the papers on the desk, and Benny suddenly stopped when his eyes landed on a notebook labeled **CURE V-XV**. "Bingo! Check this out."

Knowing their time was limited, they thumbed through the first few pages, which were medical mumbo jumbo and clearly not what they needed. Maggie skipped forward to the last five pages. "Jackpot, Benny. We hit the jackpot."

It was all about the cure. The clear yellow liquid was stored in the refrigerator along with five pre-filled syringes that were housed in a special clear container. The virus Veridian XV was stored in the slide warmer next to the refrigerator. A hazardous material warning sign was posted on the door.

At the far end of the room was a wall of thick paned glass that housed high-level safety suits. Thankfully, they appeared to be brand new and not outdated like the office equipment.

Maggie shivered at the sight of the giant circular steel vault that shined eerily in the illuminated room. It didn't require a combination. They simply had to twist the heavy wheel to open the airlock chamber.

"Well, we might as well get it over with," Benny said, moving to the area where the safety suits that looked like outer space gear were stored.

"If anything happens, Benny. Leave. Do not try to come get me."

"I'm not leaving you, Maggie. We're a team."

"No! I do not want you exposed," she replied, her voice firm. She paused for a moment, thinking. "Here's the plan. If anything goes wrong, I will tell you. Call 911 and blow the whole lid off of it. It's not worth losing one more life in the secret lab of horrors—and so, help me, Benny, if we make it out of here, I'm going to destroy this place myself. It's what Kerrington planned."

"And I'm going to help you. It'll be total annihilation."

Benny helped Maggie put on her complex, full-body, air-supplied protective suit. Donning and doffing were the proper terminology for safely putting on and taking off protective gear. BSL four gear demanded strict procedures to be rigidly followed. Both of them had formally received special training in Anniston, Alabama, at FEMA's Center for Domestic Preparedness.

Maggie and Benny inspected the thick white colored gear, and she applied disposable gloves before applying the powered air-purifying respirator. She confirmed the respirator was working correctly before applying the full-body suit. Benny helped her zip it closed. A little claustrophobic emotion surged through her heart for the first few minutes, as it usually did after getting fully geared. Still, the sensation quickly passed when Maggie noticed it was pretty easy to breathe in the suit. Maggie pulled on the heavy outer gloves, and Benny taped the edges with duct tape to ensure a tight seal. Benny inspected the entire suit to make sure the seals were secure.

They did a final communication check, and then Maggie stepped through the airlock door. It closed with the resounding sound of steel on steel. Maggie stood fascinated yet filled with terror about the tasks at hand. Up to this point, she'd not been afraid because her drive to save Kerrington was foremost in her mind.

When the next door automatically opened to allow her to enter the BSL four lab, her stomach sank to a nauseous level as she realized that what she was about to do held grave danger. The access door closed behind her, echoing with a harsh thud, catching her by surprise and making her body jolt. It reminded her to be super cautious.

Maggie's eyes at once did a slow search of the room. She blinked hard. The space was clean and shiny, and there appeared to be no sign of active work in the first room. The adjoining chamber was sizable, with a simple desk in the corner covered with files and notebooks that were organized neatly. Various steel tabletops were covered with diverse scientific equipment, which was too complex for Maggie to understand.

On the far side of the wall stood a giant commercial glass-door refrigerator next to the same type of warmer. It was clear intricate work was being done in the lab.

Maggie quickly headed over to the hybrid refrigerator/warmer. The thick, clear-glazed double doors made it easy for her to see the contents stored on wire shelves. She gasped with relief. Maggie could clearly see the prize she'd come for. The yellow liquid was stored precisely as described in the manual. She removed all of the vaccine cures, shut the door, grabbed the notebook, and put everything carefully into unique sealed bags. Maggie then scrubbed the outside of the containers with a high-grade germicidal wipe.

"You're running out of time, Maggie. Let's go." Benny warned over the communication system.

"I'm coming. I just have one more thing I must do," Maggie replied through her special microphone. She moved back over to the slide warmer and placed her hand on the temperature dial. With trembling hands, Maggie turned the dial to 167 degrees, which was as high as it would go. She smiled and said out loud to herself. "Goodbye, Veridian." The humming engine responded quickly, filling Maggie with great satisfaction. They would never have to worry about Veridian XV being on their property anymore. It would be dead before the sun came up on a new day.

Maggie exited the room feeling exuberant but exhausted. Benny awaited her exit, holding up big plastic bags. She placed the items in the double bag for extra security, and then Benny helped her remove her equipment.

Maggie was covered in sweat and quickly guzzled down the extra-large bottled water Benny held open, ready for her to drink and rehydrate. Then, they headed back to the elevator and exited the lab.

Out in the open, they both stared wide-eyed at the container Maggie had taken from the fourth level. Maggie shivered at the thought that she'd actually held it in her hand.

"I want to see it. What does it look like?" Benny queried, staring at the container.

"It's regular vials of clear yellow medication. Ming knew precisely what he was doing. At least, let's hope he did. I don't want to open it."

"Well, if you're planning on giving it to Kerrington, you need to open it sometime," Benny warned. "Now is as fine a time as any. Don't be so selfish. I want to see it. Besides, Ming carried it in his pocket. It can't be that dangerous."

Maggie opened the container, and they sat in stillness, staring at it. Finally, Benny spoke. "I need a drink."

"You? What about me? I deserve one."

Chapter 24

Dorrie Blanchard

MAGGIE AND BENNY were at a nursing conference at the hospital. They had to recertify every two years to keep their certification in Forensic Nursing. They had just finished taking the post-lecture examination and were waiting on their scores when they simultaneously received a phone call from Amelia. She had them on a conference call, which meant she considered the call an emergency. They both stepped into the hall.

"You need to come home. The school called me to pick Dorrie up. She's crying and won't talk to me. The school wouldn't tell me what happened. They insisted they could only speak to the parent."

"We'll be right there," Benny replied. "You call the school while I drive."

Maggie called the superintendent to schedule a prompt meeting. When she connected with Mr. Steven Baxley's voice, she noted that it was uncomfortably stiff. She put the call on speakerphone so Benny could hear. Baxley had usually always been open and friendly around them. Something clearly had gone wrong.

"We understand Dorrie was sent home from school today, but we don't know why. We were told you wanted to meet with us. Can we come by after lunch?"

"We don't want you coming to the school, Mrs. Blanchard. It would be best if we met via **Zoom** conference. I'll email you the link. Would four p.m. work for you?"

"Yes. Four works fine."

"Are you familiar with Zoom?"

"I am, but I'd prefer to meet in person."

Baxley cleared his voice. "That won't be possible, Mrs. Blanchard. Meet me at four."

The call ended abruptly. Maggie looked over at Benny, who had an annoyed yet greatly concerned look. "What was that all about? It's like he definitely doesn't want a face-to-face meeting. What could Dorrie have done for them to send her home? She's a straight-A student, and she's even part of the student council."

***

DORRIE RAN SOBBING into Maggie's arms before she could even get out of the car. "They kicked me out, Mom! I got called into the office for screaming in the hall, but I was so scared. Someone painted a red gravestone on my locker door with the message to get out. It looked like blood!"

At first, Maggie was caught for words. "I'm sure it <u>did</u> scare you, but you're okay now. And safe. I promise. So, settle down, and let's get in the house. Okay?"

"I don't think it's going to be okay, Mom. The students shouted at me. Go. Go. Go. I didn't do anything wrong, I promise."

Benny took her into his arms. "Like your Mom said. Let's settle down. Stop crying. I'm sure it's just a simple misunderstanding. We'll talk to Mr. Baxley and get the facts. Now, let's get us a chocolate milkshake. That always makes things better." Benny forced a smile, put his arm around Dorrie, and escorted her into the house.

***

AT FOUR PM SHARP, the Zoom conference call connected, and Maggie and Benny faced a very grim-looking Baxley. The meeting was straightforward. Baxley skipped the niceties and went straight to the point as if he'd rehearsed the conversation many times.

"Dorrie cannot return to our school. Your husband has an unusual virus, and we don't want it in our school. A lot of parents have complained and are refusing to send their children to our school. The students say they are afraid. She'll have to transfer somewhere else."

"She's not sick. She doesn't have the virus. She went through the proper quarantine."

"People say the virus came from your property, so you don't know for certain she isn't virus-free. I'm sorry if this is an inconvenience to you. We have to consider the safety of everyone, not just her. The board of directors met and made the decision. It's final. Dorrie will not be allowed to attend any of our schools."

"What do we do about her education?"

"I would suggest hiring a tutor, but under the circumstances, that might not be possible. Pretty much everyone is talking about this virus. Possibly, you might want to consider boarding school far enough away that people aren't familiar with the story of your husband's illness. I can send you a list."

Benny snapped. "We're not sending our daughter to a boarding school. She needs her family near, and we're a good family. We'll be talking to our lawyers."

"We've done that as well. Our decision, as I said, is final. We've cleaned out Dorrie's locker and will have someone deliver her items. Good day, sir."

As before, the call ended abruptly.

"What in the hell?" Benny mumbled as Maggie looked at the door to make sure Dorrie wasn't nearby. "Boarding school?"

"We have Amelia. She could tutor her."

"Amelia is not qualified to teach all the subjects Dorrie needs."

Silence hung in the air as they both sat buried deep in thought. Finally, Maggie spoke. "We'll enroll her in homeschooling and teach her at home. She's smart enough and reliable enough to do the work. Then, after all this has died down, maybe they'll let her back in."

Chapter 25

Lila's Madness

LILA HAD A METHOD to her madness. Pick up several items to buy, check them out, and walk out the door with the small-sized item in her hand. Then, if she got caught, she'd pretend she'd made an error. Walking away with a stolen item brought her a giddy feeling that was totally satisfying in a way that was hard to explain. She was a kleptomaniac, and she was on a shoplifting journey to ease her anxiety when her cell phone rang.

William Strout, Bruce's partner at the law firm of Russell, Stout, Bigham, and Finley, extended an invitation to Lila for dinner. His voice was unusually warm and friendly, almost as if they were old friends, which piqued Lila's curiosity. "It's a casual affair," he assured her, "just the two of us and my wife Becky, of course. "I'd like to catch up on Bruce," he added in a hushed tone as if sharing a secret.

Lila was caught and trapped for words because she truthfully had no desire to dine with such stuffy people. After giving it a second thought, however, she decided to accept the invitation. Her smile was smug when she ended the call, realizing how the dinner invite might work to her advantage to solve her current dilemma.

She wanted a new dress for the dinner party, and today, the stolen item would be earrings to match the dress. She didn't really want or need anything because her closet and jewelry box were filled to the brim with an endless amount of valuables, but now, she was filled with an urgent need to feel better. Stealing items that she didn't even want or need made her feel powerful. Her shrink had helped her stop her thievery for a while, but now, she was anxious and sensed a helplessness.

Although she was filled with guilt about what she was about to do, she couldn't stop herself. She joyfully picked out an expensive silk dress and new shoes to match, then paid for them. She exited the upscale store carrying her dashing earrings in her hand, saving herself a whopping three hundred dollars. The feeling was exhilarating, but later, when she got home and looked at the stolen jewels, an ugly realization swept through her mind. Bruce would be so ashamed of her if he found out. The thrill of the ride was over, and Lila was left to deal with the less happy emotions related to kleptomania.

***

THREE HOURS LATER, Lila arrived on the Strout doorstep wearing her new, long red silk dress. Yes, she was too dressed up for the occasion, but they'd just have to forgive her. She craved the beautiful feeling she always got when she got dolled up and looked fancy. With Bruce in the hospital, the dressy moments didn't come anymore.

Becky and William greeted her with a hearty welcome, and Becky complimented her on her pretty gown. Lila gifted them with a fine bottle of white wine.

Their house looked much like Lila's and Bruce's—bright white, metropolitan design, a spread-out floor plan with massive columns separating the areas, and gorgeous, large, colorful modern art decorating the walls. A glass wall overlooked a gigantic pool and gardens, blending nicely with the over-the-top modern decor. Soft, serene music played over a piped-in stereo system, adding a comfortable ambiance along with the dimmed lighting meant to set the mood for dinner.

The night was indeed low-key. Italian seasonings lingered in the air throughout the central part of Strout's house. They ate outside overlooking the sparkling pool as temperatures in Charlotte had cooled off to a beautiful eighty degrees, which made the outdoors welcoming.

A ping of jealousy struck Lila as she watched William and Becky together. They were the perfect power couple, with both of them having been born and bred in the deep southern traditions that were steeped with upper-class mannerisms and influence. William looked like the southern lawyer **Murdough**, who had recently been found guilty of murdering his wife and son. His dark blue eyes held a mysterious look, almost evil. Becky was from Charleston, South Carolina, and had the well-bred airs of aristocracy and wealth.

Lila arrived feeling nervous and queasy and had been pondering endlessly during the drive to Strout's house, wondering whether William was aware of Bruce's intention to divorce her. The worry left her body feeling stiffly tense and uncertain about what awaited her. She could feel thick tension between them. It was clear that the visit wasn't solely about Bruce's cancer treatment. There was a confident attitude about William, which made Lila wonder about the invitation to the dinner. Was she invited out of obligation rather than him being concerned about her well-being during these trying times? Lila's curiosity led to uneasiness. She stiffened her posture and held her head higher in the air. She was determined to carry on and successfully fulfill her role as a dutiful wife in Bruce's absence.

Lila hadn't even swallowed her first sip of the delightful 2008 Chateau Lafite Rothschild red wine when she realized William wanted something unique from her—as costly as the wine. Lila smiled and looked William directly in the eye. "I believe this bottle of wine runs about twelve hundred and fifty dollars a bottle—a hefty price tag to attach to your dinner menu. What's really going on here, Willy?"

"Let's forego the stiff dining rules tonight and have some more intimate chatter," William replied, wiping his mouth with his napkin and taking a pause for a sip of wine, as if he were struggling to find the right words to continue. I heard the strangest thing at the office today," William said, his eyes looking directly at Lila. "I certainly hope it isn't true because it genuinely concerned me."

Lila didn't respond because she was unsure what William was referring to and didn't want the partners to know how close to death Bruce was at the current time.

"I heard Bruce has an unusual, shall we say, hospital-acquired infection," William declared as if he knew it to be factual. "A serious infection. And a rare one."

"That is true. Bruce is quite ill," Lila responded, looking down, avoiding his eyes. "He has what many have referred to as Flesh Easting Bacteria."

Becky coughed uncomfortably. Lila smiled inside. *Shock and Awe* was Lila's favorite game to play in the world of the over-cultured, snotty people of high society. Lila didn't really give a shit whether Becky approved or not. After all, William brought the subject up.

"It's frankly a hospital-acquired infection that looks like it very well may take his life. I think you need to jump all over that, Lila."

"What do you mean?" Lila replied, feeling taken aback a bit by his boldness.

"I mean just what you think I do. You're Bruce's power of attorney, and I think a nice, shocking malpractice lawsuit should be considered. I hear there's another one in the wings against his doctor for giving blood to a Jehovah's Witness. We should strike while the iron is hot. You know. Catch them when they're vulnerable."

Lila sat quietly, secretly delighted he'd brought the malpractice issue up. It kept her from doing it herself, which she was afraid would make her look greedy. Now, Lila simply looked more like a victim. Finally, she spoke. "You are Bruce's best friend. What do you think he'd want me to do?"

"Get revenge. Sue the pants off of them," William said, staring Lila hard in the eyes.

Lila knew full well what Willy wanted. As Bruce's lawyer, he would make millions.

"Then, I think Bruce and I should have revenge," Lila responded, lifting her glass in a toast with a smile and taking a big sip of the delectable wine.

Chapter 26

Kerrington Isolation Unit

MAGGIE, BENNY, AND GLENN entered the Isolation wing. Maggie nodded, moved away from the two of them, and scurried quickly towards Kerrington's room, gripping the needle and syringe tightly. It was loaded with the clear yellow liquid vaccine she planned to deliver to her precious husband.

Glenn kept the nurses busy with patient-related questions. Benny used his jovial charm and started talking about the Carolina Panthers football season, which was about to start. It didn't take long to get everyone engrossed in the conversation.

Maggie anxiously stood at the viewing window, watching Kerrington's chest as it stiffly rose and fell in rhythm with the ventilator window. It was clear to Maggie that the ventilator was working hard to push air into his lungs. Kerrington was actively dying with each breath, and Maggie shivered at the thought of him dying before she could get the vaccine into him. She looked up at the propofol medication bottle designed to keep Kerrington sedated while on the ventilator, to keep him from fighting it. Maggie traced the white milky liquid in the IV line that traveled to his intravenous triple-lumen catheter. She checked the other medication bags. Two other lines entered the triple lumen. One was Dopamine, which kept his blood pressure up and protected his kidneys. The other line was plain normal saline. That was the line she needed to use. She made a mental note that it was connected to the brown port. Maggie thoroughly searched every nook and cranny of his ICU room, as it was pretty large. She was relieved to see there was no one else present but Kerrington. Quickly, she scanned both ends of the corridor. *So far, so good*, she muttered nervously to herself. *Let's do this*.

Maggie pushed the metal door handle and entered the anteroom. She placed the syringe on the counter and rapidly donned her BSL4 protective gear as if she were responding to a code. Then, she picked up an empty red lab carrier container, grabbed the syringe, and entered the room.

Within seconds, Maggie spotted the brown-colored cap and searched for the closest access to the line. She double-checked to ensure the line was connected to normal saline fluid. That was important because the vaccine couldn't be mixed with fluid-containing drugs as it might not be compatible with other medications. Maggie twisted the syringe into the port and did a quick pull back to confirm the proper placement of the catheter. When she confirmed that blood was present, she gently pushed the plunger and watched as the yellow-colored vaccine floated through the tubing. She deeply exhaled as it slowly entered Kerrington's body. Maggie took another deep breath and prayed Kerrington wouldn't have a bad reaction, knowing the risk was high.

Maggie withdrew the syringe, watched, and waited.

"What are you doing?" A woman's voice demanded over the intercom. She was standing outside the viewing window watching Maggie with fierce, penetrating nurse eyes.

Maggie's heart jumped violently. Her hands shook as she carefully placed the syringe in the lab box and explained, "I'm from the CDC lab. They want another sample." She was grateful for the heavy protective gear that shielded her face from clear view.

"Next time, make sure you sign in at the desk. We like to keep track of everyone who enters this room. CDC rules," the nurse dryly commented as she stared curiously at Maggie, unsure as to whether she believed her. Maggie let out a sigh of relief when the nurse simply walked away.

Maggie speedily returned to the anteroom, where she doffed her equipment.

Out in the corridor, Maggie stood staring at Kerrington for a good fifteen minutes, watching him like a hawk for signs of anything—any change, good or bad.

When Maggie finally returned to the desk, the same nurse looked suspiciously at Maggie and demanded, "Where were you? I was just at your husband's window, and you weren't there."

"I went to the bathroom," Maggie stammered.

"You should get home and get some sleep," the nurse stated, her voice suddenly filled with sympathy.

"Thank you," Maggie said before exiting the unit and heading to her car. She wasn't waiting for anyone.

Glenn and Benny joined her shortly after that.

"Any change?" Benny asked excitedly—out of breath from rushing.

"Nothing."

"Nothing?" Glenn queried.

"Absolutely nothing."

"There's still hope, Maggie," Benny said, his voice encouraging.

Chapter 27

Wickedness

L ILA SAT DUMMIFIED in her living room wing chair. William Strout was on the phone with her, updating her on the lawsuit.

"We filed the papers and have met with hospital attorneys. Things may be tougher than we expected. The hospital has cultured all the places Bruce was exposed to during his hospitalization. There is no evidence of the bacteria anywhere. They are now trying to say Bruce brought it with him on his hands or skin when he entered the facility and that he gave it to himself by touching his wound with his contaminated hand."

"Those people are freaking crazy! He got it in the hospital."

"You know that, but we can't prove, beyond a shadow of a doubt, that he got the Flesh-Eating Bacteria while in the facility. That is what the jury will want to hear. They want proof. Otherwise, we will be forced to settle out of court for a pittance of what we are suing for, which hardly makes it worth our effort."

"We're not dropping the suit. Something will come up to prove it. We just have to be patient. Don't give up on me, Bill."

William sighed. "Thirty days. They are still swabbing places. I'll demand one of our staff members be present during testing. Maybe even make them retest areas. The picture looks dim, though, Lila. I just wanted to give you a heads-up. It was a bad idea on my part – this whole thing. I'll keep you posted."

Lila ended the phone call and threw the phone across the room. *What do I do now?*

***

LILA WAS STILL ANGRY as she shoveled strawberry ice cream into her mouth while watching an episode of CSI. Thirty minutes later, the epiphany struck. Lila leaped from her chair, ran over to her pocketbook sitting on the hallway entry table, opened it, and pulled out the culture swab. Walking over to the light, she stared hard at the cotton tip stained with blood from Bruce's incision. Was the bacteria still moist enough to transfer? She lightly touched it. It would work.

***

LILA SPENT THE entire day in the hospital waiting for the perfect opportunity to carry out her plan. Twice, she had spotted Sunday in the corridor waiting for the elevator. The first time, Sunday was paged to the nurse's station. The second time when Sunday stepped into the elevator, it was too full for Lila to get in. Neither time had Sunday seen her. This time, she would be successful, she thought. She was directly behind the doctor. When the elevator doors opened, Lila pulled off her plan. She stumbled against Sunday, knocking her to the ground, scratching the doctor's arm with the bacteria-laced eighteen gauge trimmed-off needle that was tucked between her fingers and hidden by her wedding ring. *Bingo.* She said to herself. There was a long scratch on Sunday's arm.

"I'm so sorry, doctor. I must have not been looking at what I was doing. I tripped."

"It's okay. I'm fine," Sunday said as she went on her way.

Lila smiled. Sunday didn't even realize she'd been injured. Lila just hoped the bacteria took hold.

Chapter 28

Hospital Boardroom

ITHOUT WARNING, the day took a sharp turn for the worse as Maggie crossed the threshold into the OR locker room to change into scrubs. She grabbed a pair of clean scrubs off the rack and took a quick whiff of the green material, as was her habit. There was nothing better than putting on new scrubs straight from the laundry. She loved the pristine smell.

Maggie was surprised when she glanced up and saw her good friend Sybil Good, the OR Supervisor. Today, the look on her pretty face was different—grim.

"I need you to come with me, Maggie," Sybil said in a quiet voice. "Sure. What's up?"

"They want you in a meeting."

"What kind of meeting?" Maggie began to feel nervous because of Sybil's tone. She knew her coworker well, and Sybil seemed to be as uncomfortable about the situation as Maggie was.

Sybil and Maggie walked down the gleaming corridor and into the plush, carpeted Department of Surgery boardroom. The shiny, expensive, colossal conference table was filled with high-ranking officials from various departments of Saint Vincent's Medical Center: Surgery, Infectious Diseases, Critical Care Medicine, and the Legal Department. Maggie didn't recognize many of the people in attendance. It was a daunting sight. She straightened her back and lifted her head. The purpose of the meeting was clear right off the bat. It was a Sentinel Event investigation into the blood transfusion debacle that had prompted a hefty lawsuit along with claims of hospital mismanagement.

Maggie scanned the sea of faces, most wearing forbidding expressions.

She'd walked in on the tail end of a temperamental meeting. The legal eagle's eyes were piercing and hostile, indicating that many present were more focused on defending the hospital than on understanding Maggie's perspective.

A human resources representative used a simple hand gesture to indicate that Maggie should take a seat in the only empty spot at the table. Maggie had less than six months of experience in surgery and was a relatively new member of the surgical team. As such, she was ill-prepared for the complexity of the questions she predicted were sure to come her way. Maggie looked down and saw the edges of the paper in her hand trembling. Quickly, she placed it flat on the table, thinking it best she hid her bad case of overwhelming fear.

To her relief, after about an hour, the group's approach softened towards her. The Sentinel Event inquiry had gotten off to a rough start, having been blown out of proportion, likely due to the media frenzy surrounding Doctor Richardson's other pending legal cases.

It appeared that Maggie was there only because she worked directly with Doctor Richardson and not because they intended to harm her on any level. The questions pertained to all the Richardson cases, and she told the truth as best she could. One of the attorneys quickly intervened and indicated all questions should be limited to the transfusion event, which lowered the temperament in the room significantly. Maggie sighed in relief and continued forward with what was needed from her.

Yes, it was her job to review consents prior to blood transfusions. "I spoke with the patient, and he agreed to a blood transfusion," Maggie confirmed. "He was a minor, and the mother who had custody could not be reached. The patient told us his father had signed a consent during an earlier hospitalization at one of our outlying hospitals, and we went with that information. The patient was not confused. His only complaint was a severe headache. The surgery was emergent, and due to the urgency, we went with the signed consent from the father per electronic records."

The inquiry continued for several hours, and Maggie was exhausted when she was allowed to leave. Per instructions, she was not to have conversations with Doctor Richardson or anyone else about the topics discussed in the room.

***

THAT SAME DAY, Maggie got the news that a second lawsuit had been filed against Doctor Richardson and the hospital by the family of Julie Snipes, the woman who had suffered complications from the aneurysm repair. The family, having heard about patients dismissing Doctor Richardson from their cases, hired an attorney and sent a formal request in writing to have another neurosurgeon take over the care for Snipes. Per request, Sunday was removed from the Snipes case. A malpractice suit quickly followed.

The building news surrounding Doctor Richardson barreled through the hospital with mighty speed. Maggie heard from at least five surgery employees that more patients had requested to have Doctor Richardson removed from their cases.

***

BY THE END OF THE DAY, Maggie could see the writing on the wall and was not surprised, in the least, when Sybil Good notified her that she was to report to the Chief of Neurosurgery. Maggie wanted to call on Sunday to not only offer her support but also try to find out what was happening on her end. All she'd heard so far was gossip. She wanted to hug her friend and be with her.

The result was hard to take. When Maggie entered the office for the meeting, Sunday was sitting on the sofa waiting. Her eyes were red and puffy from crying. Maggie opened her mouth to at least say hello, but Sunday stopped her.

"We're not allowed to communicate."

Maggie nodded understanding and turned in time to see the door open for the meeting to start. Thirty minutes later, it was all over except for more crying. Sunday was officially suspended from practicing surgery for the next five days until the hospital's legal team had thoroughly interviewed all parties involved. They needed time to review all the patients or families involved. In other words, Doctor Richardson's surgical privileges were suspended. Maggie's assignment was altered. She was barred from participating in surgery and was told to immediately round on Richardson's patients and officially turn them over to the newly assigned neurosurgeons. Then, she, too,

146

would not be working for five days. Instead of crying, she became furious with the very institution she had dedicated her life to serving.

***

BENNY WAS NOTIFIED by Sybil Good that he'd been transferred to Section Seven, which was orthopedic surgery.

"I don't have orthopedic surgery experience. I'm not doing it," he exclaimed.

"You'll get a proper orientation," Sybil promised.

"Five days? I have zero knowledge of orthopedic surgery except for procedures I performed when I worked in the ER."

"It's where we need you," Sybil dryly replied.

"Then, I'm requesting five days of emergency time off."

"I can't approve your leave, Benny. We're short-staffed. Word has it that Doctor Richardson's job is on the line, and yours will be, too, if you decline to be reassigned. Be here at seven in the morning. Report to Jeremy in Orthopedics."

In a blaze of fury, Benny left the OR and went straight to the ER, where he burst into the Nurse Manager's office. "I need a job."

Thirty minutes later, Benny left the office with a new job working as a Registered Nurse in the ER. He was exhilarated when he walked back into Sybil's office and said, "I quit."

Grinning like a Cheshire cat, he headed off to meet Maggie.

***

BENNY WAS LATE for his daily five o'clock meeting with Maggie outside the Isolation ICU. She had spent most of the day in the visitor's lounge waiting for visiting hours. She'd been allowed to see Kerrington several times, and with each visit, he looked worse. In between visiting him, Maggie spent a good bit of time in the chapel praying. A flood of tears erupted and made their way down her face to the floor as she incessantly begged God to spare her husband.

"Where have you been?" Maggie asked, irritated that he was late.

"I'm Getting a job," Benny replied before updating Maggie about the OR trying to reassign him to orthopedics. "I'm transferring to the ER. They wanted to know if you wanted your old job back."

Maggie sat silent—her mind wrapped up in thoughts of Kerrington.

"Are you even listening to me?" Benny asked.

"No," Maggie answered simply. "What were you saying?"

"Your old job hasn't been filled. The administration changed the job requirement to require clinical nurse supervisors to have their NP license so they can write prescriptions from triage when they're overcrowded."

"Don't take this the wrong way," Maggie said. "My mind can't go there right now. It's too much for one day."

"I get it. That was bad timing on my part, but at least the ER is opening the door for you if you need a job. Let's go see Kerrington."

With dread, Maggie walked to Kerrington's window and peered inside, expecting the worst. Instead, his rash was gone. And his blood pressure was normal. His heart rate had lowered to normal as well. She put her hands over her face and cried, "It's working. I think it's working, Benny. Thank God. Thank you, God."

***

LATER THAT NIGHT, Maggie checked out the *careers* section for the hospital. Her eyes lingered on the new posting of her old job. She had to admit she hadn't been happy in the OR, and the prospect of getting her old job back filled her with a new excitement. Benny was right. She had all the new requirements, including five years of recent ER management experience.

Maggie leaned back and stared at the **Apply Here** button. Her hand lingered above the mouse. A smile broke out on her face as she recalled how demanding the work was, but truth be told, it was where she belonged. Yes, it was highly stressful, but she loved it far more than surgery. Maggie struggled, trying to sort out the truth. *Maybe things are how they should be.*

Admit it. You feel displaced in the OR, and no amount of patience will make you love surgery. Besides, you may not even have a job there in the future.

Maggie's hand hovered over the mouse for a time before she removed it. She couldn't and shouldn't apply without having a face-to-face meeting with Sunday.

Chapter 29

Blanchard House Pool

MAGGIE, BENNY, AND SUNDAY relaxed in the pool before joining the family at the table.

"So, how are you doing?" Maggie asked.

"Horrible," Sunday replied, her voice highly annoyed by the question. "I feel like I'm going to lose my sanity, quite frankly, between losing my house, my marriage, and my career—I'm pretty overwhelmed. My attorney fees are through the roof, eating up funds I've saved for the girl's college tuition. In many ways, I understand the blood transfusion issue, but Bruce's brain infection—I'll never get over how that could have happened. I'm up for making substantial changes in my life. Any suggestions?"

"I think there's more to the flesh-eating bacteria than meets the eye," Benny abruptly retorted as he cupped water from the pool and drizzled it over his chest. "It's all I've thought about," Benny said. "Bruce's wife, Lila—she is a kook job if ever there was one. The things Lila is putting you and Tess through are inhuman. She's wicked, I tell you, constantly looking for new, inventive ways to hurt people, and that's a fact. I think it gives her joy. Did you folks know she did her clinical rotations in our lab? She has access to all levels of bacteria. I definitely think she's capable of deliberately infecting him. It would make for the perfect crime—maybe even a great malpractice suit. Think about it."

"That's a pretty outrageous accusation, Benny," Maggie said, eyes widening as she took a sip of beer. "You've been watching too much **CSI**, my friend."

"It's not out of the realm of possibility, Maggie," Benny shot back. "Like I said—think about it. Just for one minute, allow yourself to imagine. Rumor has it Bruce was divorcing Lila and planning to marry Tess. We know that firsthand because Tess told us all about Bruce when she met him. We've been with her every step of the way in her relationship. Dearest Lila is a wicked wife with a doctorate in laboratory science. Also, Tess told security that Lila was out to get her because Bruce had a prenup in place, which left Lila broke in the event of a divorce. How's that for a type of ***Desperate Housewives*** story?"

"I think it's far-fetched."

"Well, we'll see about that, Miss Smarty-pants. I'm meeting with my second cousin in security tomorrow, and we're going to be looking into what little secrets the wife is hiding. Tess doesn't lie, and here she is, unemployed and thrown out of the residency program. Also, I might add that Lila sees a shrink because I followed her one day."

"Benny. Leave things alone. I don't want you to lose your job," Maggie warned.

"I'm never going to lose my job! I have way too many friends in exceedingly high places. I will never get fired."

"That's true," Sunday reminded Maggie. "Benny was born and bred at Vinnie's. He has over fifty extended family members employed all over the hospital, with many holding positions in high places. He's as protected as anyone can get." Sunday laughed and turned towards Benny. "Hey there, friend. Why don't you send a little of that protection my way? I could sure use some of that power jelly spread over my stale toast."

They laughed and left the pool for dinner. Benny became even more determined than ever to find Sunday's power jelly. She didn't deserve the rotten crap the Department of Surgery was serving her.

After dinner, Sunday and Maggie had drinks in the Gilded Bar, where Maggie finally strummed up the courage to talk to Sunday about the ER posting.

"I want to return to the ER," Maggie began, nervous about how she would deliver her news through an honest conversation. She carefully chose her words, not wanting to hurt Sunday any more than the hospital had already wounded her. "I'm not happy in surgery, and God knows when you'll be able to practice surgery anymore. I have to consider my future, and right now, it looks bleak. With Kerrington so ill, I have to keep busy, or I'll go crazy. I'm sorry, but I truly have to do this. My old ER job is still open."

"Oh, don't be sorry, girl. It's unbecoming of you to wallow around delivering me apologies. My days of being a surgeon are over, and I want it to be. I have a new job. I start next week," Sunday grinned, enjoying the shocking look on Maggie's face as she took a sip of her martini.

"Where?" Maggie's eyes widened in curiosity.

"In the Medical Examiner's Office."

"What?" Maggie laughed out loud. "You little sneak. Holding back such a secret."

"Yep. And I'm excited, so don't worry about me. I'll be operating, just not on the living."

Benny roared. "If that doesn't take the cake. Hey. Maybe I can volunteer there. I've always been curious about working there."

"Me too," Maggie chimed in. "What a turn of events. I'm in shock."

Sunday smiled, leaned forward, and took off her sweater. "It's getting hot again," she announced. "The news reported we'll be back up in the hundreds tomorrow. I hope that's the last wave."

"Ouch," Benny said with alarm. "What's with your arm, Sunday? It didn't look like that out at the pool. Jeez. It has puss coming out of it. How did you do that?"

Sunday looked down. "I don't know."

All three stared at it. "That happened fast. Does it hurt?"

"I never have pain. I'm one of those people. It does sting a little. I'll take some antibiotics. It'll be fine."

They went back to their drinks and stayed up late talking. Maggie's friends knew she needed a distraction, especially with Kerrington being so close to death's door. Maggie was happy to have Sunday living at Blanchard House. She blended in perfectly.

It was nice to have the kids out of town with friends at a Taylor Swift concert.

THE FOLLOWING MORNING, over breakfast, the girls plowed in just in time to settle at the table for breakfast.

"Why is your arm so swollen?" Dorrie asked, her voice filled with alarm.

"I have a little infection going on. Somehow, I managed to scratch my arm."

"Mommy, that looks bad," May remarked, her voice equally as alarmed enough to get Maggie and Benny's attention. Maggie leaned sideways and looked across the table, as did Benny. "Wow, girl," Benny remarked. "You need to have that cultured. Whatever antibiotics you took positively ain't working."

"We're going to the ER," Maggie said. "Grab some biscuits to eat while we wait. If we hurry, we'll be able to get in and out. The ER isn't usually terribly busy at this time of the morning."

***

THE ER VISIT was fun for all of them as friends came in and out of the room to say hello and chat. They all said the same thing when they looked at Sunday's arm: "Ugh. That looks nasty."

Sunday's temperature climbed higher by the hour, and it didn't take her long for the doctors to diagnose her with a horrific case of flesh-eating bacteria. For the first time since birthing a child, she found herself admitted to the hospital for a raging infection that seemed to have no boundaries.

***

LILA GOT TIRED of waiting for Bruce to return to his room. He'd been off the unit for testing for the last two hours. Restless, she took a walk in the hallway, where she overheard staff members talking.

"They say the doctor might lose her arm," the technician said. "I saw her in the ER. I heard she's got that flesh-eating bacteria."

"Doctor Richardson?"

"She's had so much bad luck lately. I feel so sorry for her."

"We should pray for the doctor. She needs it."

"Yeah."

Lila smiled. Ten minutes later, she had William, her attorney, on the phone. "Doctor Richardson was carrying the infection that infected Bruce. She's been admitted to the hospital with flesh-eating bacteria. It's got to be the same germ. You see the opportunity here?"

"I certainly do. A golden one."

Chapter 30

Shenanigans

THE AFTERNOON SUN gently caressed Benny's skin as he lazily floated in the Blanchard House pool, soaking up the luxuriating warm sun. The trickling sounds of the nearby cascading waterfall soothed him, enveloping him in complete relaxation. The mansion's oasis of tranquility was comparable to a high-end luxury resort—without tons of people. It held the intimacy of a private retreat.

The recent summer sun had been unforgiving, relentless, and suffocating. Benny smiled as he tilted his sun glassed face towards the sun, grateful it was gentle now, no longer giving off the feeling of being fried in a frying pan. It was blissful, this escape from the severe stress that had tied his muscles in knots. Slowly, he was escaping from the horrors of Kerrington's illness and Maggie's resulting desperate state.

Benny's serene reverie dissipated as cool droplets sprinkled over him. Benny lifted his sunglasses and watched Amelia emerge from the water. Her devilish smile was inviting and so infectious he couldn't help but grin back. Her confidence radiated, unaffected, despite her naughty behavior that had disrupted his peaceful moment. It awakened something deep inside, buried for too long a time. It was as if he was seeing Amelia for the first time. A different Amelia with a charming and unapologetic personality.

Her bronze skin glistened as she stepped out of the water. Benny found himself being held captive, unable to tear his eyes off her. Her every movement was a deliberate dance of grace and allure. She was mesmerizing. At her lounge chair, she gathered her long, black, silky hair, squeezing out the excess water. A playful smile danced across her lips.

"Bonjour," she said with a voice that sounded like a melody. "The water is refreshing, no?"

Benny nodded, his voice barely a whisper. "Yes, it is."

With a mischievous look, Amelia eased herself back into the pool. She swam towards him, her body exuding a hypnotic display of fluidity. The water rippled over her, accentuating her perfectly curved body. She locked eyes with Benny, instantly dragging him into a state of entrancement. *Had she always been like this?* What had blinded him? Benny found he was unable to break the spell of her beauty. It didn't matter anymore that their relationship was considered inappropriate; he had resisted long enough. She was his for the taking.

Amelia looked his way and boldly approached him. "May I join you?"

He stammered, "N-no. Yes, you may."

Her magnetic presence charged the air with an undeniable tension that sent Benny's heart racing. Amelia drew him into a conversation that felt timeless, flowing effortlessly with occasional laughter that came easy. They talked about everything and nothing until Dorrie's arrival interrupted the moment.

"So, there you are," Dorrie said. "I was looking for you. My friends left. Can you take me shopping for school supplies?"

"Of course," Amelia replied, her voice warm. "Let me get ready. See you later, Benny."

Benny waved goodbye, his eyes lingering on her as she walked away. He longed for her return, and every day that followed was filled with a yearning for their moments together.

***

LATER THAT EVENING, over dinner, Benny couldn't help but steal glances at Amelia whenever he could. He wanted to engage her again, yet it seemed that Dorrie interrupted every time he tried to have a conversation with her. His composure faltered when he noticed Annella and Maggie observing him. Like a boy caught with his hand in the cookie jar, their knowing looks made his face flush with embarrassment. They knew. Now what?

He kept his head low, eating in silence, contemplating his next move. He had to admit he was a lonely man, and Amelia had reignited something within him that had long lain dormant, sparking life back into his soul. Today, he was filled with emotions of joy, the kind that came from being cared for again—a man desired by a woman. She made him feel alive, and he wanted her to continue fanning those flames of excitement. He resolved to pursue the sparks that had been lit, no matter what anyone said.

After dinner, he retired to his bed chamber alone, pondering his next move. Perhaps he could buy Maggie's little blue house on Park Road and give it to Amelia. They could hire another au pair, but that wouldn't solve her resident status in America. He didn't want her ever to leave.

Benny resolved not to make any move that might take Amelia away. But in his heart, he knew she was the one, and he quite possibly wanted to marry her.

Chapter 31

Questions

O N SATURDAY MORNING, Maggie was in her bedroom getting ready to go to the hospital to see Kerrington when Dorrie entered her room.

"What's up, sweetie?" Maggie asked, her mood playful.

"Can I go with you to see Papa?"

"No. I'm sorry, honey. You can't. Papa is in a special unit that doesn't allow anyone under eighteen to visit."

"Oh," Dorrie replied as she sat on the edge of the bed, petting Dover as he jumped up and joined her. Dorrie was quiet for a minute before letting out a light sob.

"Honey. What is it?"

"The newspaper in Papa's office... it says he's near death."

Maggie stood stunned, briefly avoiding Dorrie's eyes as she struggled to pull herself together long enough to answer her child's question. Finally, she moved over, sat beside Dorrie, and embraced her tightly. "They've given him a new medication, and things are getting better. Papa is a strong man. And he'll fight hard to return to us. Pray hard for him. That's our job."

"Okay. I will," Dorrie replied, her face scrunching up with tears streaming down her cheeks. "It's hard, Mom. I keep seeing Papa in my mind like I used to see Mommy— when she was missing. I want him to come home. I need him to hug me."

It was a heartbreaking moment that followed as Maggie and Dorrie shared their grief—honestly and openly. Just as Maggie got up to leave, Dorrie asked another question. "Is Daddy getting married to Amelia?"

"Not that I know of," Maggie replied, surprised by the question. "Why do you ask?"

"Amelia always talks about him and asks me too many questions about him. She's in love with Daddy."

"What makes you think that?" Maggie was utterly caught by surprise. "If I tell you the truth, do you promise you won't get mad at me?"

"Do you <u>think</u> I'll be mad?"

"Yes."

"Okay." Maggie paused, carefully selecting her words lest they backfire. "I can't promise what my reaction will be, but the fact you plan to be honest with me is a clear sign I won't be as mad. Do you want to tell me now?"

"I read her diary."

Maggie gasped and placed her fingers over her mouth. "No. You know better than that, Dorrie. How could you? What made you do such a thing?"

"I was worried."

"Over her and Benny? Daddy?"

"It's more than that. Daddy watches Amelia all the time, and I see them making goo-goo eyes at each other. And then, the other day, out at the pool, they were flirting like the kids do at school—you know, like the kids who are in love. I don't want him marrying her. I don't want him marrying anyone."

"Well, honey. Daddy is allowed to fall in love again. That's natural." "But I don't want him to fall in love with her."   ___

"Why not?"

"She works for us. She's my au pair. I don't want her as a mother. I don't like her <u>that</u> much. I tolerate her. She'll go away, and then another au pair comes. I don't need an au pair anymore anyway. All I need is a driver to get me from A to Z. Send her away."

"It's not that simple. Amelia is under contract. And she hasn't done anything wrong. Let's just leave it alone for a bit and let me talk with Daddy, and you, stay out of her diary. You're better than that. Never again. Promise."

"Yes, ma'am."

Maggie kissed her on the forehead and left to see Kerrington. She stewed over her new knowledge. She had to admit she was angry with Benny for being so foolish. And it troubled her as to how she would handle the situation. What infuriated her more than anything was that Benny had chosen to be so fool-hearted at a time when she needed him. She needed Benny to be beside her, especially with Kerrington's illness. There were still so many problems to solve, and the thought of her being alone without Benny to help her was nauseatingly overwhelming. Maggie abruptly got up and left the table, claiming not to feel well.

***

MAGGIE FRETTED on her walk into the Isolation Unit. Every visit since she'd given Kerrington the vaccine made her anxious about what she might find when she approached his viewing window. Would the rash be back? Would he be back on the Dopamine drip because his blood pressure tanked again? She looked down at the floor as she stepped forward, not having the courage yet to look at him. Finally, she took a deep breath and looked.

Kerrington was off the ventilator and breathing oxygen by nasal tubing. Tears stung her eyes and fell down her cheeks as her lips trembled with happiness. His eyes were open. Kerrington's beautiful blue eyes were looking straight at her. He gave her a weak smile before closing his eyes. Maggie stepped away from the window, leaned her back against the wall, and cried like a newborn baby. He would live! He was hers again, back from the other side.

***

AS SOON AS MAGGIE returned home, she ran up the stairs, calling out Dorrie's name. She gave Dorrie a giant hug as soon as she saw her. "Papa is better. He's so much better. He looked at me and smiled!"

They hugged tightly and celebrated the news with a chocolate milkshake out by the pool.

After a few minutes, Dorrie looked worried as a frown gathered over her eyebrows.

"What's the matter, love?" Maggie asked.

"Papa is going to be ashamed of me when he finds out I was kicked out of school. I let him down."

"You did not let him down, Dorrie. The school let us down. It never should have happened and trust me—when he finds out—the problem will go away. Papa will make sure of that. Meanwhile, we have everything under control. You're learning, and that's what matters."

"But I need to get into college. That's what Papa expects."

"You'll get into college. Don't worry. Trust me. Papa is going to make it home, and he will fix everything."

***

AFTER DINNER AND a relaxing bath, Maggie went out to the lanai to enjoy a soothing glass of chilled white wine while she reviewed the events from the morning with Dorrie. She had wanted to ask Dorrie precisely what she had read in Amelia's diary. What was in there that had alarmed her?

A giggle drifted across the lawn. Maggie looked toward where the laughter came from. Under a tree by the pool, Maggie watched Amelia pull Benny into her arms and kiss him passionately, slowly wrapping her arms around him. Benny returned her affection.

Dorrie was spot on. Maggie was filled with rage, furious with both of them that they hadn't told her, and she had to hear it from her child. What will Kerrington say?

Chapter 32

Ming Isolation Room

BENNY AND MAGGIE struggled with their emotions as they stood at the window, watching Ming dying.

"We have to give it to him," Maggie whispered, tears edging her eyes. "We cannot stand idly by holding the vaccine that could cure him. It goes against the very grain of who we are as human beings, and especially as nurses who took the oath. The question is—who has the guts to do it?"

Neither one uttered a word as they lingered deep in their thoughts, wondering if they were willing to take such a significant risk.

Maggie stared at the floor in Ming's room. Dare she risk everything to give him the cure? If she got caught, it would blow the top off all their secrets.

Benny's thoughts reflected the same. "Just because we pulled it off once doesn't mean we can easily do it again. Dorrie's at stake here."

"So is a man's life, Benny. You know we have to do it." Benny was adamant. "It's my turn to take the risk."

"I'm doing it," Benny and Maggie both said simultaneously.

"Like I said, Maggie, it's my turn. If I get caught, I'm not saying anything to anyone, and that's that. No one can find out anything unless I tell them. It is what it is. And it's my choice."

"Maybe he'll get better. How do we know he didn't already take the cure?"

"Look at him! Does he look like a man that's on the mend? It's done."

"You know the staff at the desk, Benny. I don't. We'll do it just like we did before. I'll give it. And like you, if I get caught, I'll just keep my lips sealed."

Maggie walked into the anteroom and began putting the equipment on.

Benny shook his head and headed to the nurse's desk, glad a Panther game was coming soon. It would give him something to talk about with everyone. He was grateful that everyone on duty tonight was an avid Panther fan.

***

It didn't take much effort on Benny's part to get them all worked up about the Panther's losing streak, which made their chatter lively and non-stop.

Maggie carefully examined Ming from the window before entering the anteroom to get dressed in BSL4 gear. In her hand, Maggie carefully gripped the syringe that held the yellow liquid vaccine. Finding the proper place to inject the med would be difficult as there were dozens of lines and ports labeled with a rainbow of colors.

At long last, she figured out which line was the main one that was only saline and didn't have piggyback drugs running through it. Quickly, she dressed, entered the room, and inserted the syringe. Maggie pulled back on the plunger, confirmed the presence of blood—then, slowly injected the clear yellow fluid. Maggie then tossed the syringe in the red box. She jumped reflexively when she heard a loud knock on the anteroom window.

"What are you doing in here?" An angry, unfamiliar nurse stood on the other side of the door, staring darts at her.

Maggie was trapped and had no words readily available to explain her presence. She hadn't given any consideration to what she might say if she got caught.

"I'm here to evaluate the patient for a clinical trial. I'm part of the research team," Maggie replied, trying to shield her face from view, which was pretty easy wearing the get-up she had on.

"What clinical trial?"

"Fornlesticalyst," Maggie replied, pulling the term out of the air, relatively sure there was no such thing. "I need to hurry. It's hot in this suit."

"You got that right. Make it speedy. I need to get in there and do my thing. I have meds due in five minutes, and they can't be late."

"I'll be right out," Maggie promised, breaking out in a sweat and wondering how she might escape without the nurse seeing her face.

"I'm taking a bathroom break before I get dressed. Please be out of here by the time I get back."

"Will do."

Maggie scoured the anteroom before exiting. She quickly undressed, her hands trembling from the fear of getting caught. When Maggie finally freed herself of her equipment, she was drenched. She peered through the door, spotted an exit sign, signaled Benny at the end of the hall, and stepped into the stairwell, where she leaned against the wall to breathe a sigh of relief.

Benny joined her, and they ran down the stairs to the main floor and exited the hospital.

***

THE NEXT MORNING, Maggie and Benny entered the isolation unit to visit Kerrington. They had to pass Ming's room to get there. They slowed their pace and stopped, pretending to be talking about something serious as they both looked at Ming, searching for any sign or symptom of improvement.

A nurse exited the anteroom and passed another nurse in the hall. "It's like a miracle," she exclaimed to her co-worker. "It's just like the Blanchard man. On death's door, and suddenly, he's coming back to life. His color is back, his breathing has improved, and I was able to cut back on his ventilator setting. Best of all. His fever is gone. His temperature is normal for the first time since his admission."

They rejoiced and headed to the desk together to share the good news.

Chapter 33

Into The Woods

LILA SPENT ALL evening ruminating over Bruce and Tess and drinking rum and coke. Anger chewed at her gut as hot as if she'd eaten a giant bowl of hot chili peppers. Nothing eased the heat.

What worried Lila the most was the possibility of Bruce regaining his memory. Suppose he recalled his engagement to Tess and her kissing him in the ICU room. Daresay Bruce might even recall Lila lying to the nurse, claiming Bruce didn't know Tess. What then?

Thank goodness, the flesh-eating bacterial infection was obviously under control now. Doctor Richardson had missed the big picture when she'd tried to kill Bruce. Tess was the problem, and Lila hated her more than ever, so much so she wanted her dead. Bruce had genuinely loved Lila until Tess came along. Deep in her heart, she knew Bruce would love her again once Tess was out of the picture.

Lila stewed over her options and how she might carry out her plan. An hour later, a strategy formulated in her mind. Lila called Tess and asked her to come over to meet with her to make things right between them.

"It's a little late for that, don't you think?" Tess retorted—her voice filled with anger. "I have three days to vacate my apartment because Bruce didn't pay the rent. You know he was practically living here and you deliberately didn't pay it. Plus, they repossessed my car because I'm out of a job. So, don't be nice to me, Lila. You're insulting my intelligence."

"It's not what you think. I've had a change of heart. That's what I'm calling about. If you come to my house tonight, I will give you the money you need to restore your apartment rent and get your car back. Cash."

At 8:00 PM, having no other options left, Tess rang the doorbell. Lila greeted her with a cheerful and welcoming smile. She handed Tess a stack of one-hundred-dollar bills totaling fifteen thousand dollars. "That should take care of things," she said.

"Thank you, Lila," Tess said with a surprised look on her face. "I didn't think you'd really pay me."

"If it's not enough, you just let me know. I don't need the money anymore. See?" Lila said, holding up her hand and flashing a brilliant diamond ring she'd purchased for herself. The diamond was fake. "Bruce is all yours."

"Well, that's a surprise."

"Have dinner with me so I can tell you all about the recent turn of events going on in my life. I have a lot to tell you."

"Hmm. I was supposed to have dinner with Benny," Tess replied. "It's not a date or anything like that. It's family dinner at the Blanchard's."

"Tell him you'll join him tomorrow. Please. I really need to see you."

Tess hesitated, then ignored her intuitions, which were warning her not to go. Instead, she texted Benny and opted out of dinner with him, asking if they could take a rain check tomorrow night.

Over a luscious dinner cooked by Lila's chef, Tess listened to Lila's story, thinking how outrageous it sounded that she'd suddenly up and found a wealthy fiancé, Josh Hartwell, a real estate mogul from Asheville. Lila bragged about him buying a farm not far away and moving there to live with her, stating she was granting Bruce his divorce. "As a matter of fact, you could move in here. Bruce will be delighted, I'm sure. Truly, I'm happy for you because my new life is happy now."

Lila worked hard at her new plan. Turning Tess around was a challenge, but finally, after dinner, Lila convinced Tess to go with her to see the new farm. Lila promised to give her a ride home. Tess warned Lila she couldn't be gone long because she had a job interview in the morning and needed to rest.

"Oh, we'll have you home in no time. I just wanted to share my happy news with someone."

As they headed to the car, Tess gave in to her intuition the minute her hand opened the passenger side of the door. "I can't go, Lila. It's too late. Maybe tomorrow."

Lila came around the car. "Get in the car, Tess," she warned, pulling out a taser gun and holding it out, aimed straight at Tess.

Tess stood frozen in place. Slowly, she removed her hand from the door handle as she desperately searched for a way out.

Lila smiled. "Surprise, Tess. It's my time to get even." Lila fired the taser, sending Tess to the ground, her body jerking violently. Lila laughed as she watched with joy. As soon as Tess stopped shaking, Lila fired again without hesitation. Then, she repeated the tasing. When she was convinced that Tess wouldn't give her any more trouble, she loaded her body into the passenger seat and strapped her in place, smiling as her head bobbed over and slobber dripped, drooling from her mouth.

As Lila drove Tess down the long, dark, isolated country road, she suddenly stopped the car. Tess was awake and recovering from the shocks delivered by the taser. Lila took a map from the glove compartment, got out of the car, laid the map out on the trunk, and turned her cellphone flashlight on.

Tess managed to get out of the car; her legs trembled with weakness. She looked around, terrified. They were on deserted land out in the middle of nowhere. Tess jerked as a gust of wind suddenly whipped through the trees, creating an eerie symphony of howling sounds and snapping branches in the darkness. She took in the surrounding treetops highlighted by the moonlight. They reminded her of skeleton hands opening and closing in a horror movie. She shivered as a chill of realization crept up her spine. Lila was going to kill her. Of that, she was sure.

Lila turned the cell phone flashlight on Tess's face, showcasing the fright buried deep in her eyes. Lila raised a gun in her other hand. "What are you doing, Lila?" Tess asked, backing up, terrified she didn't have the strength to run.

"I'm going to make you barren, Tess. Then, we'll see if Bruce wants you." Lila fired the gun at Tess repeatedly, shooting Tess in the belly. "A whore who steals a woman's husband deserves to be punished. Severely."

By the time the gun chamber was empty, Lila was dripping with sweat, her rage satisfied. Lila checked for a pulse. *Good and dead*, she said to herself.

Lila dragged Tess's body into a ravine and removed the fifteen thousand dollars from her pocketbook before tossing it on top of Tess.

Lila left satisfied that she had done the right thing to salvage her marriage. No one would ever find Tess.

***

BENNY BECAME SUSPICIOUS of Lila when Tess said she was having dinner with her. *Why would Tess agree to hook up with Lila?* Something wasn't right. After giving it sufficient worry, Benny decided to drive by Lila's house to see if Tess was okay. He was surprised to see both of them leave Lila's house. Tess was getting into the car, on the passenger side, when Lila met her at the car door. Benny strained hard to see what they were doing. *Are they struggling?* Benny questioned. He was ready to drive the car up behind them when Lila closed the door and got into the driver's seat. They drove off before Benny could make a move.

Benny decided to follow them, still suspicious as to why Tess would go anywhere with Lila. He followed them for a long way and became genuinely concerned when Lila headed deep into the countryside of Albemarle County. Lila turned onto a dirt road. It was hard to keep track of the car without raising suspicion that he was following them. When Benny lost sight of the tail lights, he pulled over and got out of the vehicle.

The air was hot with a thick, suffocating darkness, making it impossible to discern the roads. Benny estimated he'd been driving for well over forty-five minutes. He leaned against the car, not knowing what to do next. Where would he drive? Should he text Tess—or would that set Lila off? He waited patiently, searching and listening for any sign of a car.

The night sounds normally relaxed Benny, but tonight, under these circumstances, they reminded him he was deep in the countryside, isolated and vulnerable. He checked his GPS. As of now, he could easily find his way back because he'd taken the roads that were on the map.

Benny retreated to the safety of the car and was just closing the car door when he heard a round of gunfire that sent a sudden jolt through him. It was nearby, remarkably close to him. He jumped back out of the car and listened hard, trying to discern which road led to where he thought the gunfire came from. Lila and Tess were nearby. He could feel it in his bones. Had Lila shot Tess? Benny was just about ready to crank the engine and turn on the headlights when he heard a car approaching from a side road. He waited. The road was no more than fifty feet ahead. He watched as Lila's car appeared, and she was in such a hurry she didn't even stop at the end of the road before turning left and gunning the engine, driving quickly away from where he was parked. Tess was not in the car.

The second the car was out of sight, Benny turned down the road Lila came from. He turned his lights on bright and drove slowly towards where he estimated the sound of gunfire came from. His eyes desperately searched both sides of the road for any sign of Tess's white sweater. At long last, he got out of the car, activated his cell phone flashlight app, and searched all around him. He screamed Tess's name and listened. Again, he called out.

Benny was about to get back into the car and move further down the road when he heard a soft moan, followed by another. He turned the beam of light towards the cry when he heard it again. Finally, the light landed on a bloody white sweater. Tess was off to the side of the road, lying twisted and severely bleeding.

The night quickly turned to chaos. Benny activated a 911 call for help and went to work, trying to control the bleeding. Tess was barely conscious when she whispered, "Lila shot me."

Benny was so grateful for their cell phone's GPS; it pinpointed their location in the woods. As he waited for the emergency response, which arrived quickly, he offered Tess reassurances despite the fact she might not hear them.

His chest rose with a deep sigh of relief when he heard the first sound of sirens, which were quickly followed by a massive response of police and ambulance lights as they burst onto the scene. Tears burned in his eyes as he watched the response team take over, giving emergency aid to Tess. Blue police lights shimmered through his tears as they danced amongst the trees. He held his head low and wanted to cry openly, fearing Tess's thought might very well be right. She was definitely dying.

BENNY MADE HIS WAY HOME and told Maggie the news about Tess. They then went to the ER and waited with the ER staff to hear what news there was about Tess. They had been forced to institute the massive transfusion protocol because she'd lost so much blood, and they quickly took her to the OR in an effort to stop the bleeding. The injuries were severe.

***

LILA RETURNED HOME and had a stiff drink, followed by several anxiety pills. She was delighted at first, but then her self-loathing and reprehension took over, making her terrified of herself. *What have I become? I'm a monster. That can never be fixed.*

Chapter 34

Maggie And Kerrington

MAGGIE QUIETLY entered Kerrington's room. That morning, the doctor blessed her with the beautiful news that the virus was miraculously gone from Kerrington's body. All lab tests continued to show no presence of the virus, so quarantine and isolation precautions were lifted.

"Kerrington?" Maggie softly called his name.

Kerrington opened his eyes and looked at her. She'd waited and prayed so long to see his stunning blue eyes again. He smiled.

"You're going to be okay."

"I know."

Maggie took a seat in the leather chair beside the bed. She took his hand in hers and proceeded to tell him everything from the beginning to the end. She told him about visiting the laboratory and finding a hidden floor where dangerous projects were going on. "With a deadly virus."

"I know," he whispered. "That's how I got sick. When I discovered the hidden elevator, I went inside."

"I did, too," Maggie said. "That's where I found the cure. We followed the scientist Ming home. Benny and me. We spied on him and overheard him talking with someone about how the vaccine he discovered cured monkeys. We went back into the lab, secured the cure, and gave it to you. Well, I did. Benny kept the staff busy, so they didn't see me entering your room. It worked."

"That happened in our lab? How brilliant," Kerrington said, his face beaming with pride.

"The scientist was Ming Fu. There was an argument with the man at his house, and the man stabbed him with the virus. Apparently, Ming had purchased it from him. Ming almost died, and we gave him the cure, too. He lived. He's right down the hall. I didn't want you to hear all this from someone else. We did what we had to do, the two of us. Please don't blame Benny. The majority of the plans were mine."

"It's what I love about you, Maggie. As I promised you, the lab will be destroyed as soon as I'm out of here, but I'm going to be straight up with you. I'm building another lab, a much bigger one, and I'm going to hire that brilliant scientist to head it up."

Maggie sat stunned for a moment before she stood, walked over to his bed, and hugged him gently. "I'm behind you, whatever you do. You are truly the love of my life, Kerrington, and I'll never, ever take your love for granted."

They sat together for over an hour as Maggie filled him in on Dorrie, how people became afraid of her at school, and the eventual decision to have her removed from the property. "She was devasted. It broke her heart, not just being banned from the property but the way they carried it out. It was so brutal, the way it all came down. They wouldn't even meet with me and Benny. It had to be done by Zoom."

"By Zoom?" Kerrington repeated, astounded by the thought. He stayed quiet as he comprehended the impact such a thing could have on his child. "Is Dorrie okay?"

"We raised a strong girl. She's being homeschooled. We enrolled her into an official program." Maggie went on to tell Kerrington about Amelia and Benny and all the other events that had taken place in the household during his absence.

"I can't wait to get home."

Chapter 35

Tribulations

THE NIGHT BEFORE the start of the trial, Sunday entered Maggie's room after everyone had gone to bed. "Have a drink with me, Maggie, please," she said with the tone of a beggar who needed help. Immediately, Maggie got up and slipped into her robe. It was late, but she couldn't turn Sunday down no matter how sleepy she was—Sunday sounded desperate.

Maggie poured two screwdrivers and took a seat beside Sunday at the bar. Her gut wrenched as she watched her friend take a swallow, wearing a bewildered look on her face.

"So, you got me out of bed to talk. What's going on, Sunday?"

"Tell me what's NOT going on, Maggie. I've run out of positive things to say. I mean, don't get me wrong. I thank God every day that you're my friend and for the gracious way you've welcomed my family into your home. It seems like every single thing I try to do to put my life together goes to hell in a handbasket like I'm doomed or cursed with some evil spirit."

"Now that, my friend, is gloom and doom talk. First of all, you don't have to burden yourself with a place to live. And you are welcome to stay here forever. I'd love that. The house gets so lonely sometimes because it is so big."

"Think about it, Maggie. I've lost everything. My house. My things. My work. I miss the hospital and the feeling of security I had living in that environment. I miss my friends, the people I've worked with forever. My girls are growing up too fast. What do I do with my life? Meet with lawyers. Look for a house to buy. A house I can no longer afford. Where do I go? What do I do?" Sunday began to cry by the bucketfuls, and the more she talked, the more Maggie became at a loss as to how to comfort her.

"It won't always be this way, Sunday. I thought I would go bananas when

Kerrington was dying, but then I finally resolved that I would have to take life one step at a time. One moment at a time. One day at a time. I know that sounds like an overused philosophical line, but it's tried and true. You've allowed yourself to be buried in your thoughts."

"I'm overwhelmed by all the what-ifs. It's snowballing out of control."

"Are you thinking of hurting yourself or having thoughts that you don't want to live?" Maggie asked with great concern.

"Oh, hell no. I still have a tiny bit of hope left. I'm not that far gone."

"That's a relief."

"Betrayal is an evil thing to deal with, you know. Paul. I still shake my head sometimes, wondering how I missed the signs. Well, that's not accurate–I didn't miss the signs; I failed to acknowledge what I saw. I didn't want to deal with it. I hoped it would pass, like the seasons do. I saw them together many times at parties. I saw shared looks between them but lied to myself that they were just friends. Partners. Hah! They were partners, all right. If I had asked him, he would have told me the truth back then because he's that kind of guy. Direct. Instead, I chose to go on living a lie, knowing inside it was all going to blow up in my face sooner or later."

Maggie felt it was best not to say anything, knowing her friend needed to talk about the lies and deceit to get it off her chest before stepping into the most critical court battle of her career.

After taking another gulp, Sunday continued. "I remember when he went to the conference in New York City. It lasted a week, and when he came home, he was a new and changed man, happy, singing in the shower like he used to when we first got married. I felt robbed. Like was a thief coming into your house in the middle of the night—I let that woman come in and rob me of everything. She took it all, and now she's going to play mommy to my children. I hate her like I've never hated anyone. I feel rage and imagine horrible things happening to her, not that I would hurt her or anyone, but there, I said it. I've never felt such anger."

"I honestly don't know what to say to you, Sunday, because there is nothing, I can do to help you. Time is the only thing that can help. It will fade in time. Until then, I think you need to apply some rules to your thinking.

You can stop those feelings and images if you work at it. When you catch yourself thinking about her—him—or them, stop yourself and force yourself to think of something else."

"That'll be hard. It's like I'm consumed. This woman will be in my life forever, living my life with my children."

"Let go, Sunday. Stop downplaying the importance you play in your role as their mother. You're their only mother, and they know it. Children don't forget a mother's love." Maggie could feel her voice escalating, yet she knew the situation required a little bit of bossiness on her part. "It's time for you to pick yourself up by your bootstraps and get a hold of yourself. You're better than this. Yes, you lost your house, but you can replace that. The things inside it are just things. Those can be replaced, too. And Paul—he is also replaceable. It's a matter of perspective, Sunday."

"Paul," Sunday repeated before a smile broke out on her face, so big that Maggie thought it looked like she was beaming. "Replaceable."

"Yes, replaceable. As for your children, they will be off to college in no time, as they are meant to be. They will start their new lives, as they are meant to do. Life goes on. Your battle was never with her. It was with Paul. It's a fact."

Sunday kept the smile on her face, and relief joined in. For a moment, Maggie could see the old Sunday returning. "You're awesome, you know. My God. You are a prestigious neurosurgeon. I stand in awe when I watch you so steadily take people's brains in your hands and fix them! No one can top you and your talent, and I'm so incredibly proud to say that I worked for you."

"Thank you, Maggie. It feels good to be reminded of my value. You've broken everything down so simply. I love you."

"I love you, too. Now, as for tomorrow, you can only fight one battle at a time. Do it well, girl, like I know you can. Stop robbing yourself of the joy of being with your children. Enjoy life here, where you are safe and secure, no matter what happens out there in the world." Maggie reached across the table, took Sunday's hand in hers, and squeezed it as if to force her friend to dig deep down and fight.

"I'll be okay. Now. I just got lost in all the noise."

Sunday stood and gave Maggie a hard hug, as only friends knew how to give. Then she straightened her shoulders and said good night. "We both need to go to bed."

Maggie's heartstrings burned inside as she watched Sunday leave the Gilded Bar and head upstairs. She'd given Sunday the best advice she could, but it was simply just that in the end. Advice. She was just as worried as her Sunday. The battle facing her friend tomorrow would indeed be a brutal one, and she wasn't sure if Sunday would win.

Chapter 36

The Trial

BRILEY BARNES, a stout man with a cannonball belly, was the attorney representing the law firm for Marlena Smith. He opened the trial by stating in a robust and bellowing voice, "Today, we are here to examine the case brought forth by Marlena Smith against Doctor Sunday Richardson. The plaintiff seeks compensation of fifty million dollars, alleging that her son, Bobby Smith, a seventeen-year-old Jehovah's Witness, underwent a blood transfusion without consent. Doctor Richardson ordered this blood transfusion. As we delve into the details of this trial, let us approach the facts with a clinical lens."

By the third day of the trial, Sunday was exhausted and sick to her stomach with fear. She sat at the defense table, wringing her hands nervously in her lap, keeping them carefully out of view of the jury. If she lost the case, it would be a financial catastrophe for her entire family. First of all, her malpractice coverage only covered twenty-five million dollars, and she certainly didn't have the other twenty-five million dollars to pay the judgment if she lost. From her point of view, things looked dismal.

Marlena Smith seemed to hold the jury in her hands as she testified, tears streaming down her face. Through her testimony, she painted an image of a tortured soul who had lost her child to the 'other side' when Doctor Richardson deliberately stripped her of her religious freedom to choose what was in her son's best interest. "She is not God. No one but the true God can know the time of death until it occurs, and in my son's case, it did not happen. We don't know if blood saved his life. God does that, and we don't know if he would have sent a miracle of life to him. Doctor Richardson couldn't have known he was going to die because she is not God," Marlena said, breaking out in sobs. "She has robbed my family of everything meaningful."

Sunday was devastated by her testimony and knew Marlena Smith would be a hard act to follow. How could she possibly defend her actions?

Cecil Locker followed Maggie's testimony. The elderly Congregational Leader was a skinny, well-dressed man who served on the Governing Body of the Jehovah's Witness Church. Cecil looked confident as he took his seat before the microphone.

"Mr. Locker," Briley asked, "Please explain to the jury the belief of *Jehovah's Witnesses* regarding blood transfusion."

"Certainly, sir. They forbid blood transfusion for Jehovah's Witnesses, and this comes from the doctrine of **The Watchtower Bible and Tract Society,**" Locker explained, his voice firm and strong. "We believe that Jehovah's Witnesses who receive blood *may receive immediate prolonging of life—but in the end, it will cost them their eternal life in the presence of God.*"

Barnes paused with confidence, observing the individual faces of each jury member before pacing authoritatively in front of the stand and pursuing his line of questioning.

"What is the role of the parent in the case where the blood recipient is a minor child?"

"Witness' parents are expected to prevent their children from undergoing a blood transfusion. In addition, the child is required to carry an ID in their wallet, which...."

"Objection! Your Honor, Barnes snapped back. "I did not ask the witness about ID cards."

"Your Honor, the explanation is relevant and applies to the responsibility of the parent," the opposing attorney, Max Martin, defended, waving his arm in Marlena Smith's direction.

"Sustained," the Judge replied, striking his gavel harshly against the block. "Mister Locker, you may continue."

"As I was saying," Cecil Locker proceeded, "The parents must make sure their child carries an ID card just in case they present to the hospital unconscious. Most hospitals are familiar with the church's standing on the issue."

Barnes asked Locker several more intricate questions about biblical passages, such as Leviticus 17:10, Genesis 9:4, Acts 15:28-29, and Deuteronomy 12:23, which were interpreted to mean that Jehovah's Witnesses do not allow the ingestion of blood in any form.

"So, Mr. Locker, exactly what punishment did the patient Bobby Smith undergo in his community as a result of receiving a blood transfusion?"

"Mr. Smith was called before the Governing Body to account for his failure to follow church law, and he was advised in writing that such an act could result in ex-communication or disfellowshipping."

"What were the results of that hearing?"

"Unfortunately, Bobby did not comply with our request to meet, so he was excommunicated, which cost him his eternal life."

As the hours rolled by, people came and went to the witness box, trailing like ants carrying food and crawling into a hole. The testimony, compiled together, documented the complex opinions that would test the very fabric of society's understanding of medical responsibility and religious freedom.

Marlena Smith, Bobby Smith's mother and legal guardian, tearfully asserted that she explicitly expressed her objection to blood transfusion prior to her son's surgery. She dramatically paused before claiming, "The medical team, led by that evil Doctor Sunday Richardson," Marlena cried out, pointing her finger towards Sunday. "She deliberately disregarded my wishes and went ahead with the transfusion. She gave my son another person's blood, which will certainly condemn him to burn in hell, as is my belief."

Maggie watched the jury, noting that many were near tears by the end of Marlena's testimony. It was obvious that many jurors appeared sympathetic, ready to deliver a handsome reward to the mother for such an awful act. Maggie's heart ached for her friend Sunday, who was buried in the troughs, sure to lose her cherished reputation forever. She was certain Sunday was overly embarrassed by testimony that painted her as having acted in such an uncaring and wicked manner.

Maggie could hardly look at her friend when they called her to testify. The stakes were terrifically high, and the price of failing hung heavily on her shoulders, filling her with great dread as she approached the witness stand.

For four hours, Barnes pursued Maggie, grilling her about the events surrounding the transfusion decision. He started by asking her mundane questions about her career, education, grades, and where she lived. That went on for too long a time, and Maggie realized he was trying to wear her out early.

When Barnes began to ask questions about the transfusion event, he became relentless in his examination of the facts. Maggie was convinced she sounded like a broken record repeating for the umpteenth time her tale of the events that occurred in the OR during Smith's brain surgery. It was clear that Barnes was trying to make her trip on her own words of testimony, looking for any small thing he could pounce on and make her look unreliable.

Hour after hour, Maggie stayed consistent. "He gave consent. He was adamant that he wanted a transfusion rather than die."

"He was a minor!" Marlena shouted across the courtroom, waving her fist in the air. Other members of the family echoed her, causing confusion and dismay over the fact that he'd been a minor child at the time of the event.

"Sit down," Judge Smart ordered, slamming his gavel down with a loud thud. "I will not allow chaos in my courtroom. If there are any further outbreaks, you will be removed from the courtroom."

Maggie tried her best to be a strong and compelling witness in her delivery of the facts that occurred in the operating room that day. When Maggie was through, she prayed the jury understood how close Bobby had come to death and how fast the events occurred.

She used a firm, steady voice when she shared the emotional journey into the decision-making process that occurred that day, hoping the jurors might grasp and understand how close to death the boy had come. "It's always difficult when a parent declines a much-needed transfusion. Healthcare workers suffer great sadness and grief when a patient needlessly dies from a lack of blood. We thought his heart might stop, and we based our decision on what the patient told me prior to surgery. He was truly clear about accepting the blood."

Maggie watched the jury closely. For a brief moment, silence hung over the jury box as a few women wiped tears and men looked uncomfortably down at their empty hands as if they held something precious. She hoped her clinical expertise and calm demeanor presented a clear picture of the situation, including the emotional rollercoaster ride they had experienced as they rode the railway between life and death, dispelling any confusion that anyone had acted with impropriety.

Sunday was the last person called to the witness stand. Her lawyer had insisted she not testify, but Sunday insisted, feeling she was the only person who could set the record straight in the minds of the jury.

It turned out to be a catastrophic move on her part.

After confirming she was the neurosurgeon in charge of Bobby Smith's case, they moved on to his age at the time of the incident.

"He was seventeen at the time due to turn eighteen soon," Sunday said.

"So, let me ask a simple question," Barnes said in a loud, argumentative voice. "Did you, or did you not willfully violate the religious rights of Bobby Smith and his mother, Marlena Smith, under the law?"

Sunday felt caught by the unexpected question. "I did."

"So, you admit it."

"I did."

Her attorney came to her rescue. "Can you tell the jury how you made your decision?"

"My job is to save lives no matter what. My patient asked me not to let him die, even if it meant giving him blood if he needed it. Things went so fast. His mind was clear when he made that choice, but the type of brain bleed he had caused him to lose consciousness quickly. It was a matter of choosing to listen to his wishes. That's how I made the decision. It was a risk. One I was willing to take – for him. It is not in my nature to stand by and watch him die."

On redirect, Barnes went for the final blow. "Would you make that same decision today, Doctor Richardson?"

"In a heartbeat," Sunday answered. The three words were fitting, she thought, because they were true. She had not been willing to watch his heart stop. Sunday felt like the end was near. The jury seemed to look at her in great dismay and disappointment at her actions.

In the hushed and solemn courtroom atmosphere, everyone gasped when Max Martin, the attorney representing Sunday, called Bobby Smith to the stand.

"Objection," Barnes called out. "I was not notified about this witness."

"Your Honor, Mr. Smith turned eighteen yesterday, making him an adult. He only came to me early this morning requesting to testify."

"He was a minor at the time. It's not relevant," Barnes argued.

"He's not a minor now, Your Honor," Max Martin defended. "He has facts that haven't been presented here. Please allow him to share it."

"I'll allow it," Judge Smart stated in a loud, firm voice. "But tread carefully."

As Bobby Smith swore his oath, Sunday looked down, unable to face him. He would be the nail in the coffin of her career. Marlena twisted uncomfortably in her seat.

"Mister Smith. Did you sign consent to receive a blood transfusion?"

"Yes. I did. I requested to be allowed to sign my consent. My father has signed one, too, but it was at another hospital a year earlier. I had no objection to receiving blood. I may have been a minor, but I considered myself fully capable of making adult decisions."

"Mr. Smith. Why did you request to be allowed to testify today?"

"I have to tell the truth and set the record straight so everyone can know what happened that day. I love my mother, but I'm afraid I have to disagree with what she has done in my name. Although I respect her right for my mother to practice her personal beliefs, I do not believe she had my true interest at heart. She knew how I felt about receiving blood. When I arrived in the ER after my accident, I knew that I was hemorrhaging, and I also knew death was going to take me out of this world if I didn't do something. I made sure before I went under the knife that the doctors knew I would accept a blood transfusion if I needed it. I texted her and told her what I had done and why. Still, I felt my mother would stop them from giving it to me because of her faith, but I am not a Jehovah's Witness."

Max stepped closer to the stand, turned, and faced the jury as loud conversations of shock broke out across the courtroom.

"Can you repeat that, please?" Max requested.

"I am not a Jehovah's Witness. I am a member of the Baptist church and was baptized when I was sixteen. My father was present. That's why I came here today. I have begged my mother to drop this lawsuit many times, and we always ended up in a fight. Over and over. I'm tired of fighting. It's important to me that I tell you what really happened so this will all end. Doctor Richardson saved my life, and she should not be punished. I want reporters to stop writing falsehoods about me and my doctor."

Marlena jumped to her feet and yelled at her son. "You are NOT Baptist! I forbid it."

Judge Smart slammed his gavel with frustration and ordered peace, again warning that further outbreaks would result in removal from the courtroom.

Max paused before continuing, making a deliberate effort to look into the eyes of each jury member. "Mr. Smith. Would you please explain to the jury how you feel about having received blood?"

Sunday fought tears when Bobby looked straight at her and gave forth a genuinely big smile. "Just knowing that **strangers** saved my life is a beautiful thing. Someone I didn't know—a stranger—cared enough about my life to donate blood to save my life. Doctor Richardson, also a stranger, dared to follow my request. I deliberately stopped carrying the ID in my wallet because I wouldn't have chosen to die." Bobby looked at Sunday, nodded, and said, "Thank you, doctor, for everything you've done. I'm sorry my mother put you through this."

Buzzing voices rang out behind Sunday as she bit her lip and held her breath. Maggie placed her hand over her mouth in shock.

Max Martin recalled Marlena to the stand and hammered away at her with questions he insisted she answer. "Did you receive a text on your cell phone from your son Bobby Smith that informed you of his decision to receive a blood transfusion?"

Marlena stared at him with a vile look before she finally answered. "Yes. I did."

"That will be all."

***

THE FOLLOWING morning, Max Martin stood up and firmly stated, "Your Honor, at this time, I'd like to call for a dismissal as there is no evidence of malpractice at this time, as the mother no longer has jurisdiction over her son's legal affairs."

A wave of relief swept through Sunday when Judge Smart dismissed the case as requested by the defense attorney, Max Martin. Sunday buried her face in her hands and cried openly without shame as Maggie moved to sit beside her, giving her friend a huge hug.

***

BENNY MET MAGGIE and Sunday in the corridor outside the courtroom. Maggie caught the lousy news written all over Benny's face the minute she saw him.

"Tess coded this morning. They took her back to surgery."

Chapter 37

The Awakening

IT WAS MIDMORNING when Bruce was awakened by the sunlight edging its way beneath the blinds. He bristled when he spotted Lila sleeping in the visitor recliner with a People magazine lying face down in her lap.

"Lila. Wake up."

Lila sat up at attention.

"Where's Tess? She should have been here by now. She said she would see me when she got off. Why didn't you wake me?"

Lila was too stunned and terrified to speak. Bruce had recovered his entire memory, and he was no longer amnesic.

Bruce picked up his cell phone. "Well, at least you kept it charged for me," he said, motioning by waving the phone her way. "Take a coffee break. I need some privacy."

Lila, relieved she didn't have to talk to him about Tess, stepped out and made her way to the cafeteria. Her head did a double take when she saw Sunday enter his room wearing a visitor badge.

***

WHEN LILA RETURNED less than thirty minutes later, she found Bruce on the phone. "I demand to speak to the Chief of Neurosurgery now. I want my doctor back. Now," Bruce ended his call, turned his head, and glared at her. "What do you have to say for yourself? You fired my doctor? You allowed Tess to be taken away without telling security the truth? Plus, you didn't even bother to tell me she'd been shot and might be dying somewhere in this hospital. My God. I don't know you at all."

Lila moved to her chair to sit.

"Don't you dare sit down! I have calls to make—to try and clean up the shitstorm you created. Get some more coffee. Better yet. Just go home. I'd start packing if I were in your shoes because you, my lady, are in the poor house. Things will be moving real fast."

Upon her exit, Lila passed William Strout, entering Bruce's suite. He was carrying thick folders and looked right at her, yet he didn't speak. The snub was clear. He was afraid of Bruce, and it was a matter of time before Bruce found out about the malpractice suit, she'd filed against Doctor Richardson. Lila backed up to allow William's entry. As she did, she took Bruce's phone. Meeting with partners typically lasted hours upon hours. Bruce wouldn't miss it. He would be exhausted and too tired to talk on the phone after their meeting was over. She didn't want him calling Sunday.

***

SUNDAY RETURNED to Bruce's case that afternoon when she received an apologetic call from the Chief of Neurosurgery. Her suspension was over, effective immediately. Before agreeing to return to her position, Sunday demanded a considerable compensation package, a public apology in front of the board to make up for damage to her reputation, and grief. Needless to say, the chief gave in to all her demands. He would do whatever it took to appease Bruce.

Bruce smiled big with relief when he saw Sunday entering his room. "Hello, friend. Welcome back."

Sunday faked a smile she didn't feel after reading Bruce's latest MRI. "Hi, Bruce," she said, starting the beginning of what would be a painful and challenging conversation.

Bruce made sure Sunday knew about all the noise he'd made upon hearing she'd been suspended and kicked off his case. Sunday nodded and listened. She even took a seat beside his bed, making clear eye contact with him, knowing that patients reported feeling that their doctor cared about them when they sat while talking to them. They also liked it when the doctor looked them in the eye.

The doctor let Bruce talk as much as he needed. She'd rearranged her schedule so she could give him a lot of time. Eventually, the right time came.

Sunday straightened her posture and softly but directly delivered the tragic news: "Bruce, your battle is over."

"Never. I'm just getting started with Lila. I've had enough."

"I'm talking about your cancer, Bruce. Your latest MRI shows the tumor has multiplied. It's expanded across your brain. The chemo is no longer working as effectively as it did. At this point, it's no longer operable. I'm so sorry."

Bruce bit his lip as his eyebrows furled so hard that they seemed to be joined together. "What now? What about clinical trials?"

"I've gone through them all. You don't qualify," Sunday replied, wanting to look away from him. He had grown to be one of her favorite patients over the years. It was always so painful to deliver such devastating news. Experience had taught her that such sad news was best received by being direct and not colored with unnecessary words that could get misinterpreted, thus slighting the impact of the news.

"It's over?"

"Yes. Again, I'm so sorry."

"You're sure there are no clinical trials available?"

"Positive."

"How long do I have?"

"A month. Maybe two. Maybe less."

"Is it from the infection?"

"No. The tumor has invaded all the major areas of your brain."

Bruce stared out the window as Sunday stood up and prepared for her exit to give him personal time to reflect and digest the news.

"I understand. Could you do something for me, Doctor Richardson?"

"Anything," Sunday replied.

"Sit with me for a time. I need to talk—while I still can."

Sunday sat back down and listened for over an hour as Bruce talked about anything and everything. He shared many of his trial victories and even told her about his funniest moments. They laughed. Then, finally, he cried like a lost little boy. He'd been so brave for so long and had given life a hard fight. Sunday stayed with Bruce until he was worn out and finally fell asleep. When she left the room, she was filled with great sadness, feeling like a failure once again. She'd failed in her private war against yet another tumor.

Chapter 38

Blanchard Family Dining Room

MAGGIE WAS HAPPY and smiling as she slipped into her chair at the family dinner gathering. The ritual was comforting as it always served as a time for bonding, connection, and lively personal conversation. Tonight, things were strikingly different. A looming change flitted about in the air that was indeed unsettling and concerning.

Maggie watched Benny and noted a change. He definitely wasn't his warm, regular, and cheerful self. Benny appeared nervous and avoided eye contact with her. It was like he'd become a stranger overnight.

Benny kept his focus on Amelia as if she owned him. She, too, seemed to have evolved into a new person since last night's dinner. Maggie noted Amelia's dress was new and designed to impress. It fit her like a glove, and Maggie knew that was why she'd chosen it. She was dressed to impress her man. It was also expensive–the kind of dress Amelia could certainly not afford to buy on her salary.

Her heart sank. Their lives were all about to change. In that sad moment of realization, Maggie's heart ached for the loss that was certain to come. The bond she'd once shared with Benny might never be the same again. Dorrie had pegged his relationship with Amelia—with spot-on accuracy.

Maggie turned her attention to Amelia. She didn't like the way Amelia looked at Benny, as if she thought she was in charge of everything. Maggie tried to intervene by starting a light conversation. Dorrie jumped right in with her jokes.

"Dorrie," Amelia interrupted as if she was annoyed. "Not tonight." Amelia's abrupt interruption instantly quelled Dorrie's jokes. She looked down as if she'd been cut to the core.

"Later, sweetie," Benny said, smiling at Dorrie. Then, he stood and raised his glass. "Amelia and I have an announcement to make."

Amelia stood and held her glass up as well before railroading Benny's news. "We're to be married. Benny and I are engaged."

"That's delightful," Sunday said. "I'm so happy for you, Benny." She added Amelia's name only as an afterthought.

Maggie's jaw dropped as Benny looked right at her, his eyes questioning and then turning to disappointment. Her heart skipped a beat when Dorrie dropped her fork. The heavy eating utensil landed on her China plate with a loud clang, breaking Maggie's private glance at Benny.

"Don't bother inviting me because I'm not going." With that having been said, Dorrie stood and placed her napkin on the table with visibly shaking hands. "May I be excused?"

"No. You may not," Benny replied. "Not with that kind of attitude, young lady. Sit down," Benny demanded.

"I'll not sit down. This would never have happened if Papa was here. I feel like I'm going to throw up," Dorrie replied before she dramatically bolting from the room.

Benny followed her, but Maggie beat him to the door, stopping him.

"Now would not be a good time."

Maggie followed Dorrie and found her in her bedroom, lying on her bed, crying.

"I hate her."

"Dorrie. Stop."

"He didn't even bother to tell me. He announces it like, *Oh, it's no big deal telling Dorrie. She doesn't matter.* But I do matter! I don't want him marrying that woman."

Benny knocked on the door. "May I have a word with her?"

"Sure," Maggie replied before getting up from the bed.

"Don't go, Maggie. I don't want to talk to him."

"Dorrie. You are being disrespectful," Maggie scolded.

"Me? Am I being disrespectful? I have nothing to say to you, Daddy."

"Dorrie," Benny said. "I love Amelia, and I want you to be happy for me. It's important to me for you to be happy for us."

"Well, I'm not happy, and I never will be. You didn't tell me about Amelia before tonight. You never thought it important enough to tell me? All this time, you've been sneaking around—lying! It's pretty clear. I mean nothing to you."

"Benny," Maggie said, trying to intervene.

"Maggie. Stay out of this. This is between me and Dorrie."

"Mom," Dorrie turned towards Maggie, tears running down her cheek. "I will never come around to being happy about their marriage. I will not go anywhere with Amelia. She will no longer be my au pair. I have nothing to say to her, and I want her removed from the room next to me. I want her out of my life. I wish Papa were home. He would protect me and my feelings about this."

Maggie was trapped in the middle and found herself at a profound loss. She was unable to mediate. The rift was too deep, too raw, to heal with words—not tonight. The dynamics within their once-close family had rapidly shifted. Maggie viewed the path ahead, and it was like a part of her died. The future of their family was now filled with emotional landmines, and they did not have Kerrington to guide them.

"Benny, maybe you should leave," Maggie said, her voice filled with great sorrow. She looked up and caught his eyes, noticing he, too, was hurting from the crushing event that had taken place. Exchanged in the swift glance was his recognition that it was too late to turn back the clock and the impact of the dinner conversation on his family may never be healed. It could never be undone.

Benny's shoulders sank, and his eyes closed as he gave out a painful sigh. In quiet resolution, he turned and walked out the door, closing it gently behind him.

***

THE NEXT MORNING, Maggie began looking for a replacement au pair for Amelia. Breakfast was another nightmare, with silence cutting the air into pieces and filling it with hostility.

Dorrie remained silent, not offering up a single joke or riddle. At least Benny had used good taste by not inviting Amelia to breakfast.

Maggie later took Dorrie to South Park Mall, which turned out to be a disaster. Dorrie simply moped around with sagging shoulders, not interested in looking at anything. They ate at the Cheesecake Factory, which was Dorrie's favorite place to go. She even refused her regular dessert. They walked and drove in silence as Dorrie stared out the window.

When they returned home, Benny was gone. Ronnie reported he had taken Amelia shopping for wedding things.

The overwhelming, invisible power of sadness filled the air all through the mansion.Unable to bear the sensation, Maggie headed over to the hospital to see Kerrington. Before leaving, she ordered Ms. Pretty to move Amelia's things to a room at the other end of the house, far away from family—which also meant far away from Benny's quarters.

Chapter 39

Visitors

MAGGIE DEEPLY SIGHED as she entered Blanchard House through the side door to drop off items, she'd picked up from Earth Market for the chef.

After washing her hands, Maggie headed out to the small greenhouse to check on her newly planted broccoli micro-greens. She smiled, happy to see how much they'd grown overnight. She pinched off a small handful and ate the veggies raw—satisfied with the fresh, powerful nutrients she was ingesting.

Maggie thought of Kerrington. The roller coaster ride was getting the best of her. Just when she thought Kerrington was out of the woods, his skin turned yellow with jaundice. He was headed for liver failure, which could be bad.

Bonnie tried to reassure Maggie, telling her that his color was better than it had been earlier in the morning. Also, his labs had improved as well. Maggie didn't know how much more she could take. It wasn't that she was feeling sorry for herself—she simply wanted it over with and for Kerrington to walk back in the door and stand beside her, eating broccoli stems with her.

As Maggie reached for a new batch, her hand froze, startled at the sound of a man's voice nearby. No one should be on the property, at least this part of it. A feeling of fright raced through her as she quickly looked for a way to escape. Then she heard Amelia's voice talking to the man in French. Maggie then heard a camera click several times, followed by Amelia's laughter. She peeked around the corner. The man was taking pictures of the house with Amelia in the foreground. She was throwing a kiss into the camera. Maggie became enraged.

"What are you doing?"

"Oh. Hello Maggie. This is…"

"I don't care who he is; get him off my property now. You are not allowed to bring strangers into our home—much less allow them to take pictures of the property. Kerrington is strict about those rules. Does security know he's here?"

"They don't need to know. I live here, and he is my guest."

"Security needs to know about anyone who enters. They are here to keep this home safe—to keep us safe. This is not your house to come and go and do what you want. You are an employee who is setting a bad example for everyone who works here. You are not special. Now get him out of here at once, and then I will see you in the library."

"This is my brother, Maggie! He's not a stranger. I was telling him about the wedding. We're going to hold it in the garden."

"Amelia. We'll talk about this inside. Privately."

Maggie sauntered into the main house, and Amelia followed her, infuriated and yelling, "Don't you think it's a little too late for privacy? How dare you embarrass me in front of my family? That was humiliating, Maggie. Who do you think you are?"

"I am your employer, Amelia. I would gladly have invited him over if you had bothered to ask. That's how things are done in our home. You are a guest here."

"I am marrying Benny, Maggie—like it or not—and this is my home. I'm having his baby, and that makes me a bit more than just a guest. So, you need to get over yourself."

"Don't you dare talk to my mother like that," Dorrie screamed as she ran down the stairs."

"Dorrie, it's okay," Maggie said, holding up her hand in peace. Amelia was just showing her brother out."

Having overheard the entire charade, Ronnie eased across the room and stepped out the back door. He returned with security and Amelia's brother, who was escorted out of the house.

"Wait," Amelia said, "I'm coming with you."

"Mom. Are you okay?" Dorrie asked, hugging Maggie around the waist.

"Honey, I'm fine. We just disagreed."

"But she was yelling at you. That's disrespectful."

Benny entered the front door with Ronnie. "What's happening here? Amelia told me I needed to get my house in order before she would come back. Maggie. What the hell happened?"

"Amelia screamed at Mom. That's what happened."

"What? Amelia never screams," Benny replied, his face lighting up with astonishment.

"Then you don't know your future wife very well."

Benny tilted his head and looked at Maggie as if she'd better have a good explanation for the altercation. "She's going to be my wife, Maggie. What could have made you two behave like banshees? In front of Dorrie, no less. That's not like you. What's going on?"

"She broke the rules. Plain and simple."

"What rules? Dorrie, honey, why don't you head up to the movie room? I'll join you in a bit. Maggie and I have to work this out privately."

"Yes, sir," Dorrie replied, looking back, not wanting to leave.

"Everything is okay, Dorrie," Maggie said as she turned and headed to the gilded bar. Uncontrollable tears burst from her eyes. "I can't take anymore Benny. Not one more thing! I feel like I'm having a nervous breakdown."

"Hey, girl. Calm down," Benny said, hugging Maggie. "Let's talk through everything. We'll sort it out."

"I'm sorry, Benny. Amelia surprised me. I didn't know he was her brother," Maggie explained, pouring herself a glass of wine. "I needed to be alone because I was worried to death about Kerrington. I was so stirred up I thought I might self-implode. It was bad timing."

"I'll talk to her."

Maggie hesitated for a moment, wondering if she should confront him with her truth. Then, she made the hasty decision to spit it out. "As your friend, Benny, I can't lie to you. I believe you're making a giant mistake, and you're headed for heartbreak."

"Well, Maggie, as your friend, I have to tell you I love her. I can't leave her. She's pregnant."

Unexpectedly, Amelia returned to the house and came around the corner with her arms folded, fury written across her face. "Maggie, you will not do this."

"Amelia. Please. Not now," Maggie begged. "Please."

"You're not taking Maggie's side, Benny."

"It's not a matter of sides, Amelia," Benny replied, his voice raised. "Please go back upstairs. We need to finish our discussion."

"The hell it isn't. I know when I'm not wanted. I'm going all right. I'm going straight home to France, and you will never, ever see your child. Good riddance to both of you. I quit."

Neither tried to stop her. Finally, Benny spoke, "I need to go after her. She can't take my child away from me. We need to work this out, Maggie, for the sake of our friendship. Can you not see what this could do to us?"

***

DINNER WAS AWKWARD. Amelia's empty seat spoke volumes. Dorrie acted almost giddy. Maggie assumed she figured out something was up. Or maybe Benny told her what happened. Annella and Glenn didn't bring Amelia up—as the tension coming from Benny was palpable—so thick one could carve it with a knife.

Sunday lifted the mood by talking about her latest visit to Kerrington. "I went by to see him just before dinner, and the yellow color was practically gone. And guess what else? Maggie. Dorrie." Sunday paused for dramatic effect before saying, "His brilliant blue eyes were wide open. And he looked straight at me. He smiled. He knew me!"

Maggie joyfully threw her hands to her face. Dorrie instantly burst from her seat, ran over to Maggie, and hugged her hard.

AS THE FAMILY exited the dining room, Maggie, Benny, and Dorrie halted. Amelia's brother was back, carrying suitcases down the stairs. Amelia followed him, holding a carry-on bag and pocketbook. She glanced at the three of them and quickly looked away. Amelia never looked back, never said goodbye. She simply walked out, got in her car, and drove away.

Benny excused himself and retreated upstairs as Maggie tried to explain the situation to Dorrie, but she stopped Maggie. "Daddy talked to me. I know it all. And much more, but I didn't tell him."

"What do you know?"

"I'd rather not talk about it, Mom. I don't think Daddy would appreciate it. He's unhappy enough with things being the way they are."

***

TWO DAYS LATER, Amelia moved back in and acted as if nothing had happened. Maggie and Dorrie sat stone-faced at the table. Benny had simply approached them an hour before her arrival and announced that Amelia would be moving back in. "The wedding will go on as expected, and Dorrie, you <u>will</u> be there and behave yourself. Maggie, I'd like it if you could pull yourself together, if for no other reason than to preserve our friendship."

Like a soap opera, life went on after the initial shock. Amelia made the first move to recover broken relationships by apologizing over the dinner table. Maggie followed suit, as did Dorrie. All for Benny's sake.

Chapter 40

Trapped

MING WAS AWAKENED by voices outside his window. His new resident physician was talking with a man with a bold, bossy voice. He looked at the wall clock. It was ten in the morning. Ming strained to see who the man was. He looked like a cop of some sort. His demeanor was firm. The tag on his suit boldly displayed **FBI** in bold letters.

"We've decided the risk of this patient eloping is very low," the detective said. "He is officially in our custody, but since he's in such a secure area, we won't be posting an officer at the door. Here is an FBI custody form signed by me," the detective handed the legal document to the physician. "It advises the hospital that Mr. Ming Fu is not to be discharged without us being notified ahead of time. We need to interview him as he has information that is crucial to our investigation. We'll need to get an officer down here to escort him off the premises. Mr. Fu, at this point, is considered to be a severe public safety threat. Would you make sure this is passed along to all oncoming staff?"

"I certainly will, sir. Are you leaving now?"

"I'd like to interview him, if possible."

"As long as he's under the influence of sedative medications, we can't allow you to do that at this time."

"Here's my card. Call me with any information related to the patient's impending discharge."

"Will do. I have to get back to my patients, sir."

"Thanks for your time."

Ming absorbed the severity of the conversation he'd overheard. He could not allow them to take him to jail. In desperation, his mind whirled with options. He couldn't afford a lawyer. Remembering scenes, he'd seen on Law & Order, he decided he shouldn't speak to them. That would be it. He would pretend that he couldn't talk or write. Just at that time, the door opened, and a doctor entered.

"Good morning. I'm Doctor Lee, your new doctor. Today is your lucky day. You are off the ventilator, as you can breathe on your own now, and your fever is gone. We'll be stopping your sedatives as your muscle spasms have disappeared. It's a miracle, for real. You were at death's door; then, suddenly, you recovered. Bloodwork of your viral load has determined you are no longer considered to be infectious. Like I said, it's a miracle. There is no sign of the virus being present in your body anymore. We will follow you in the clinic. It's essential you keep our appointments and never miss a visit. We will discharge you in a couple of days."

"Where is Doctor Sheng?" Ming asked, unable to stop himself despite his decision not to speak.

"Oh. The doctor finished her rotation here and has moved on to her next assigned area, probably Neuro ICU."

"So. I won't be seeing Doctor Sheng again."

"Maybe in the clinic at some point when she does her rotation there. But not here. Like I said. You can go home now."

After the doctor left, Ming sat by himself, wondering how he might ever see Doctor Sheng again. After all, he wanted to marry her.

***

THE NEXT MORNING, Ming got out of bed filled with renewed energy. After searching the room for his belongings, he remembered his clothing had been cut off during his emergency care. Thoroughly bummed, he climbed back into bed and paged his nurse.

Thirty minutes later, Ming was dressed in sweatpants and a generic grey tee-shirt, ready to carry out his plan. He asked if he could walk in the hall to regain his strength. "The doctor said I'm not infected anymore."

During his walk, escorted by a tech, Ming checked out his surroundings, explicitly looking for exit doors, careful to determine where they led. He was puzzled as to where he should go until he saw two staff members enter from a side door, carrying Starbucks coffee cups—meaning that the door led to the main hospital.

***

AT MIDNIGHT, Ming walked down to Kerrington's room and stood outside the viewing window, briefly observing him. Kerrington was awake, sitting on the edge of the bed in the dimly lit room. Ming stood unsure of himself and weighed the pros and cons of what he was about to do. The need to apologize to the man who had almost died from his virus had bothered him throughout the day. It was his only chance, and it was the right thing to do. The proper thing. One day, his parents might discover what he'd done, and the fact that he'd apologized would go a long way toward eventually getting their love and respect back.

Ming searched both sides of the corridor. He'd overheard the staff talking about being short-staffed, and seeing no sign of any workers, he entered Kerrington's room. Ming didn't bother to dress in protective gear because the danger of getting the virus was gone. He also overheard that Kerrington received a miracle. Signs of the virus were gone from his body.

Kerrington looked up as he entered the dimly lit room. "Who are you?"

"My name is Ming Fu, sir. I'm here to apologize for making you so sick. I work in the lab on your property."

"You were working on the virus?"

"I created a cure, sir. I'm very proud, but I didn't expect anyone would get sick from it."

"You didn't give the virus to me, son. Congressman Brightman told me about his investment. I went into the lab myself and looked around until I found the elevator to the secret floor. I entered and exposed myself. I discovered a leak in my suit after handling the virus."

"I'm so happy to hear that, sir. I mean, I'm not happy you got sick, but I'm pleased to know it was not my carelessness that led to you almost dying."

"I want you to work for me, Mr. Fu. I own GlixMorganthal Laboratories, and we have many complex development projects. You are a genius, and I need someone of your caliber to run a new laboratory I'm building. The current lab will be destroyed at once. Would you consider my proposal? You will receive a significant salary, and you can live in one of the suites at my house until your office is built. I will pay off your loan to the Congressman, and he will be severed from our lives. I want the work to start tomorrow."

Ming was stunned. This mighty man he'd always heard about wanted him, Ming Fu, to work for him. It was his dream come true. "Yes, sir. I would be honored to work for you."

"Great. Pack your things and report to my head of security, Mr. Lamar Floyd. He will have you escorted to your living quarters and new office. I'm pleased to have you on board."

Ming bowed at the waist and exited the room. He then walked out of the Isolation Unit unseen. Ming quickly found the stairwell and descended it as safely as possible, hurrying all the while. The stairs led him to the main entrance of the hospital, where he walked straight out the door.

***

AFTER MING LEFT the hospital, his mind went into chaos. In his haste not to be discovered by the staff and thus the FBI, he'd forgotten to tell Mr. Blanchard about him being wanted by the FBI. He didn't dare casually walk up to the house and report to security as ordered. He had to stay hidden until he could contact his future boss and tell him about him being a wanted man. Ming decided to go to the lab to retrieve his belongings and serum.

Ming fled on foot, walking several miles to get to the lab. He smiled with satisfaction at going back at his lab. Ming would make it quick, real quick. He would grab the vials of the vaccine cure and secure his notebooks. Swiftly, he trotted down the steps, entered the back elevator, and entered his private BSL 4 lab. After donning his protective gear, Ming opened the vault leading to the room that held all his valuable belongings. When he stepped over to the refrigerator, his breath caught in his chest. Everything was gone. All of it. He checked the virus. Someone had unplugged the warmer. It had been destroyed—meaning he couldn't even recreate the cure. His lifetime of work was gone. He would never be able to get his hands on the virus again. It was way too expensive. That thought made him shiver—without the virus and his cure, he would not make money off his work, which meant he had no way to pay back the money he borrowed to pay for the virus. Even if he had taken the job with Mr. Blanchard, he wouldn't have had that kind of money for a long time. It wouldn't be long before Mario's men came looking for him.

After leaving the BSL 4 lab, Ming sat in a chair and wondered what he might do. Where might he stay? How might he reach Blanchard? Ming didn't even know how to call him. He had no money. His wallet, which probably had his driver's license, bank card, and credit card, was in the hospital safe.

Ming finally settled on trying to make it to his brother Tron's house, which was not far away. However, it was problematic as it was daylight, and he was sure the FBI had issued a **Be on the Lookout** order. They probably had a description of his new clothing, too. He made his way through the woods in the direction of his brother's house until he came to a clearing, glad for the opportunity to rest. It hadn't taken him long to realize he'd lost a lot of strength during his hospitalization.

He stood for the longest time, looking at Tron's house. He was home because his car was parked outside. What would he say? Should he tell him about the FBI? Had the investigators already visited him? Were they watching the house? Ming was paralyzed with fear and found himself unable to make a move. Instead, he sank into the bushes surrounding a tree. He leaned against it and fell into a deep sleep.

It was after dark when Ming was awakened by the sound of mosquitos hovering around his face. He stood and quickly made his way to Tron's door, looking around, praying he wouldn't be seen. He knocked softly. The house was silent. He assumed Tron was in the back bedroom watching TV. Ming repeated the knock. This time, it was louder. Again, he looked around at his surroundings. The neighborhood was quiet.

Tron finally opened the door. "What are you doing here? You're infected. Get away from me. You have people looking for you."

"I'm no longer infected. The doctors said the virus is gone. I'm okay. I wouldn't come here if I were sick. The last thing I would ever do, brother, is hurt you."

Tron opened the door just wide enough for Ming to step across the doorframe. Then, he slammed the door and locked it.

"You can't stay here long. Are you hungry?"

"I am. Thank you, brother."

"You want a beer?"

"No, it's best I don't."

"What did you do to make the FBI come looking for you?"

"You know about Veridian XV?"

"Every scientist knows about it, especially now, since it emerged in Charlotte. Don't tell me you're involved with that, man."

"I am. Did you know that there's a fourth floor in the lab?"

"You sure about that? Where?"

"There's a secret elevator door hidden behind that big ugly painting on the back wall of the third level. It takes you to a BSL Level 4 lab. I got a loan and bought the Veridian XV virus off the black market. I discovered and made a vaccine cure."

"You're a genius. I knew you had such a thing in you. Where is it? The virus. And the cure?"

"Someone stole the cure and also destroyed the virus. It's gone. Everything."

***

OVER a meal of rice and milk, Tron asked a lot of questions. "Did you kill him? Mario? Are they going to be coming after you for murder?"

"No. I didn't murder Mario. I was defending myself. That's how I got the virus. He claimed I betrayed him by letting it get out of the lab. He said men were coming after him. They wanted the virus back. They didn't want to go to prison."

"Well. It seems to me—it's going to be really hard for the FBI to do anything. Mario is dead. He can't talk. And all the proof—the cure and your notes, they're all gone. The virus is dead. All you have to do is remove it from the lab and clean the place with Clorox, and you'll be free and clear."

"I'll take care of that first thing in the morning."

"How about now? I'll go with you and help."

"No. You're involved enough."

"I'll drive you. You got two hours to take care of things."

***

TRUE TO HIS word, Tron took Ming to the lab and dropped him off at the back of the road leading directly to the lab.

Ming entered and made his way downstairs, where he scrubbed the area nice and clean. Tron had reminded him that he didn't have to worry too much if they found a fingerprint here and there because he had a right to be in the building as he was actually employed there, albeit upstairs.

Ming secured the virus and left the lab, burying it deep in the woods behind the exit so that no one would ever be harmed by it. He took off his gloves and was ready to leave when a voice called out from behind.

"May I ask what you're doing here?" The bright light of a flashlight blinded him. He couldn't see the man's face but assumed it was security from the property.

"I was walking, and I got lost. I had to go to the bathroom, so I used the woods. I was burying—it—you know—my bathroom stuff."

"You're lying. I know who you are and what you're doing here. See the camera?" The flashlight shined on the hidden camera. The man wasn't alone. There was a woman with him. He'd seen them both before. They were standing outside Mr. Blanchard's window in the hospital. "What's your name?" Maggie called out.

"Ming Fu," he answered, his voice quivering in fear.

"My name is Benny. This is Maggie. We live here."

"We have what you're looking for. It's locked up tight and secure in our basement," Maggy said. "We discovered it, and we had to steal it. My husband was dying, and he needed it. We gave it to him—and we gave it to you. You're both alive without a trace of the virus in your blood."

"You are a mastermind," Benny cried out. "I would like to shake your hand. You do us proud, man—just knowing all this happened on our land."

Ming held his arm out and shook Benny's hand with vigor. "Come up to the house with us, and let's have a drink."

"It's buried there," Ming confessed, pointing to the spot where he was digging.

"We know, we watched you," Benny said, holding out his cell phone. "We recorded it. All the camera movement."

"But, no worry," Maggie said, walking towards the house. "The virus is good and dead. I killed it."

"I lost much money on that, but when I told your husband about everything, he offered to pay off my loan. I don't have to worry about being in the poor house."

***

MING, LIKE everyone else who walked through the door of Blanchard House, stood staring in wonder in the entrance hall. Benny led him into the Gilded Bar, where they sat and talked for a long time.

Maggie was bold when she bluntly asked Ming, "Exactly how much money did I cost you by destroying the virus?"

"Half a million dollars," Ming replied, hanging his head in shame.

"My husband called and told me about your conversation. We have a room waiting for you upstairs. There's also a new cell phone on your desk so you can call your brother."

After Ming was taken to his new quarters by a security officer, Maggie and Benny lingered behind.

"It's like old times," Maggie said with a smile. "I've missed you, my friend."

"Nothing has changed, Maggie. Ever. Things will never change with us because I won't allow it. Even if I marry Amelia, I'll never leave this house. I'll never leave my family. If she wants to be a part of it, she'll have to work at it just like we do."

"But Dorrie," Maggie said with a frown.

"She'll adjust. Kerrington should be coming home soon, and all will be well again. He was a way of guiding Dorrie in the right direction."

"You're right. You know, we might be a strange family, but the way we fit together works really nicely. Good night, my friend."

Chapter 41

The Pillow Fluffer

ERRINGTON MOVED cautiously from his bed and into the bathroom. He stood for the longest time, looking at his reflection in the mirror. His once firm, tanned, and smooth face had been replaced by hollowed-out cheeks and skin that was withered with a sallow hue. It was now a shadow of its former self. Kerrington couldn't help but wonder how much weight he'd lost. The muscles that once defined his physique were now hidden beneath layers of wrinkled skin. Even his eyes, which used to sparkle with vitality, had dulled. The reflection staring back at him resembled a character from a low-budget horror movie, a haunting reminder of the toll time had taken. He placed his hand on the sides of the sink and braced himself. Kerrington typically didn't allow himself to become saddened over vanity issues because he'd made it part of his daily routine to keep himself healthy-looking. Now, he had a severe problem. There was no way he should be seen in public. It would destroy his businesses. Confidence in him would be lost.

Kerrington closed the door to his room, sat on the edge of the bed, picked up the phone, and dialed the Patient Concierge Officer. The nurses often called them the Pillow Fluffers. As a hospital donor and board member, Kerrington was entitled to certain privileges. He paid a good bit of money to join the VIP treatment program and mainly became a member to help the program be successful. Many donors and high-profile members of the community asked that the board have such a program so they might keep the spotlight off of them during their hospitalization.

Valerie responded at once and personally to his room. Kerrington liked the way she exuded confidence. He could tell she was good at her job. "May I help you, sir?"

"Call me Kerrington. Please. I need your complete confidentiality. As you can see, I look sick. It's been a prolonged illness, and I need recovery time—and privacy. As a businessman, I can't let anyone see me this way. I'm being discharged, and I don't want to be seen leaving the hospital."

Valerie quickly formulated a plan. "I've coordinated this many times, Mr. Blanchard. I know who you are and what you do, and I agree you have unique needs. It would be best if you remained in your room with the door closed at all times. At five in the morning, I will bring your discharge papers and get you to sign them. Then, we will exit the hospital by wheelchair through the VIP tunnel, where a private car with tinted windows will pick you up and take you home. A private-duty male nurse will go with you. He is discreet and can be trusted."

"The doctor felt I might benefit from having such a person take care of me at home until I get my strength back."

"If you don't mind wearing a baseball cap pulled down over your face, I think it would be helpful. Staff will think you're a Panther player."

Kerrington eagerly agreed.

"I have another suggestion you might like," Valerie said, pulling a card from her leather professional notebook. "I've referred patients to this facility. It's pretty far from here, and it's quite expensive. It's an advanced treatment center that is designed to take care of all your medical needs and help you quickly regain physical strength. They're located in Switzerland. Patients I've referred there have given me glowing reports, especially as it pertains to privacy. If you would like me to arrange a transfer, I'll make the call."

"Baumann Clinic? I have private transportation to get there. If you could call them for me and get me in, I'd be grateful. I think it's perfect for me."

"It's hard to get into because they stay full, but I will see if I can pull some strings."

Valerie smiled when she left, giving Kerrington a sense of safety.

The following day, Valerie pushed Kerrington through the extensive underground tunnel that appeared old, like it was built with the original hospital. It went a long distance, which Kerrington estimated was over a city block. His car and the male private duty nurse, Keith, were waiting. The nurse was quiet and strong-looking—like he could manage anyone.

Chapter 42

Kerrington Blanchard

KERRINGTON EXITED the chauffeur-driven limousine parked directly in front of the estate doors, refusing help from his private nurse. Ronnie, the trusted butler, was prepared for the big event. Both of the massive, tall front doors hung open wide, awaiting Kerrington's entrance.

Two strong men from security, plus Keith, met Kerrington with a wheelchair, which Kerrington promptly refused. Maggie exited from the other side of the vehicle to help him, which he allowed. Kerrington held his head high all the way up the stairs. Maggie was keenly aware of his breathing. She could tell he was struggling to hold it together. Kerrington was a proud man and would be thoroughly embarrassed if he fell in front of anyone, much less his employees.

When he reached the top of the stairs, he warmly hugged Dorrie for a long time. "Papa," she cried out, burying her head in his chest. "I missed you so much."

When he released Dorrie, Maggie led him to his library, where he told everyone in no uncertain terms that he wished to be alone. "Including you, young man," he said, pointing to the nurse.

Maggie lingered behind, hoping she wouldn't be dismissed. After he sank into his luxurious leather wing chair, he looked up at her. "I mean no offense, Maggie. It's been so long since I've had true privacy. I would appreciate alone-time to reflect and gather my thoughts."

"No problem, honey. No offense taken. Call me if you need me. I'll be across the hall." At the door, she paused. "I'm so glad to have you back home. I need you."

"I love you and need you too, Maggie."

She smiled and closed the door.

THE SILENCE in the parlor that afternoon suffocated Maggie as she patiently waited to be with Kerrington. It was so quiet she could hear the ticking of the clock on the wall. Each passing minute added to her mounting anxiety. *What if something happened to him? What if he needs me? How would we know?* Maggie wondered quietly. She had to respect his wish for solitude. Maggie understood his need for it. Her fingers twisted nervously in her lap as she waited.

Maggie lightly gasped as a soft, familiar melody filled the house and stirred her heart as it had so many times before. Kerrington had the record album **Could I Have This Dance** by **Anne Murray** playing in his room so loudly that it echoed through the house. She wanted to cry aloud at the sound—music had been absent in the house for so long while he was gone.

Their love song instantaneously transported Maggie back to that first magic moment when she'd stood nervously beside Kerrington on the Blanchard House balcony. She'd been innocent, not knowing how much he cared for her. The night sounds played lightly around the estate beneath the backdrop of the Charlotte night skyline. Bright stars twinkled above, setting her up for the romantic moment that would allow love to bloom.

Kerrington had pulled Maggie into his arms as the song played softly overhead, the soft melody adding perfect magic to the moment. They danced, swaying gently and slowly, lost in each other. As he gently brushed a strand of hair from her face, he whispered the lyrics in her ear. "Could I have this dance for the rest of my life?"

"Yes." Maggie barely murmured her response, having been filled with such tremendous happiness it caught her off guard. She smiled up at him and sank her head deeper into his chest, marveling at the fact that this sensitive, loving, gentle man was hers.

It was as if he were calling with his music without saying her name. Maggie could feel her heart beating hard against her chest as she stood and made her way down the hall, filled with excitement. She felt drawn to him by the words of the sweet, lilting love song. His love was back, and it was rekindling the intense fire inside her. The feeling of first love came alive again—that kind of magic moment that takes you by surprise and takes your breath away.

Slowly, she opened the door and found him standing alone in the center of the room, smiling and waiting for her with open arms.

Maggie felt as if she were floating as she moved into Kerrington's arms, sinking her face against his neck. The warmth of his embrace enveloped her, and the familiar scent of his cologne brought a sense of comfort and belonging. They swayed gently to the beautiful love song, each step perfectly in sync as if they were truly made for one another. Her precious love had come back to her. Everything would be fine once again.

***

THE DINING ROOM was filled with excited chatter, reflecting their great appreciation that Kerrington was home and all was well once again. They, too, felt life return to the mansion through Kerrington's music, which he played all day, hour after hour until dinner. He had had days like that from time to time, where he sought music to ease his soul.

Dorrie beamed with love for her Papa. From time to time, he would reach over and hold her hand and give her a brief smile.

The house staff confirmed their happiness as well. Miss Pretty had been overheard humming in the hallways while she went about her work. Ronnie opened the front door with a newfound lilt in his voice as he greeted guests. Yes, Blanchard's household was back to normal. It was as if not one moment had gone by since Kerrington's was last home. The grief hanging in the air, stifling life and happiness, was instantly lifted the moment he walked through the door. Dorrie told another riddle or two, providing entertainment as always.

Annella and Glenn sat next to each other, having mended fences through counseling.

Kerrington abruptly stunned the entire table with an unexpected announcement. "As all of you can see, I'm not my normal self. Not yet anyway. I'm going to have to go away for a bit to get the treatment I need to return to my former self. I'll be gone for a month, maybe more, to a clinic in Switzerland. It's a place where I can recover quietly out of the public eye. Can we please keep this within our family?"

"You're going away?" Maggie asked, stunned. "So suddenly. When?"

"I just found out an hour ago. They made room for me."

"You're too sick to be traveling."

"I need this, Maggie. I leave on the first of September. I'll take our private jet, and my nurse has agreed to accompany me. It's a vigorous special treatment therapy that will help me regain my strength."

"But you can get that here," Maggie argued.

"Charlotte doesn't offer this program, Maggie, and I can't continue to look sick. I'm skinny, weak, and dizzy sometimes. Look at my skin. It looks unhealthy. People get nervous when they're doing business with a sick-looking man. I'm going to change that."

"May I go? I've never been to Switzerland," Maggie asked.

"No. My love. You can't. This isn't a vacation. Please don't ask." "Okay. I won't."

Kerrington hugged Maggie and held her in his arms for a brief moment before leaving the room. Maggie's heartstrings pulled for him as she watched him walk away. He had grown so thin and weak. She could see it in his every step. Yes, he needed to go. He could not let the Wall Street financial world see him the way he was—so skinny, pale, and fragile.

That night, Maggie prayed for her sweet love that one day he would come walking back through the door, back as a strong man, deliberate in his every intention, a leader once again.

****

MAGGIE WAS filled with worry about Kerrington going away. It had consumed her thoughts all night. She entered his private library to spend time with him, alone, craving more time. She was stunned when Ming entered, bowing his head to Kerrington.

"Come in, Ming. I've been waiting for you. Maggie, would you like to join us?"

After they were seated in the library, Ming stood and bowed again.

"As you know, I've hired contractors to destroy the lab, and I wanted to make certain you have removed all your property, Ming."

"Everything is protected. The lab is empty."

"Is the cure safe?"

"I don't have it, sir."

"I do," Maggie confessed. "I removed it to keep it safe. I also took his files, and they have been returned to him."

"I want the property safe for my children to run around it to their heart's content," Kerrington said, giving Maggie a warm smile.

"I've taken care of your problems with the FBI, Ming. All the proper paperwork has been filed for your creation, and our government is relieved that we have a cure for a severe biological weapon. They want more."

"I'm not going to jail?"

"No. The FBI closed the investigation. And, as for your friend, Mario, don't feel bad for him. He tried to kill you and destroy all your work. If it hadn't been for you, a virus would still be out there threatening the world. That threat is gone, thanks to you."

"Maggie," Kerrington turned to address her specifically. "Ming has done extraordinary things, and I believe he can change the world through his scientific work. If he needs more space to work while I'm gone, please make sure he gets everything he needs."

"I plan to take a bride, Mr. Blanchard," Ming quietly announced. "If she wants to work in research, would she be able to work with me when the new lab opens?"

"Certainly. Your wife can collaborate with you on the project here. She can even live on the property if you like. It'll make it convenient. And you might liven up our dinner conversations. When you're married, we'll give you a proper family suite. It has a private living room, three bedrooms, and three baths on the second floor. I promise you will love it. Think of it as a gift—a thank-you gift from me."

"I am so proud to say I live here. That is gracious, sir. It will allow us to save and build our own home when we have children."

"You won't have to do that. You are always welcome to stay at our home for as long as you like. Children. Grandchildren. They are welcome as well. It's time you invite your parents here. I would love to meet them. Your brother, as well."

***

THAT AFTERNOON, Kerrington contacted his media teams. They met in Kerrington's office with his public relations manager.

"What's going on?" Maggie asked Kerrington the first chance she had to get him alone.

"There's a perception problem that needs to be addressed. We have to change people's minds about me and the virus and let everyone know the positive outcome of events." Kerrington invited her to attend.

The meeting was intense, as more media personnel jumped into the discussion with ideas; many often stepped out of the room to make phone calls. Each returned with promising news that made Kerrington happy. Maggie watched the progress with amazement. The energy Kerrington brought to the meeting was captivating and motivated everyone present.

Just before the meeting adjourned, the secretary, Mrs. Dobbs, summarized the events that would be taking place over the next immediate days. News outlets, big and small, agreed to print stories about the fantastic scientist superstar Ming Fu. Following the press release, they would tell the world about a young man's determination to make the world a safer place. News anchors were scheduled to meet and interview Ming. As word spread around the media outlets, more big press outlets called to get in on the media hype.

For the next month, Ming's face would appear on the cover of major magazines, and his story promised to become an Internet sensation. The first tweet published went viral before the meeting even adjourned. Other news stories would be published about Kerrington Blanchard's battle with the virus and his new biological lab that would explore other deadly viruses that threatened the world.

Everyone agreed that perception would change overnight, and the pace of the story would be relentless.

After everyone left, Kerrington chatted with the school superintendent and demanded that his daughter be invited back to the school. Dorrie's school called her personally and apologized for the poor manner in which they handled her right to education. The school agreed to meet with the parents regarding their complaints of danger. They would be advised that the school is safe and that if they still have concerns, they could take their children elsewhere. Kerrington promised to match the cost of any funds lost through tuition.

***

THE DINNER brought a night of gaiety and celebration. All of their hospital friends joined them for an Italian dinner feast at Benny's suggestion.

Sunday, Glenn, Benny, and Maggie, along with several senior ER residents, made a toast to Tess. Hospital chatter flew around the table. Even Dorrie joined in, as she had been binge-watching **Grey's Anatomy** for the past year. Maggie smiled inside, proud of her little girl for knowing so much about the medical world. She hoped she would follow in her mother, Willow's footsteps and become a nurse.

All of the senior residents were uncomfortable at first being in Kerrington's presence. One even did so much oohing and ahhing over his accomplishments, including being a member of the hallowed and sacred Board of Directors of the hospital. Kerrington graciously stopped her and made a significant effort to make her feel welcome and relaxed. He wanted to be seen as just an average man. He did so with incredible grace, and Maggie was so immensely proud of him in that moment.

Ming fit right in. Every topic that centered around a research project one of the residents was involved in, he jumped right in on the conversation excitedly, proving he belonged in Blanchard House.

Kerrington made another toast to everyone at the table. Then, he addressed each resident personally, asking where they came from, where they currently lived, and what they wanted out of life. All reported living in cramped apartments and struggling to make ends meet.

"I'm going to make each of you an offer—a small gift that will lighten your stress and make your lives a little easier. We have an entire wing of empty suites, and I grow weary of having such a house that stays mostly empty. I'd like to give each of you one, rent-free, plus a driver to take you to and from the hospital. It would be nice to liven up the place with educated people."

"What about the movie star? Doesn't she live here? Will she be okay with us?"

"Annella? She does live here between filming. She has other homes around the world, and she's as grounded as I am. She's married to Glenn Sloan over here," he said as he motioned to Glenn. She loves people all kinds of people. She's what some people refer to as cool. She doesn't like being treated differently.

Carolyn Wells was the first to accept, followed quickly by the rest of the doctors.

Just like that, Blanchard House became alive more than ever. Kerrington took Maggie's hand and held it; they were both quite happy with the sudden turn of events.

***

THE FOLLOWING MORNING, Maggie awakened to find Kerrington's side of the bed empty. She called his name. He didn't answer. Maggie quickly got up and got dressed, noting his cell phone was on the nightstand next to his bed. She assumed he had gone to breakfast early. *Good*, she murmured to herself. *Maybe he'll eat a lot. If his appetite returns, perhaps he won't have to go away.*

When breakfast came and went without Kerrington, Maggie grew concerned and went about looking for him. Everyone at the table confirmed her reason for worry when they denied having seen him. Maggie checked the entire first floor without finding him. She hesitated notifying security because she didn't want to make a big deal about it, but she gave in. Lamar, as head of security, always knew of Kerrington's comings and goings. He would know if Kerrington had left the property.

Lamar's look of surprise was alarming, and he took immediate action, ordering all security officers to search the entire house. For the first time, Maggie was made aware of the emergency response system that had been installed in the house. Lamar explained it was for tornado warnings or other such emergencies. She noticed an urgency in his voice as he picked up the locked phone box and paged Kerrington's name overhead.

Kerrington still couldn't be found. He didn't respond to the overhead page. Maggie felt useless, so in an effort to help, she headed to the panic room to look and came up empty-handed. Even Benny, Glenn, and Annella were looking for him. Benny had sent Dorrie to do her homework and told her not to worry. Dorrie did what teens do: She started crying and went to her room.

Maggie looked at Benny. "The lab?"

"I don't know why he would go there, but let's go take a look."

The two of them, trying to stay out of others' eyesight, hid behind hedges and eased over to the lab. There was no sign of Kerrington.

They stepped into the elevator, hoping he might be on the fourth floor. When the door opened, there he was, drenched in sweat, spraying foam insulation everywhere. Cases of the spray containers lined the entire back wall.

"What are you doing, Kerrington? We've been looking everywhere for you!"

Kerrington turned to face her, eyes ablaze yet not connecting. He was clearly baffled. "I'm fixing a problem," he said, shaking his head as if to clear it.

"He's not himself," Maggie whispered to Benny. "Call Glenn. Tell him to bring his emergency bag."

Maggie carefully and slowly made her way towards Kerrington, not wanting to cause him to become alarmed. Her mind raced. *What could be the cause of his confusion? Drugs? No. He wouldn't use mind-altering substances. Head injury? No. Hypoglycemia? Possible! He'd been given an untested medication. Could hypoglycemia be a side effect? Maybe. He hadn't been eating much since he'd been home. He just picked at his meals. Bingo. That's what was wrong.* She was certain. Maggie picked up the wall phone and called Benny. "Bring some orange juice and sugar. Hurry."

"Get back!" Kerrington shouted. "You don't want to get hurt. This place is filled with things that can kill you. Move!"

Maggie's heart raced, knowing he could easily become violent. She'd seen outrageous and ferocious behavior in people when their blood sugar levels fell to dangerous levels. He was still a strong man. Benny would have to help her force him to drink the juice.

Benny bolted into the room, carrying a pint of orange juice and a bowl of sugar. He was shaking the bottle, mixing the sugar as he ran. Glenn was directly behind him, carrying his black bag.

They all flew into action just as Kerrington dropped to the floor. Glenn pricked Kerrington's finger and performed a fingerstick blood glucose test as Maggie lifted Kerrington's head. "Drink the orange juice."

Maggie sighed when Kerrington did as he was told, barely able to swallow.

"His blood sugar is 42," Glenn called out. "I'll get the gel glucose tube ready in case we need it."

The response was immediate. First, a look of recognition returned to Kerrington's blue eyes, and he slowly raised his head. She made him drink more juice. Then, he asked, "What happened?"

Eventually, they got Kerrington out of the building and put him to bed, where Glenn did a thorough examination and declared, "He's out of danger, so there's no need for the hospital. He just has to eat. Regular meals with plenty of calories for now." Glenn looked firmly at Kerrington. "That's my order. Do you understand, Kerrington? You have to eat."

"Yes, sir," Kerrington replied, shooting off a salute before grinning at his brother-in-law.

***

KERRINGTON SEEMED to be back to himself and even came to the dinner table. Benny had slipped out of the house and bought a blood glucose testing kit. The *DexCom Powered AID*. Kerrington could quickly check his glucose as often as he wanted. No more worry.

Along with Glenn and Benny, Maggie did a thorough investigation of the clinic in Switzerland. They promised aggressive physical therapy, advanced nutrition, careful monitoring, and, of utmost importance, privacy. Glenn approved all of the doctor's credentials, and quite simply, Maggie was impressed with the place.

Kerrington's glucose was stable as a rock, and Glenn blamed the hypoglycemia issue on the fact that Kerrington had stopped eating. He now looked better than ever after putting some of the lost weight back on his bones. He still had a long recovery ahead of him, but she felt hopeful that all would return to normal.

Maggie gave him a deep hug before he walked down the stairs and headed to his silver helicopter, which was waiting on the landing pad behind the estate. It would scoop him away to the airport to board his private jet. She felt comfortable about him going away for a while. It wouldn't be forever.

Chapter 43

Jazzi

ENNY MET HIS cousin Jazzi Maxwell from security for lunch in the park. Jazzi and Benny were the same age, having grown up together—and thus were far better than just close friends, which Benny was banking on. He'd thought long and hard before asking Jazzi to eat with him because of the seriousness of the dining topic he planned on bringing up.

"So, what's up, Cuz?" Jazzi said, removing his security hat. Jazzi was a big, solid, muscled Black man who had been in security since the day he started. Now, he was high up in the department and the Chief of Information Services, Access Control, Crime Prevention, and Video Management of the property, which was what Benny needed from him today.

"I need help, Jazzi."

"Oh, Lord. Don't tell me it's help of the last kind when you got involved with a serial killer."

"Maybe not of the serial kind."

"I was kidding!"

"I'm not. Something serious has happened in our hospital, and I need you to keep mum about it. Doctor Richardson—one of our docs, is in serious trouble. She's a great surgeon, and I'm afraid she might lose her license to practice if we don't get to the bottom of what I think may have happened. I'm positive a crime has been committed. I'm sure of it. Attempted murder."

"Here in the hospital?"

"None other," Benny replied, taking a bite of his pepperoni pizza and wiping his mouth with a napkin.

"Who knows about it?" Jazzi asked, with his eyes widened.

"Nobody but me and my imagination. I think Maggie might be suspicious."

"Maggie's involved? That poor girl's middle name is Trouble, with a capital T. It follows her around like a sick puppy dog. The two of you together don't know how to stay out of it—and now, you've managed to drag your surgeon in on it. That pour innocent soul." Jazzi let out a light laugh.

"Seriously, Jazz. We're trying to clear the doctor's name. She really is innocent, and this is dangerous stuff. No joke. I think a visitor may have poisoned her patient."

"For real! Wow. How so?"

"It's complicated but try to follow. The wife's husband has brain surgery. Then he gets an infection from a rare bacterium, otherwise known as flesh-eating bacteria— it's called that because it typically can eat the flesh at a rate of up to one inch an hour. I was in on the case in the OR, and I'm trying to figure out how he got such an atrocious infection because I know for a fact that Doctor Richardson demands a sparkling clean operating room," Benny said, pointing his finger for emphasis on the park table. "The surgical suite was spotless because I personally always go behind the cleaning crew – just to make it spic 'n span. Operating on the brain is serious stuff."

"So, how do you think he got the infection if he didn't get it from some germs lying around?"

"Well. I'm not exactly sure. I was digging into the wife's past just because she's a weirdo. There apparently was a new woman waiting in the wings, and you know how vicious divorces can get. Last night, the witch tried to murder the woman out in the woods. Shot her six times! I think she tried to do her husband in with an infection because now it appears she's filed a malpractice lawsuit against the doctor for millions and millions. She is a desperate woman willing to do anything to stay a rich woman."

"You're going by your intuition, then."

"Exactly. Well, it turns out the wife, Lila, has a PhD in Microbiology. That, in and of itself, is interesting since Hubby managed to get such a badass infection. And then I found out she did her college clinical nowhere other than our very own microbiology lab. Are you catching up with me here?"

"I sure am."

"Turns out there's another case in the hospital."

"How do you know that?"

"I have friends. That's all I can say. Just like you do after all these years."

"So. It looks like you already have what you need."

"Far from it. I need proof. I need video footage of a blond female entering the lab after hours, on explicit dates of entry, specifically the micro lab section. And if she did, what did she do when she entered? Where did she go? What did she touch? Did she take anything with her? Did she talk to anyone? Then I need to know if she was in the VIP Neurosurgical ICU room right after that. I realize it's a lot to ask of you, Jazzi, but I must get this information."

"Whew. That's a lot, cuz," Jazzi said, dramatically wiping his forehead. "It may be hard to get."

"I'll make it worth your time," Benny replied, reaching for his pocket. "One grand. Two grand. Five grand."

"No. Stop. Don't reach into your pockets. Are you crazy? I don't take money. And I can't get caught taking what could be considered bribery. I'm an honest man. You know better than that."

"I'm sorry, dude—but I'm a desperate man."

"I will help you, but only if it's the right thing to do by a patient. And if we think someone is going around poisoning our patients. Then, it's the right thing. Mum's the word. I'll get it done."

Benny hugged his cousin hard. "You the man, Jazz. You the man."

After finishing lunch, Jazzi agreed to call Benny after he'd had sufficient time to look into things—privately, you know, after hours. It's a lot of footage covering a lot of stuff, but I'll see what I can come up with as soon as feasibly possible.

BENNY TOOK ADVANTAGE of the free time and grabbed a bite with Maggie downstairs in the crowded hospital cafeteria. Benny was updating Maggie on the Tess situation when his phone went off. It was Jazzi. He had good information. Benny excused himself and raced off to meet his cousin.

***

BENNY TOOK GREAT CARE, not to be seen by anyone, as he made his way out of the elevator and down the hall to Jazzi's office.

He was impressed by the sight. The oversized room had no windows. Conference tables lined one side of the room. The walls facing the tables were solid walls filled with various-sized video streaming screens, with one large screen centered in the middle of both walls. Benny estimated there had to be at least a hundred video screens in total. The room appeared to be soundproof as well. Benny's tension dissipated.

"So, what's up, Cuz?" Benny asked.

"Have a seat up here beside me. There's a lot of stuff to review," Jazzi remarked as he shuffled a couple of lists together to get them in the correct order.

"Okay. First up," Jazzi started in. "This is the back employee entrance to the lab on the night in question. Center screen. Rear Point of view. A woman with blond hair uses a key card to enter. The name on the key card is Lila Russell. As you can see, she heads to the Micro lab, looks around suspiciously, and acts like she's afraid she will be found. She slips on a pair of gloves and searches through what I believe are called Petri dishes. It appears she's looking for something specific. On the first round, she passes it by but then swings around later and stops at the sample, carefully reads the label, and looks around cautiously before grabbing some type of cube stick."

"That's a culture swab," Benny reported excitedly. "She's opening the swab cover, careful not to contaminate it. Then, she opened a petri dish and rubbed the Q-tip over the specimen really well before placing the specimen back into the tube holder. We got her. She has the specimen in her hand. Can you stop the camera and get a close-up of the label?"

Jazz adjusted the camera view for a close-up. "Can you read it? It's a complex name."

"*Streptococcus pyogenes—a Group A Strep* also known as *Necrotizing Fasciitis,*" Benny remarked, letting the complicated terminology slip off his lips like he said it every day. "That's it! Flesh-eating bacteria. Lord, have mercy, we got her red-handed."

"You're positive? Then, write down the exact description of the pocketbook she put the sample in while I move the tape forward. She almost gets caught, and I don't think it's worth spending our time reviewing it. Blondie hides under the desk, but the entering lab employee doesn't see her. We also didn't get a good look at the woman either, but we can grab her name and picture from the ID scanner she used when checking in and out of the lab."

"Next," Benny called out after completing the documentation of the description of the purse.

"Give me a few seconds while I get the footage up of the ICU. Okay. Now. Take a good look. Blondie is pressing the visitor's button to be allowed entry. And here she is, going toward the VIP suite, waving all nice to the nurses. Then, she goes into his room and takes a seat beside her husband, who is asleep. Now hold on while I get a better view, where you can see her better."

"Oh. Please. Please. Please," Benny prayed out. "Tell me you got her."

"Take a good look at this, Cuz. Here she is. Watch! Close. She puts on gloves. She pulls the stick out of her pocketbook and removes the swab from the container. And look at what she does."

"That Bitch!" Benny howled. "She's sticking it under the dressing and rubbing it hard to make sure she contaminates his wound really well. How evil!" Benny said, covering his mouth with his hands in disgust.

"Then, the tech removing laundry almost catches her, but she drops the swab in time and distracts him by saying something," Jazzi notes. "Watch again. After the tech leaves, she recovers the swab and puts it in her bag."

"That's nasty, putting something like that in a pocketbook that carries lipstick."

The two men stare at each other in amazement, and Benny breaks out with a victorious laugh. "We got her—hook, line, and sinker."

"You were so right, man."

"What is the next step?" Benny wonders aloud.

"Well, the hospital has to report it through the appropriate channels once I notify them."

"That will take too long. I have a homicide detective friend I can call. He's in the hospital several times a day. He knows all the ins and outs and how to make this crime stick. I say, don't share it. Please, Dude. The last thing we need is to have this tied up in the legal department. Promise me you'll keep this to yourself. My detective friend will obtain it legally and make sure we follow the chain of command so it will be properly admissible in a court of law. He also has to do an investigation and a crime report."

"That sounds like the right thing to do," Jazzi replied.

"Thank you, Jazzi!" Benny joyously replied, giving Jazzi the high five.

Chapter 44

Detective Mark Hanes

B ENNY SET UP A MEETING at Blanchard House with Maggie, Sunday, Jazzi, and Mark Hanes, a homicide detective. Hanes was Maggie and Benny's close friend, having worked together often on murder cases in the ER. He helped clear Maggie's name when she was accused of murdering her patient years ago.

Jazzi bent his head back, looking around the Gilded Bar in awe. "I cannot believe you live here, Cuz."

"Me either, sometimes. But after a while, it grows on you, and you get comfortable with the peculiar lifestyle."

"Like the butler and chef?"

"Yeah. That did take some adaptation."

They were waiting for Hanes to arrive and seated themselves around a large circular table. Although a homicide hadn't occurred, Benny needed Hanes's guidance on how to proceed with the evidence he and Jazzi had uncovered. Maggie already knew everything, but Sunday would be hearing it for the first time. They opted out of letting Glenn in on things because he was so heavily connected to the administrative arena of the hospital. "His involvement will only complicate things," Benny argued.

"You guys have me curious. Why am I here?" Sunday asked, looking around the table.

Benny never got to answer her question because Ronnie entered with Hanes and ushered him to the table.

Sunday looked at Hanes with building curiosity. When she saw his gun and badge, she raised her eyebrows alarmingly at Maggie.

"Don't worry. He's not here to arrest you Sunday. Chill. You'll see,"

Maggie said before lowering her voice to all but a whisper. "You're safe but take a deep breath–this meeting will blow your mind."

Maggie turned to Hanes. "This is Doctor Sunday Richardson. She's a neurosurgeon, and one of her patients is threatening to have her charged with homicide."

"I know all about it. The patient called me. Have no fear. There's no case being brought against you." Hanes looked as fresh as ever without a wrinkle on his shirt. His light brown hair was bleached blond from being out in the sun, neatly combed as always. When he pulled out his well-beaten leather notepad, Maggie intuitively knew their conversation would be well-documented.

Sunday looked at Hanes with new eyes. He was dashing with his sun-tanned face that held a telltale shadow of wearing sunglasses a lot. He definitely was a hot cop in her book. She eyed the gun strapped to his tight, trim waist beside the golden detective badge clipped to his belt.

"You can take the gun off if you wish," Maggie said, patting the seat beside her.

"I'd rather not, if you don't mind. It's safer where it is." His eyes widened with delight when the chef loaded the table with upscale snacks.

The meeting started on a high note as Benny and Hanes chatted about the latest ER homicide investigations. It was Benny's favorite topic of discussion with Hanes. Maggie smiled. Benny was definitely back where he belonged.

A certain excitement spread around the table, and Maggie was glued to the conversation. Hanes was a delight to be around after one got to know him. She looked at Sunday who was staring at Hanes, completely mesmerized by his every move. Hanes also seemed to be taking Sunday in, not with cop eyes but manly eyes. Maggie sensed a strong attraction building between them and she was glad; Hanes needed someone in his life, and so did Sunday.

Maggie briefly told Hanes about the case involving the three of them on that fateful day in the OR.

"Geez. Flesh-eating bacteria? That sounds horrid." Hanes remarked.

"It is," Benny said. "Sunday just got over it."

"You don't look sick." Mark remarked smiling Sunday's way.

"It was awful," Benny remarked. "That's part of why I asked you here. We need advice on a developing situation at the hospital. At my urging, my cousin Jazzi, found disturbing security footage at the hospital. We believe Bruce Russell's wife, Lila Russell, tried to kill him with the bacteria. Unlike Sunday who has a strong immune system, Bruce was weakened with cancer."

Sunday gasped and covered her mouth.

"Doctor Richardson is hearing this for the first time, Mark. I believe Lila, methodically set out to destroy Sunday's career so she could sue her for malpractice and get a wad of money. Additionally, to boost her malpractice case, I think Lila deliberately bumped into Sunday and gave her the same bacteria in order to link Sunday to Bruce's infection. It that crazy or what?"

Benny proceeded to tell Hanes everything – starting with how he became so distressed over Bruce getting the infection and his strong belief that the bacteria hadn't come from either the OR – or the ICU. Together, Jazzi and Benny laid out all the evidence, slowly and carefully, so Hanes could fully understand the complicated infection of **Necrotizing Fasciitis**.

Maggie couldn't help but break out in a satisfying smile as she listened and watched Hanes scrupulously taking notes, furious and fast–as he always did in the ER when he was investigating a homicide.

Sunday sat, shaking her head in shock as she watched the films of Lila stealing the bacteria from the lab. "That is so disturbing. Lila actually plotted and planned such an evil thing and then methodically carried it out with such malice in her heart."

"She's never acted like a normal person," Maggie added.

"I can confirm she has a Borderline Personality Disorder," Sunday said, looking at Hanes. "Her husband Bruce told me in confidence. He hired a private investigator to learn everything about her after he caught her lying to him. I don't know if that helps. Bruce said he discovered she'd been hospitalized for mental illness several times during her life."

228

"We have enough to open an investigation," Hanes said, "But not for homicide. How close did your patient, Bruce, come to dying?"

"Very close," Sunday said. "He won't die from the infection though. Sadly enough, I've been told by reliable sources that he's had an explosion of tumors occurring throughout his brain. He won't survive the cancer."

They both looked at Hanes. "Then, that's it," he said, closing his leather pad. "I'll still be in touch, but a different detective will be assigned to the case, depending on what charges they want to pursue. I ask all of you to keep this under your lid. We mustn't tip our hat."

"We're not done, Mark," Benny announced as Hanes stood up. "You might want to sit back down. It gets a lot worse. It's about Bruce's girlfriend, Tess. He planned to divorce Lila and marry Tess. You might know her. She was a resident physician in the ER. Lila tried to kill her."

"I know Tess. Are you kidding me?" Mark reopened his notepad. "How so?"

"Lila tricked Tess into going for a ride. I was following Tess because she told me she was meeting Lila, and I was alarmed, so I went to Lila's house. I saw Tess enter, and not too much later, the two of them got into Lila's car. From where I was sitting, it looked like Lila forced Tess into the car. I think she tased her. I followed the car deep down into the country in Albemarle County, where Lila shot her six times. I didn't actually see the shooting, but I heard it. Tess told me Lila shot her. Medics claimed they found taser wires still attached to her, so I suppose you can add kidnapping to the charges. I think that's how Lila got her into the car. Tess is up in the ICU on death's bed. I know it's not a homicide, but can you follow up on her case? For me?"

When Hanes's phone abruptly rang, he answered it using his cop voice, firm and businesslike. They watched him closely as his face took on a grave look. He stepped away for privacy, and the conversation became inaudible. The call lasted less than two minutes when Hanes returned to the table. "I'm sorry to tell you this, guys, but Tess just died. So now, it's officially a homicide. I've been assigned to her case, so I have to go. I'll get back to you. Officially–I'll need more information from you, Benny."

The meeting converted to mourning as they talked about Tess and shared fond memories of working with her. The drinks became stronger to help dull the grieving stage.

Chapter 45

Homicide Investigation

HANES FOUGHT his tiredness by drinking stale coffee. His anger towards the Lila girl kept him going forward throughout the night. He looked through the crime scene photographs. Tess was beautiful, even in death. He read through his notes again, pouring over every detail. People spoke highly about how much potential she had. Co-workers held Tess in high regard and cried when they heard she'd been murdered. Hanes could have ended his investigation sooner at the hospital, but he was driven to hear more. Tess was one of those few homicides that would stay in his heart for a long time. He'd often noticed her moving around the ER in constant motion, going from room to room. She was the type of doctor who didn't let grass grow under her feet. Hanes wasn't one to get deeply involved emotionally with murder cases, but this one was different.

When he was done with Lila, there would be nothing to save her. He would not leave one single stone unturned in his effort to get the goods on Lila. He would be patient, not moving ahead too fast. Hanes would dig until he had a rock-solid case that would lock her away for murder for the rest of her life. What she'd done was hard-core evil. He had a hunch that many more malicious deeds had yet to surface, and usually, his hunches turned out to be spot on. Hanes had perfected the art of patience. He would move with deliberate intention, but only when the time was right. He needed much more than what Benny had told him.

Chapter 46

Wicked Lies

A FTER MUCH PAINFUL worrying, Dorrie decided to play the part of the dutiful daughter who loved the idea of her Daddy marrying her au pair. Nothing had changed, though. She didn't like Amelia, and if she had to pretend to love her to make her daddy happy, then she would act excited about their baby and become best friends with Amelia.

Dorrie got dressed for school, joined Amelia in her bathroom, and sat on the closed toilet seat to watch Amelia apply her makeup.

"So, do you know if it's a girl or boy yet?" Dorrie asked, genuinely wanting to know.

"I do. But I can't say. I have to tell Benny first."

"Why don't you tell us together? I mean, it's my brother or sister. Please," Dorrie begged.

"Let me think about it," Amelia said, throwing her makeup sponge in the trashcan at Dorrie's feet.

Dorrie wanted to grab the sponge to see what Amelia's makeup would look like on her. Maggie wouldn't buy her any, saying she was too young to wear it. Still, Dorrie was curious. Instinctively, she reached for the bin when her eyes caught a pregnancy test beside the sponge. She jerked her hand back. She'd learned all about pregnancy tests in school. The pregnancy test was definitely negative. Dorrie stared hard at it, wondering *how it could be negative if she were pregnant.*

Amelia overlooked Dorrie's actions as she was pretty engrossed in applying eyeliner. Dorrie looked up at her, not knowing what to say or if she should say anything at all. *Why would Amelia tell everyone she's pregnant when she clearly isn't?*

Dorrie said she'd meet Amelia downstairs and fled the room. At the foot of the stairs, Dorrie ran into Jenny Pretty, the chief housekeeper.

"They need to empty Amelia's trashcan. It doesn't look like it's been emptied lately," Dorrie said, assuming the pregnancy test was old.

"I beg your pardon, Miss Dorrie. I check every family member's suite during the dinner meal to ensure every room passes inspection before everyone retires for the night. It was emptied last night."

"Oh," Dorrie said, surprised. "I must be wrong. I apologize."

Dorrie wanted to tell Maggie but didn't dare to confess she'd been snooping. From that moment forward, she vowed to find out precisely what Amelia was up to, even if it meant reading Amelia's diary despite Maggie's warnings not to do such a thing again. Dorrie vowed to make it a morning habit to visit Amelia when she put on her makeup so she would check the trashcan for more evidence.

She didn't have to wait long. Every morning, when she sat beside Amelia, a new test appeared—negative. Dorrie began to watch Amelia's every move and read everything she could find about pregnancy.

"Can you feel the baby move yet?" Dorrie asked. She planned to ask many questions, one after another, until she was satisfied. "Didn't they give you a picture of the ultrasound? Did you tell Daddy the sex of the baby yet?"

"No, no, and no. I feel what I think are gas bubbles, but I'm not sure if it's the baby. And I've decided not to tell him the sex of the baby. I want him to be surprised."

Dorrie finally grew weary of talking to Amelia about the baby and let it go. One thing was sure: her belly wasn't growing. Dorrie was left with the same unanswered question. *Why would a pregnant woman take a pregnancy test every day if she already knew she was pregnant?*

***

DORRIE COLLECTED evidence. Every morning, she searched the trash, and every morning, a negative pregnancy test was there. After Amelia left to go to breakfast, Dorrie put on gloves and retrieved the tests, storing each one in a zip-lock bag and placing them in a shoe box in her closet.

By the time the wedding was less than a week away, Dorrie was worrying incessantly about her father and was troubled about what she should do about it. What made it so hard was that her father seemed to be very happy about his upcoming vows. Thinking about it made her ill. She was too afraid to confront Amelia alone.

***

DINNER WAS TRANQUIL. Annella Wryn was eating uptown in a fancy restaurant with Glenn. Dorrie missed her lively chatter and was stuck trying to feel happy at the table. She was also out of fresh, new riddles. Dorrie was working hard to keep her thoughts about Amelia to herself, but at the same time, she felt driven to mess around with Amelia.

"I can't wait till you start showing, Amelia. When do they think you'll start poking out there. It's time, isn't it?" Dorrie said.

Amelia dropped her fork and reached for her napkin, clearly biding for time. "The baby is small."

"Is everything okay?" Benny asked, suddenly concerned. "I want to go with you on your next visit and get them to take an ultrasound."

"Better yet," Maggie piped in. "You could come to the hospital, to the ER. We can do the ultrasound secretly by ourselves."

"Yeah!" Dorrie said, clapping her hands. "Maybe you could get me a picture to put on my dresser."

"No. We're not doing that. I don't want anyone knowing the sex of the baby until it's born. The baby is fine, and that is that."

***

Benny sought solace in his sitting room, seeking private time with his thoughts. He wanted to be actively involved with his baby. He wanted to be present for ultrasounds so he could see it and watch it grow. Amelia was selfish and made all these rules of her own. He had rights as a father, but he felt ignored. He wanted to know if it was a girl or a boy so that he could imagine his life with him or her. It didn't matter what sex the baby was; he simply wanted the opportunity to daydream in specifics. Amelia should tell him.

"You look worried, Benny," Amelia said, her French accent heavy as it always was at night.

"It's just hospital stuff," Benny said, annoyed by her interruption. Lately, she'd become suffocating by interrupting his thinking time. So much was happening all around him, and sometimes, he simply needed to be alone. The biggest thing he wanted to think about was the wedding. He didn't feel the same way about Amelia as he did Willow. The more time he spent around her, he began to see things he hadn't seen before.

Willow had always filled him with joy, providing him with beautiful love and deep friendship. Amelia was that way at first, but since she'd found out about the baby, all the love and caring faded away. He didn't know if he was being overly sensitive. Still, it seemed like every single moment he got Dorrie alone to have father-daughter time, Amelia appeared and deliberately inserted herself between them.

Benny looked over at her, and his stomach fell. "What are you looking at?" Benny asked, pointing to the magazine she held in her hand. "You look serious yourself."

"I am. I'm looking at houses," Amelia replied. "I want you to buy us a house. I want to have my own mansion."

"We don't need a house, Amelia. We live here."

"But I want my privacy. A place where my family can live. I want them here in America. You have plenty of money. You can easily spend three or four million on a house for me and the baby."

"Amelia," Benny replied, his voice edgy, filled with astonishment. "There are over twenty empty suites on this floor alone. There's plenty of room for your entire family and more. I'm sure Maggie wouldn't mind. Besides, this is Dorrie's home. Kerrington, Maggie, and I are all parents to Dorrie, and we agreed to live here together as a family."

"I don't want to live here, Benny. This is Maggie's house. I want my own mansion. Why can't you buy it for me? You have well over sixty million dollars, and you never spend anything. I deserve my own home."

"How do you know how much money I have?" Benny asked, his voice filled with building anger. "Only Kerrington knows about my financial matters."

"I know about them. I read your statements. They're right out in the open, lying on your desk. I couldn't help but see them."

"You went into my office and went through my private things?"

"Yes," Amelia's response was straightforward, as if she believed she had every right to invade his privacy. "We're getting married. I have a right to know."

Benny turned to face Amelia. "There's something we need to iron out before getting married. First, I insist on my privacy. You shouldn't be going through my private things. People don't do that in America. Marriage does not entitle you to do it. Also, when I'm having private time with my daughter, I don't want it interrupted. My family is just as important to me as yours is to you. You're welcome to bring them here with Kerrington's permission, but I want to clarify one thing. I will not leave my family for any reason. I will not buy us a mansion. We will always live here. And our child will live here. This is our home."

Amelia glared at him. "We'll see. You'll see. Maybe we won't get married then, and your child will be born a bastard." Amelia got up and stormed out of the room, slamming the door behind her, something that was never done in the Blanchard House.

The following day, Amelia refused to come out of her room. She called the housekeeper, Ms. Pretty, her supervisor, and told her she was ill. Amelia wouldn't answer her door and remained in her room, watching television with the volume on high. She insisted her meals be delivered and left outside the door.

The following day, when Amelia returned to the family table for breakfast, she appeared to be fully recovered. She acted as if nothing was amiss and chatted wildly about the wedding.

Dorrie abruptly excused herself from the table and took the elevator to her floor, dashing into Amelia's room to check out the trashcan. Sure enough, another negative pregnancy test was visible. Dorrie retrieved it and escaped to her room, hid the zip lock, washed her hands, and returned to the meal table, explaining she had to take care of something.

Maggie looked at her curiously but didn't say anything. She'd heard from a nurse friend that teenagers were odd creatures who acted strangely and often kept things to themselves. It was part of growing up.

Chapter 47

The Shoebox

ORRIE PICKED UP the shoebox and carried it to her mother's room, where she found Maggie propped up in bed reading a nursing journal. Dorrie's hands began to shake as she approached the bed, afraid to do what she knew was the right thing to do.

Maggie looked up and slowly grew both curious and concerned. "What's the matter, honey?"

Dorrie stood very still. All the practicing she'd done for this very moment had proven to be useless. Dorrie found herself tongue-tied and terrified about telling her mother what she'd done.

"What's in the box?"

"You don't want to know."

Maggie couldn't help but laugh. "Let me get this straight. You walk in here looking like you're terrified, holding a box, and I'm not supposed to ask you anything about it?"

Dorrie moved her hand to hide it. "Don't laugh. It's not funny." Things weren't going as she planned. She wanted to run.

Maggie studied her daughter. "No. I apologize. I guess it's not something to laugh about, is it? Show me, Dorrie. What do you have in the box?"

Dorrie moved towards Maggie and slowly opened the top of the shoe box, revealing the hidden contents.

Maggie's eyes popped wide open. "You're having sex? You are way too young. Oh my God, Dorrie. How could I miss the signs that you're sexually active? Are you pregnant? They all look negative. What's happening here?"

"They're not mine. They belong to Amelia. I took them from her trash can."

"Amelia's? That can't be. She's supposed to be very pregnant."

"No, she's not. Have you really looked at her? Her tummy is flat; she just wears baggy clothes. I read her diary. She takes the test every day, hoping it will be positive, but I've seen them all. They are all negative. Every single day."

"You reread her diary after I forbid you to?"

"You're changing the subject, Mom. She's lying to Daddy. I can show you what I read. She's not really pregnant but wants to be, so he will marry her and buy her a big house. Amelia wants to move her family to America so they can live with us in another place without you. I don't want to live anywhere else. This is my home. I don't want to leave. She's not a nice person."

Maggie jumped from the bed and pulled Dorrie into her arms, livid after hearing the news. "You're not going anywhere, and you're way too young to have to worry about adult things. Leave this to me and promise me you will not say a word."

***

THE MINUTE BENNY entered the house; Maggie approached him in the entrance hall beside the elevator door.

"We have to talk."

"Not now, Maggie," Benny replied curtly; his voice was filled with impatience and irritation. "I need to get out of my scrubs, and then I have to meet with Amelia. I'm late. It's not a suitable time and likely won't be for the rest of the day. It has to wait." The elevator door opened, and Benny stepped inside, reached his arm out, and pushed the button. As the doors began to close, Maggie became desperate.

"Amelia's not pregnant. I have proof."

Benny's arm shot out and punched the *Door Open* button, leaving them to face each other. Maggie was crestfallen for her friend as she watched his face fall.

"What did you say?" Benny asked, his voice barely a whisper. He exited the elevator and motioned Maggie to join him at the Gilded Bar. Maggie followed him, feeling like a heel for hurting him.

Benny led her to their usual spot at the back table, where conversations couldn't be overheard from the doorway. Stalling for time to make sense of what she said to him, he stepped behind the bar and mixed two stiff screwdrivers without even asking if she wanted one. When he returned to the table, he whispered, "Tell me what you know and how."

Maggie told him about all the negative pregnancy tests that Dorrie had obtained from Amelia's trash.

"Dorrie knows about this?"

"I'm sorry, Benny. I know Dorrie shouldn't have been snooping, and we'll talk to her about that later. For now, you have bigger fish to fry. So sorry."

"Oh, we're going to be frying a lot of fish. This is the best news I've had in a while. I so do not want to marry her—not now, not ever. You were right. I was about to make a colossal mistake."

Maggie held her drink up in a toast. "No more sex with her."

"Oh, that's been over for a bit. Never again."

***

BENNY CLIMBED the staircase, carrying the shoe box. At the top of the stairs, he ran headlong into Dorrie. She was crying; worry was plastered all over her face. "Don't, honey," Benny said, giving his daughter a long embrace. "I do want you to be sorry for snooping into Amelia's diary and spying on her, but I don't want you to be sad for telling Maggie. It's over now." He kissed Dorrie on the forehead and sent her off to her room to give him privacy. Then, Benny walked the long hallway leading out of the family quarters. He stood silently outside Amelia's door, summoning up his courage before finally knocking.

Amelia called out, "Come in."

Benny looked over at Amelia, who was sitting in the middle of her king-sized bed, covered with her silk comforter. She was flipping through a real estate magazine. "We need to talk," he warned before plunging ahead. "You can put that away," he said, motioning towards the publication. "We won't be buying a house because we won't be getting married. I know you aren't pregnant."

"What are you talking about?"

Benny placed the shoebox on the bed, opened the lid, and poured the contents on the bed. He spread the zip lock bags out to prove his point that her deceit had been a repeated act of lying and deceit. "These pregnancy tests came from your bathroom. You lied to me."

Amelia stared down at the evidence, unable to meet Benny's knowing eyes.

Benny kept the conversation brief. "I don't want you in this house one more day. I want you to pack your things and go to a hotel tonight–never to return. Ms. Pretty will have your belongings sent." Benny handed her an envelope from his pocket. "That's a thousand dollars in cash and plane tickets back home. It would be best if you kept it safe because that's all you'll get from me again. You are not to have any contact with Dorrie ever again."

"It's not what you think," Amelia said with a tone of desperation.

"It is what I think. You're a liar who got caught. What were you thinking? Have you been having sex with someone else, trying to get pregnant because we haven't been intimate in weeks? What kind of person are you that you really thought you could pull this off?" Benny turned and left. Before closing the door behind him, he gave her a deadline. "You have one hour to leave willingly, or I'll have security remove you. The car will be waiting downstairs."

As Benny descended the stairs, he resolved never to put Dorrie in such a situation again.

Chapter 48

Ming's Search

MING STOOD in the middle of the opulent suite, taking in the breathtaking surroundings of Blanchard House. The room filled him with gratitude and euphoria. His new residence radiated a sense of grandeur and filled him with wonder. Was he merely caught in the midst of some great, beautiful dream that would end at any moment? He turned around in a circle, taking in each piece of elaborate art, such as he'd never seen before. His heart swelled with the realization that this breathtaking space, indeed, was now his home. It was a dream come true.

In the afternoon, Ming took his daily work break and took a bus to the hospital, where he wandered, searching for his future wife. He made the same trip every day, hoping that by some stroke of luck, he would find her. It was a shift change. After an hour, he headed for the nearby Starbucks, where he ordered his favorite beverage, a chocolate latte—seeking a drink that equaled his latest indulgent experience living at Blanchard House.

The aroma of freshly brewed espresso, richly woven with velvety, sweet chocolate, usually filled him with delight. Still, after taking his first sip, he leaned back in his chair and sighed with disappointment. He'd come up empty-handed again.

Ming wiped a tiny bead of the frothy layer of steamed milk from his lips and closed his eyes, trying to find comfort as he basked in the warm sunlight streaming through the glass. He smiled. Life had indeed brought him full circle in such a brief period. Was it just last week that he felt destined to be living in a prison cell?

Opening his eyes, he watched the vibrant, pulsating lives of the world pass by on the sidewalk. As he absentmindedly gazed at the passersby, his heart skipped a beat.

It was her—Doctor Sheng, the beautiful Asian doctor who had been his savior as he lay dying in the hospital. A rush of hope surged through Ming's veins as he abandoned his drink and hurriedly fled from the coffee shop— rushing to catch up with her and get her attention.

Breathless, Ming got close enough to call her name. "Doctor Sheng. It's Ming Fu, your patient. Do you remember me?" he stammered, his voice barely above a whisper. She stopped, turned to face him, and instantly, she took his breath away.

Sheng's beautiful, russet brown eyes were magnificent. They drew him into her and seemed to swallow him whole, making him incapable of talking. They widened with surprise at the sight of him. "You're alive! You made it," she exclaimed delightfully, her voice filled with genuine relief.

"Lucky me, indeed. The nurses called it a miracle," Ming replied, a nervous smile playing over his lips as he searched for something else to say, anything they would hold her in his presence a little longer. Time could quickly slip away and take with it all the hopes he had in his heart. Before he could stop himself, he blurted out the truth. "Doctor Sheng. I want to spend time with you. Will you share a drink with me? And more importantly, will you marry me?"

Doctor Sheng briefly looked taken aback, her gaze flickering between disbelief and curiosity. Ming felt suspended in time, held captive by her extraordinary beauty. He watched the sunlight shimmering in her silky black hair, which delicately framed her flawless ivory complexion. Holding his breath, he awaited her response.

A smile slowly spread across Doctor Sheng's face, illuminating her features. It was a smile that spoke of possibility and revealed, more importantly, that he had successfully stirred her emotions. "I would love that," she murmured, her voice gentle and filled with hope. "Both that of sharing a drink with you—and maybe even becoming your wife. Call me Mei-ling."

The two of them boarded a bus and fled the bustling hospital neighborhood. They found a quiet café in South Park. Ming's heart soared the entire trip. It had been love at first sight for him, and now fate favored him once again. It appeared it may have been love at first sight for her as well.

Over dinner, their conversation effortlessly flowed as Ming revealed his deepest aspirations and his triumph over the virus that nearly took his life. Hesitant yet hopeful, he confessed, "I invented the cure."

To his astonishment, Mei-Ling's eyes shimmered with pride and admiration. She gently grasped his hand, her touch conveying unspoken understanding. "I am so proud of you, Ming. Your courage and determination are truly remarkable," she murmured, her voice laced with admiration.

***

TIME DIDN'T MATTER as they sat together, getting to know one another. When Ming looked at his watch, hours had passed. It was almost dinner time at Blanchard House. He couldn't be late. Ming invited Mei-Ling.

Dinner served as the official beginning of their journey together. The night was filled with jubilation as he introduced Mei-Ling to his loved ones and announced his intention to marry her. The evening stretched on, conversations flowing, laughter echoing, and the undeniable magnetism between them growing more substantial.

After dinner, Ming walked Mei-Ling to the car that Maggie arranged. With a warm smile, he handed her his cellphone number. "Call me whenever you want. You mean everything to me," he whispered, his voice brimming with overwhelming love.

As Ming ascended the stairway to his lavish suite, he could think of nothing but Mei-Ling and the memory of their love story and how their lives their lives had intertwined—as if destiny had played a hand in it. From that day forward, he knew they would navigate life's ups and downs together with love as a beacon of hope and a testament to the power of genuine connection.

***

WHEN MING TOOK his seat at the table for breakfast, Maggie looked at him with curiosity. "Did I see you getting on a bus yesterday?"

"Yes. I always take the bus. Taxi fare is too high."

"I don't think Kerrington would like you taking buses. Security likes to control the property, and it bothers them to see someone walking through the drive."

"Oh, Ming said."

"I'm asking you to take our car service. That's why we have it."

Ming didn't say anything because he didn't know what to say. He wasn't used to his new lifestyle, and it seemed too lavish, but he didn't want to argue with Maggie. Technically, she was his boss. He simply nodded his head in compliance.

"Ronnie. The butler can call the car when you need it," she added.

Benny saw Maggie through a new lens. She was no longer the woman living in the little blue house on Park Road. Blanchard House had changed her as firmly as it had changed him. They had adapted.

He thought about their future. They would have to fight to remain who they were. Benny knew he would never leave the ER again, and neither would she. They'd tried that once by working in surgery. The experience had been awful. The ER was perfect for them. It was a place for seekers of random, new experiences. He looked around the table. He liked the change he was seeing at Blanchard House, and he liked that Kerrington felt the need to shake things up. Glenn, Sunday, and all the hospital residents dining down the hall were proof of good things.

Chapter 49

The Laboratory

KERRINGTON DIDN'T have to be home to get things done. Lamar notified Maggie that the back of the property was temporarily closed for three days but didn't say why. She found out the next day when she spotted a construction crew near the lab. It was over almost as soon as it started, and the crew departed the property, having transformed the space where the lab had stood. On top of the space was a new helipad. The older one closer to the house had been removed. The nightmare was gone. Her future children could safely roam about any place on the property.

On the far left of the property, a new, colossal gazebo had been built, and the older one became history. In the new pavilion, memories would be made with new people.

***

Chapter 50

Hunting With Hanes

D ETECTIVE HANES was relentless in his pursuit and had spent days digging into Lila's background, convinced there was more to Lila than met the eye. With nothing much to go on but a history of Borderline Personality Disorder, the search was problematic from the start. What stuck out to him the most was that Lila seemed to be an intelligent girl when it came to carrying out her devious activities.

The thing that stumped him was the fact that Lila appeared to have come out of nowhere, arriving in Charlotte fifteen years ago, which would have made her twenty-one years old. Her marriage license listed her birth name as Davenport. A deeper dive into her maiden name revealed a lengthy line of addresses from Orlando, Florida; Atlanta, Georgia; Las Vegas, Nevada; Society Hill, South Carolina; and Charlotte, North Carolina.

His work would be cut out for him. He started with the *National Crime Information Center*, looking specifically for aliases, outstanding warrants, or criminal records. His next search landed him in the databases of *LexusNexis* and *Accurint* to search for public records, past addresses, property records, divorce records, and birth records that might indicate she had a child somewhere. Deep in his bones, Hanes felt he was on the right track. He pulled credit reports and obtained her social security number from the Social Security Administration.

Hanes didn't have time to read and digest the information so he printed it out to study later. During his brief glance at some of the details, he had found several things that caught his eye, facts that might lead him somewhere useful. There was nothing Hanes loved better about his job than hunting. It was like digging for gold. So far, the stack of printouts stood two inches thick. He got utility records and court records and went through the driver's license database in all the states in which she lived. Interestingly enough, two of the photographs were brunettes.

The phone rang as it often did, interrupting his investigation. It was always a call to investigate a homicide somewhere. Disappointed, he was forced to leave the hunt, time after time. By the third call late in the day, he stuck his information in a briefcase and took it to his car. He'd have to go over it later.

Then, a nice call came over his cell phone. It was Maggie inviting him to dinner. Eagerly, he accepted on the spot and promised to be there as close to seven as possible. Maggie wanted to have drinks before dinner.

Chapter 51

Surprise Discovery

A S HANES DROVE to the crime scene involving a gang shooting between three other gang members, his mind wandered back to Lila. He had a lot of questions. How did such a successful man, Bruce Russell, end up with Lila? How did they meet? Maybe it was time to talk to close friends of Bruce's. Men were preferable because men tended to share intimate details of the relationships, at least initially when the relationship started.

Dinner at Maggie's. They had drinks in the Gilded Bar, which was surprisingly crowded. Hanes soon discovered that many of the people present were Emergency Medicine residents from Saint Vincent's. They apparently all resided at Blanchard House. The environment was lively. He casually listened in on conversations, not intentionally, but more out of a habit that had grown more out of being a detective. He found Sunday's conversation by far the most interesting. She was talking with Maggie in the corner, and in a faint voice, she told Maggie her divorce papers arrived. It was official. She was a free woman again. Hanes raised his eyebrows. He liked that news.

Hanes was the only cop in the room and didn't really get into a lot of the resident's chatter because it was full of medical mumbo jumbo that went far over his head. Hanes eased over to Sunday's side and asked her how she liked living at Blanchard House. He didn't really care about that; it was merely an opening line to get her talking. That was his talent. He could get anyone to talk to him, many times when they didn't want to. He had a way of getting people to spill their guts unwillingly; however, he wanted Sunday to be a willing conversationalist.

He hadn't found a woman who could hold his interest for long, but there was something about her that drew him to her. First of all, he could tell by looking at her that she was brilliant. It was in the way she looked at things with her eyes, the way she seemed to sum people up quickly, and what she chose to talk about with them. Her voice was soft, southern, almost musical, but steady.

Hanes asked if she'd like to walk in the garden before dinner to get away from the noise. Sunday grinned and said, "Lead the way. You've been here enough to know your way around."

Hanes found he didn't have to work to have a conversation with her. Sunday jumped right in, and he was delighted. He could tell she wanted to get to know him. "I heard all about the trouble Maggie and Benny manage to get themselves involved with. I also heard about how you managed to get them out of it every time. They're good people."

"I know. I choose my friends carefully. Maggie may appear to be a sunshine goodie two shoes, but that girl would've made a great detective. She took me on a mean ride trying to keep up with her when she went after the serial killer. Almost got herself killed in the process, along with Kerrington and Benny."

Sunday laughed. "Yeah, my friends are something else."

Out of nowhere, raindrops fell from the sky and quickly became a downpour. Mark grabbed her hand and pulled her into the gazebo. By the time they got inside, they were both drenched. They ended up in the new pavilion just as it started to rain. The smell of the nearby roses was tantalizing and would become a part of this memory of being with her.

Sunday grabbed a hand towel from the bar and handed Hanes one. She lightly giggled as she dried off. "How did we not see that coming?"

"Maybe we were distracted by each other," Hanes replied. He searched her eyes and said what was on his mind. "I'd really like to kiss you."

"Then, go on. Do it."

When his lips met hers, it was all over and done with because he felt it all over, the giant spark. He never wanted to leave Sunday's side. He kissed her again and again.

Sunday gently pushed him away. "I would definitely like to do that again, but it's time for dinner. The rain has stopped. We have no excuse to be late."

Hand in hand, they walked back to the house and joined the family table. Hanes missed not seeing Kerrington. "Where is everyone else?"

"They're in their dining room. You're special; you get to eat in here with us," Benny said with a chuckle.

Maggie caught Sunday's eye. "I see you two got caught in the rain. How was it?"

"Wet," Sunday replied. They broke out in laughter, and the night became magical. Love was clearly in the air, and Maggie was happy for them.

Chapter 52

Mary Margaret

IT WAS MIDNIGHT when Hanes began the long journey of reading through his research on Lila. She indeed, had been to many places. She'd worked many jobs as a waitress mostly.

As he read on, he discovered she had an alias: Mary Margaret Lee. The name change occurred in Las Vegas, so something happened between Atlanta and Las Vegas. Who was Mary Margaret Lee?

As it turned out, Mary Margaret had gotten married in Atlanta. No children. The marriage had been brief. Her husband, Ollie Barrett, died. Eye drops had poisoned him. According to the prosecutor, Mary Margaret (Lila) had placed the drops in his ice water.

Somehow, she managed to make bail and promptly fled the area. Hanes leaned back joyfully in his chair, pounding a fist into the air. That's the piece of the pie that was missing. Hanes filled with delight. First thing in the morning, he'd make a call to the prosecutor.

It was like taking candy from a baby. Julius Michaels had an outstanding record of winning his prosecution trials. Not only did he tell Hanes what he knew, he sent him the evidence papers.

The medical examiner in Atlanta found tetrahydrozoline in lethal doses in the victim's body. An eye drop bottle was found in the trash dump. It was fingerprinted. Homicide secured the fingerprint from a drinking glass. The prints matched. The motive: Mary Margaret, aka Lila, made a cash withdrawal from their joint banking and savings account totaling over $700,000. She claimed the money was hers and that she'd given it to Ollie. Paper trails proved the cash belonged to Ollie. He'd inherited his mother's estate.

All Hanes needed was Lila's fingerprint so he could compare it to Mary

Margaret's. That would be easy, peezy. Hanes assigned a detail to follow Lila, and they obtained her fingerprint.

When Hanes pulled up both prints, they were an exact match. Lila and Mary Margaret were the same person.

Hanes walked down the hall to the DA's office and pled his case. He left the room with an uplifted gait. Finally, he'd gotten what he wanted.

Chapter 53

Alias

L ILA WAS ENJOYING a glass of wine, sitting on her sofa in pajamas, watching a pre-recorded episode *of General Hospital,* when the doorbell rang. She pulled her robe tight around her waist and opened the door.

Hanes stood on the porch, holding his badge in the air, grinning. "Hello, Lila. Or should I call you Mary Margaret? We have a warrant to search your property."

Lila's face fell. Her hand flew to her face, causing the wine to splash onto her robe. Hanes handed her the warrant and waltzed into the house as if he owned it. A trail of law enforcement officers, crime scene investigators, and forensic technicians followed in tow.

"You're under arrest for the attempted murder of your husband, Bruce Russell, and the murder of Tess Larken. It appears that Atlanta has been looking for you for some time now. Did you skip bail? That was not a smart move. It complicates things and leaves me a bit disappointed. Under the *Uniform Criminal Extradition Act*, you will be transported to Atlanta, Georgia, to stand trial first for the murder of Ollie Barrett."

Lila felt her heart skip a beat before she fainted, landing hard on the floor. She soon awakened to the obnoxious whiff of a broken ammonia capsule being held under her nose by a medic. She was strapped to an ambulance stretcher. Her hands were handcuffed to the side rails. She caught the glare of a female police officer's stern eyes. Lila was taken to Saint Vincent's Emergency Room.

After several hours of testing, Doctor Glenn Sloan walked into her room and nodded to the police officer in attendance. "You apparently had what we call a vasovagal reaction. You received shocking news, and you simply fainted. You appear to be stable, but we'll observe you for a few hours and then discharge you into police custody."

"Can you get them to take these things off? Lila asked as she moved her hands about trying to get out of the handcuffs."

"I'm afraid I can't. That's up to the officer here," he replied. "Close your eyes and rest. I'll be back later to check on you."

***

BACK AT Lila's house, the search revealed damning evidence against her. They found the gun that Lila used to kill Tess. Blood splatter found on the gun matched Tess's blood sample. Lila's fingerprints were present on the weapon. Carpet samples taken from Lila's car had the same blood splatter evidence that matched samples found on the bottom of one of her shoes found in the closet. Most damning of all was Lila's Gucci pocketbook, hidden high up at the top of her closet. Inside, they found a culture swab. Lab analysis found it to be covered with Streptococcus pyogenes, the bacteria that had been used to infect Bruce.

Chapter 54

Final Rounds

S UNDAY STOPPED in to see Bruce on rounds. He was the last patient she had to see before going home.

He was alone and dying. His lips were dry, so she grabbed a mouth swab from a cup, wet it with water, and swabbed his mouth. Sunday didn't have it in her heart to leave him, so she took a seat beside his bed and put his hand in hers. It was cold. Like a mother hen tending to her young, Sunday tightened the blanket around him and tucked it close around his neck. If his hands were cold, then so was he.

Bruce suddenly opened his eyes and smiled. At first, she was surprised to see him so perky, with life in his eyes, but patients did that occasionally. Not long before death, for some reason, life would shoot through them as if nothing was wrong with them. Nurses often compared it to a rose, calling it the final bloom before the petals fell off.

"Where's Lila?" he asked. His voice was weak and raspy.

"She stepped out to get coffee," Sunday lied. She didn't have the heart to tell him the truth. Hanes had told her the whole story about Lila. All her crimes and that she'd killed her former husband.

"I wanted to tell her... I changed my mind." Bruce paused for a breath as if driven by some force to say his last words. "Tell her I said I love her. There will be no divorce."

"Sure," Sunday replied.

Bruce took his last breath and closed his eyes.

It was hard for Sunday to sit holding his hand, watching his head fall to the side. It was such a small move, but it was his last. His body became very still. She waited for a few minutes to make sure he was dead. His pulse was gone.

With profound respect, she whispered in his ear, "Goodbye, Bruce. My friend forever." Before leaving the room, she pulled the sheet over his face, covering it. He wouldn't want people seeing him in death. He didn't even want a funeral. Everything was laid out clearly in his *living will*. He had given her a copy to put in his chart. His last wish was for Sunday to call his partner, and he would take care of everything.

She was sad as she left the room, pulling the door closed with such finality. She would never forget the sound.

Sunday told the nurses so they could call the funeral home listed in his documents. As she filled out his death certificate, she recalled Bruce as he was when she first met him. He was so brilliantly funny at times with his humor and sought to bring positive feelings to the awful situation facing him. He worked hard to lighten Sunday's worry, managing to get a chuckle out of her from time to time simply by laughing. He'd been so contagious with his laughter.

When there was nothing left to do, Sunday left and called Hanes as she strolled down the freshly vacuumed carpet. She couldn't look up when she passed his room.

***

HANES ANSWERED on the third ring, saying he was glad to hear her voice. Sunday asked if he would take her to see Lila.

"She's downstairs in the ER. She fainted when I served her with the search warrant. Better see her now if you're going to. She won't be going home. I can meet you in the ER."

"Good. I'd love to see you, but more importantly, I have to break some bad news for her."

***

TWENTY MINUTES later, Hanes met Sunday at the entrance to the ER, and they walked to Lila's room. The light was off, and Lila's eyes were closed.

257

Hanes greeted the officer and had him step outside, where he briefed him on the situation.

Sunday woke Lila up and told her Bruce had died. The response she got was far from what she expected. Lila went off like a rocket after hearing about Bruce's death. She screamed at the top of her lungs and didn't stop thrashing about on the bed. Yelling out and calling the medical staff killers. Nothing seemed to settle her down. Glenn finally ordered a sedative.

Hanes raised his eyebrows. "I can't question Sleeping Beauty now."

"Want to come to dinner?" Sunday asked.

"I would love to."

Chapter 55

Paul

THE FOLLOWING AFTERNOON, the house phone rang in Sunday's suite. It was Ronald. She had a visitor at the door. "He says he's your husband."

"We're divorced," Sunday advised Ronald. "Show him to the parlor."

Sunday took her good, sweet time preparing to meet Paul. She was irritated with him for showing up at her door without calling.

Paul sat on the sofa with his head in his hands. When he looked up, his eyes were red. He looked like he'd been drinking. His clothes were rumpled and messy.

"The girls are not home. You should have called to save yourself the trip."

"I'm not here to see them. I'm here to see you."

"Well, then, get on with it. What do you want?"

"I made a mistake. A big one, Sunday. I moved with haste without thinking things through."

"So, what—you want to start over? Is that what you're saying?" Sunday sat down on the sofa, intentionally leaving a distance between him. She'd thought about this moment so many times—she craved it, actually. She'd imagined being ugly to him. Surprisingly, though, she didn't have the heart to be cruel. It was typical of Paul to think the grass was greener on the other side.

"We can't go back, Paul. What's done can't ever be undone. You broke my heart. What's worse is that you were brutal and cruel in the way you went about ending things. You can never take back those words and the way you spoke them."

"Sunday. Please. Hear me out. I bought Ally Billingsly's share of the partnership, and she's out of our lives. She's going back to New York."

"I don't care where she goes, Paul. You should have stayed with her because you're certainly not welcome in my life."

"We had a good life, remember. For many years, we were happy. We just got lost building our practices. We lost sight of what was most important."

"You lost sight, Paul. Not me. I was always there, waiting for you to come to your senses and stop ignoring me. It's what you did. You made me feel like a stranger in my own house. You didn't even look at me when I walked into the room. Those are the things that mattered, but they don't anymore. I've moved on."

"What do you mean, you've moved on? Like with another man?"

"Yes. That's exactly what I mean."

"Just like that. The ink wasn't even dry on our divorce papers, and you moved on? How long has this been happening? Were you seeing him while we were married?"

"No, unlike you, I wouldn't have done that to you. I would have had the common decency to end things before seeing another person, much less falling in love."

"You love him?"

"I do. Very much. We'll probably marry soon."

"You're getting married? Another man will be raising my children?"

"Ah. Now, the shoes are on the other foot, but I'll ease your pain there. You will always be the father of my girls. Mark would never intrude on your space. He'll be good to them, but he would never assume he could take your place. He's too smart for that?"

"Is he a doctor or something?"

"No. Actually, he's a homicide detective."

"What an ugly thing to bring into my children's lives. Murders? Killing? I can't believe you. You're marrying a working-class man. Unbelievable."

"Yes. It was unbelievable that I actually found someone as great as he is. Our time is up. There's no more for us to talk about."

Paul got up and walked out of the room. At the door, he turned and said. "Bitch!"

Sunday expected it. How had she gone so long without seeing who he really was as a person? She was glad to see him go.

Chapter 56

Wall Street

MAGGIE THOUGHT her heart would stop when she saw the front cover of a newspaper on the shelf in the Barnes and Noble bookstore. She was horrified by the picture of Kerrington. Someone had captured his picture through a long lens camera on the morning he boarded his private plane to Switzerland. The headlines seared *Wall Street Mogel Dying*.

The picture was taken almost a month ago. Maggie assumed it had taken a bit of time for them to see it. She couldn't get home fast enough to gather his media team, but it was too late. It was all over but the crying. Maggie sat in Kerrington's office, with all the television channels glued to the financial networks, which ran the same photographs repeatedly. All of Kerrington's holdings dropped so fast that the market had to stop trading.

Maggie wondered if he knew. He told her the clinic where he was staying was so remote it didn't have cell service. She looked into his top drawer and found a business card with the Blumann Clinic number. It took a long time for Kerrington to come on the line.

She chose her words carefully and told him what had happened. He told her not to worry that he would take care of things.

***

TO SAY THAT Kerrington was devastated was an understatement. He called for his private jet and made his way home. On the trip, he contacted all the CEOs, analysts, and media. Was there a corporate raider trying to take over his assets? Had they gotten ahold of the picture and released it? Who was buying? Who was selling? His mind calculated his losses and gains. He was caught in a bloodbath. Finally, he called his traders and gave them the order to buy everything, no matter the cost. "Don't break any laws." If someone were really raiding his financial holdings, he would make it hard.

Before getting off the plane, Kerrington arranged for a media team to meet him, including reporters. Then he held his breath, went into the bathroom, and looked at himself. He'd done the right thing. Over the weeks of his treatments, he hadn't allowed himself to look in the mirror, but he had watched his body during his grueling workouts that took place three times a day. He'd followed the nutrition program diligently and never sent any food back on his tray. It had worked. He looked healthier than he had before he'd gotten the virus.

Maggie stood on the tarmac, waiting with all the reporters. He was glad to see her as her presence alone would make him strong. He stood and waited for the door to open, then held for a moment to gather his courage. He would win this battle. He would prove to the world that they could not mess with Kerrington Blanchard.

When he exited the plane, he was careful to stand still for a moment. Then, as his beloved Annella had taught him, he smiled and waved, looking the reporters in the eyes and allowing them to get good photographs. "Show off your beautiful tan and your brilliant blue eyes," she advised. He did exactly as he'd been taught. He played the cameras and the people. He'd gotten his charming mojo back and knew one thing for sure. This image would stun the world. People who had dumped his stock would feverishly fight to repurchase it. He smiled to himself. Before all was said and done, he'd have more significant financial control of his assets than ever.

When they entered the back seat of the limousine, Maggie melted in his arms, and he held tightly onto her. He would not let her down, not at any cost.

***

KERRINGTON skipped family breakfast and retreated to his penthouse office uptown, which overlooked the Charlotte skyline. He watched the sunrise, which always comforted him unless it was raining. His personal assistant gently knocked, quietly entered and placed a fresh cup of coffee in front of him. She put all his favorite newspapers on the table. All the headlines were welcoming news touting about how healthy he looked. Upon reading the articles, he was happy to be given the delicious news that some reports believed the photographs of him in a dying state had been possibly AI-generated. Yes, it was a beautiful new day.

He smelled the rich aroma and thought to himself. *I am a lucky man, and I will never be foolish enough to put my life at risk again.*

He savored the excellent news and waited patiently for the market to open. It was just as he predicted, and recovery came swiftly.

***

KERRINGTON CAME home early that afternoon. He'd called and told everyone to be ready. They were going to the rodeo. With renewed enthusiasm, Kerrington slipped into his blue jeans, put on his rodeo shirt, pulled on his leather boots, and walked to the entranceway where Maggie, Dorrie, and Benny were dressed like proper rodeo fans. He loved the feeling it gave him. He felt like an ordinary man, just like every other cowboy he would meet that night.

Tears filled his eyes when he took off his hat and placed it on his chest as he listened to the Star Spangle Banner and heard the words of prayer. It helped him realize all was well in their world. People still loved America, and they still loved God.

Chapter 57

Doctor Glenn Sloan

ANNELLA WAS packed and ready for Rome and came to the dinner table excited to see Kerrington back home sitting at the head of the table. She kissed him on the cheek before taking her seat beside him.

"I'm glad your film had to delay shooting. I didn't think I'd get home in time to see you," Kerrington said, beaming at her.

The minute Glenn staggered in the door, a thick gloom and doom invaded the air. Even Dorrie caught his foul mood. Maggie instantly became alert to his change in personality. She thought he'd pulled himself out of his dark thoughts, but it was obvious he had not because he'd clearly been drinking a lot. She heard the slur in his speech, and his anger was palpable. When he drank too much, he became a changed man, filled with rage.

"Where have you been?" Annella asked. "I've been looking for you."

"Why would you care where I've been? You're leaving to go God knows where because I'm not important enough to you to want to stay home."

"We're not doing this again, Glenn. Not tonight."

"Why not? Because the family doesn't want to hear it? The family that keeps all these hidden secrets."

Kerrington cleared his throat, making things worse.

"So, let's tell her, Kerrington. You want to know where I've been? Let's bring it all out here in the open. Let's talk about the hidden thing in the back of the estate."

Benny immediately got up and led Dorrie out of the room. "I'll have someone bring you dinner if you could take it in your room or to the TV room upstairs."

Dorrie looked at Benny with concern. "It's not a good moment for you to be here. Everything is okay. We need adult time tonight." Benny was glad the residents living in the house were in the far wing, along with Sunday.

Glenn stared darts at Kerrington. "You think you know your brother, Annie? I think not. Did he tell you about the laboratory out in the backyard? Did he tell you he brought the virus into our lives?"

Annella's eyes changed from bright blue to dark blue as she digested Glenn's accusation. She turned to Kerrington and shot him a questioning look. When he lowered his eyes, her face registered the crushing blow.

"Oh. It goes deeper than that, girl. Everyone sitting at this table is involved. I wouldn't have found out if they hadn't called me for help when dear Kerry collapsed." It was as if Glenn heaved a giant sword into the table, dividing it into pieces.

"Kerrington, what is going on?" Annella said, her lips trembling.

Glenn poured another glass of wine, gulped it down, and slammed his fist on the table. "I just told you what was going on. Why do you need to ask him? Do you not trust me?"

Annella's eyes became cold and harsh when she turned to face her husband. "I think it's time for you to go, Glenn."

A hidden buzzer, present in every room, was buried under the carpet beneath Kerrington's seat. He pressed his foot on it just as Glenn got up, grabbed Annella around the neck with his hands, and planted a harsh kiss on her lips.

Several security officers entered the room at once and took Glenn to the floor.

"Remove him from the property," Kerrington ordered. "Drive him to the closest hotel and get him checked in where he can hopefully get sober." Kerrington looked to Annella for support. "You want him removed?"

Annella nodded her head and looked down, too ashamed to face anyone.

"When you've recovered," Kerrington said. "I will tell you everything. I was only trying to protect you and Dorrie. It was not my doing."

"If you knew about it, that makes you a participant." Annella then looked at Maggie and Benny. "All of you betrayed me, and I don't know that I will ever forgive you."

Slowly and with as much grace as she could muster up, Annella left the room.

***

LATE THAT night, Annella crept into the library where Kerrington sat sipping his Brandy. They stayed locked in the room, talking into the wee hours of the morning. Wounds were mended between brother and sister. Glenn's attempt to divide them would never happen; they promised each other to forgive and forget. Annella shared her plan to divorce Glenn. "I love him—almost too much, but I can't help him—and I can't live with what he's become.

***

UPTOWN, GLENN sat in a chair by the window of a swanky hotel room with uncontrollable tears streaming down his face. The realization that he had successfully self-destructed couldn't be ignored anymore. His life was as paralyzed as a man who had severed his spinal cord. "There's no going forward, and there's no way back," he whispered to himself. "I don't want to be here. Not anymore."

On the table lay a letter saying goodbye to Annella. "Talk to Maggie," he explained. *She's the only one who understands what happened to me. I'm sorry. I will always love you, even in death. Love, Glenn.*"

Glenn took a revolver from his lap and held it to his head, aiming at just the right spot that would end his pain forever. Then he pulled the trigger.

Chapter 58

Intuition

MAGGIE SAT bolt upright in bed as if she'd witnessed Glenn's final act. She felt his presence lingering in the darkness, if only for a brief second. Dread entered her heart. It was an intuitive thing. She knew he was gone.

Maggie stepped into her slippers and walked downstairs. There, alone in the darkness, she thought of Glenn. The sound of his laughter encircled her heart, owning it and bringing profound pain.

There were so many great moments when they had worked side by side, moving around each other, working a trauma—carefully dancing around each other, knowing each other's moves, and predicting them.

Hot tears stung her eyes as a tight knot grew in her throat. Her life would never be the same without him. He was the only one, anywhere, who knew her true fears and the very dark moments they'd shared on the floor of the ER. That was the day she'd lost him. That was the day his life ended.

Maggie waited in the stillness for the news to come. She knew it was coming because she couldn't feel him anywhere. All she felt was the steady beat of her heart.

***

IN THE early hours, Maggie heard the knock on the door and saw Ronnie rushing towards it, still dressed in his robe. She stood up to see Lamar and two police officers on the doorstep. Maggie didn't want to hear. She couldn't bear it. Her heart dropped, sinking deep inside, as she fell to the floor.

***

THE NEXT MORNING, the mansion became filled with a profound sadness. After receiving the news, Kerrington and Annella called a meeting of everyone in the house, where they announced the news of Glenn's death. Grief overcame everyone, and chatter decreased to whispers.

Time slowed to a stop as everyone's clothing changed to black in memory of a great man whose life had been so tragically ended.

Chapter 59

Justice Is Served

LILA SAT IN her jail cell, her nerves in a tangle. She wanted to die, but here she sat staring around at what the rest of her life looked like, and it all started because of Tess. She wished she'd made her suffer more, maybe even beg for her life. If she had it to do over, she'd beat her within an inch of her life and leave her in the woods for the bugs to crawl all over her while she died.

All the things she'd done in the name of trying to save her relationship with Bruce had been useless. He was dead, and without Bruce, nothing would be normal again. Her life and happiness had evaporated as if it had all been a beautiful dream. However would she go on? People hated her. They called her a murderer. A black widow. Cell mates screamed for her to go to Atlanta and not come back. Some even threatened to kill her if she ever stepped foot in Mecklenburg County again.

Lila would end it all. She would not live like this. Somehow, she would find a way to end her life—or piss someone off enough that they would violently stab her to death while in confinement. That would pay them all back. Imagine the chaos her death would cause.

Chapter 60

Another Day in the ER

IT WAS A WILD MORNING, and it felt like Maggie had never left the ER. Memories of her adventures in surgery were like one big blur she didn't want to relive.

A trail of ambulances lined the driveway and greeted her on her arrival, promising a day of hectic activity.

Maggie barely made it through board rounds with the new attending physician, Garrett Rockingham, a nerdy-looking genius with whom she had instantly made friends—when the radio blared at the desk, announcing a pileup on I-85.

"We have fifteen victims; how many can you receive?"

Benny, the assigned Trauma Nurse, quickly joined them at the board.

"The Trauma Room is empty," Maggie started. "That's one. Move rooms 2, 3, and 4 to the assigned ICU beds upstairs. Rooms 7, 8, and 10 can go to the Observation Unit."

Garrett advised, "I'll discharge rooms 1 and 18. That makes room for nine patients." He picked up the radio and confirmed the ER could take nine. Maggie, meanwhile, called the ICU charge nurse and advised them to come to pick up their patients. "STAT. We have a lot of incoming," Maggie said.

Benny was already in the Trauma Room, dressed in a yellow protective gown. Beneath it was a heavy lead apron to protect him from x-ray radiation. The ER galley was soon filled with moving medical personnel from all over the hospital. The news spread quickly, and Trauma Pagers went off all over the hospital, calling for immediate response. People knew what to do, and they would all make it happen.

Colorful fall leaves covered the stretcher sheets and fell to the floor during the rapid movement of patients. Beautiful brown, orange, and green colors dotted the floor before blood erased their beauty, turning them red.

Not even thirty minutes after the disaster response was completed, three cardiac arrests arrived one after another, all requiring extensive CPR resuscitation. When the third came, Maggie and Benny locked eyes before breaking out in a smile. The message they secretly exchanged needed no words. They were in their realm of happiness. They were finally back to where they belonged.

THE END

ACKNOWLEDGEMENTS

Thank you to Kenny Maxwell who allowed me to use his image as a muse for the character, Benny Maxwell. In real life I worked with Kenny at Carolina's Medical Center Main Emergency Department, now called Atrium.

When I originally created the character Benny to carry story forward – I recalled the images of Kenny as he worked in the ER and related to doctors and nurses. He became the perfect muse for one of my central characters. I can never thank you enough, my friend. What a beautiful and fun journey it had been.

I send deep gratitude to my husband, Michael Sowyak, who has been my mentor. My guide. My champion. He's been so generous with his time, providing me with perfect edits. I love you so much.

Here's a big shout out for my daughter Sunday Richardson who said, "Mom. I want to be in your book. Make me a doctor." She made a great neurosurgeon whose life gets shattered and put back together. Thank you for your patience and allowing the freedom to create her story.

Thank you also to Sunday's husband Jason, my grandchildren Anna, Ella, and Wryn. Also I send gratitude to my siblings, Sidney, Pam, Sheri, Greg, and Kathy, who cheered me forward and patiently listened as I talked about my book.

Beta readers are the spine that holds up my book. My deep thanks go out to Maggie Jackson, Tony Jackson and Kathy Mason for their in-depth editing and advice. Thank you, Tony, for allowing me to use your name as a character in my last book.

And finally, I would never have authored a book had it not been for Gwen Hunter, a giant author who inspired me to write my first chapter of Crematorium. At the time, I only knew scriptwriting and did not believe I had the talent to write a book. Thank you, Gwen, for believing in me and pushing me forward.

ABOUT THE AUTHOR

Marilyn Benner Sowyak was one of the entertainment industry's most sought-after medical consultants for over twenty-five years. Her credits include Emmy winners: As the World Turns, One Life to Live, Guiding Light, and Another World. Benner was the Medical Advisor for Law & Order and was also the Medical Coordinator for over twenty-one major feature films.

"I've become a master at creating medical stories and bringing them to life on the screen," Sowyak says. "Now, I tell my own stories.

Marilyn Benner Sowyak is a registered nurse who has worked in the Emergency Departments of New York City's Bellevue Hospital, Mount Sinai Medical Center, New York Hospital Cornell, and Saint Vincent's Hospital. She has also worked in the ED at Orlando Regional Medical Center and, most recently, was the Clinical Nurse Supervisor for over a decade in the Emergency Department at Atrium Main Medical Center in Charlotte, North Carolina. "I understand the heartbeat of hospitals, patients, and medical professionals. I love writing about them."

Review of her work: "Sowyak's grasp of human hurt and healing deepens this terrifying novel's lasting impact." Kirkus Press.

Go to Amazon.com to purchase her psychological thrillers. Crematorium, Locked Inside, and Revenge. Locked Inside is also available at Ingram Sparks and Barnes and Noble.